# Last House Burning

## KATY SCOTT

Herringshaw Press

ISBN-13: 978-0-994-16770-5

www.katyscott.org

To Dylan, who always believes in me.

# A Patient Man

The man stared at the massive map of Australia that was pinned to the wall of the office. He turned as his assistant came into the room.

"They touched down in Sydney an hour ago," she said. "The car hire records say they're going to the Blue Mountains."

"Thank you, Daisy," said the man.

"Do you want me to find out which town they're staying in?"

"No. I already know."

The man selected a pin from a china bowl on the desk, and carefully drove it into the map next to a small dot labelled *Carmenton*.

"How did you..?" The assistant trailed off.

"Oh, just a feeling," the man smiled darkly. "I'm rather familiar with that place."

"Is there anything else, sir?"

"That'll be all."

The assistant left the room, and the man sat down at his desk. He unlocked one of the drawers and pulled out a photograph.

"I'm glad you're safe, my dear," he told the small child who was smiling into the camera. "But right now, I have other places to be."

He stood, straightened his emerald-green tie, and walked out into the corridor towards the elevators. The doors opened smoothly and he stepped inside, leaning over to press a small shiny button on the bottom of the panel.

He gripped the railing tightly as the lift dropped with a jerk and plummeted down into the depths of the Earth.

# - CHAPTER ONE -

# A Patch of Darkness

Ben Fletcher shoved his phone into his pocket with a sigh of defeat. It was official: there was zero mobile phone reception out here.

"This is definitely the wrong road, David," he heard his mother say to his father. "We should be there by now."

"Should I turn around?" David asked, easing his foot onto the brake pedal. "This is your area, Susan. Do you know where we are?"

"Kind of," she said, squinting at the map in her hands. "Just keep going. This side road should get us there eventually."

Ben slumped back in his seat. Could this trip get any longer? Next to him, his little sister started to sing softly, and he squeezed his eyes shut.

"Tia," he growled. "Can you please. Just. Stop."

She grinned to herself and started singing even louder.

"Tia!" he yelled. "Shut up!"

Susan twisted to face her children. "Ben, don't speak to your sister like that!" she snapped, a crack in her voice. "You're not helping things. Neither is that singing, Tia. Can you both just cut it out?"

"Sorry," Ben muttered, folding his arms and staring out the window.

"Ben," his father soothed. "This'll be our last family holiday for… probably years. It'll be great! Once you're at university we might not have these times together anymore."

"Yes. Yes, I know."

"And look," David continued in an irritatingly cheerful tone, "I think we're almost there! We should get into town any…"

His voice trailed off as the long grass at the sides of the road thinned out then disappeared abruptly. He slowed down as the car's headlights lit up the sides of buildings ahead.

"What the hell is this?" Ben hissed, twisting forward to stare through the windscreen.

"Language, Ben…" said his mother, then paused as she caught sight of what was in front of them.

Lining the street were large houses that seemed to have sprung from the black soil. Their chimneys twisted eerily into the sky, and moonlight reflected off patches of roof tiles. Jagged stone walls cast black shrouds around the front porches and yards. The shadows surrounding the houses seemed to swallow up most of the light, and the beam of the headlights looked weak in the darkness.

As they drove slowly between the houses, it struck Ben that he couldn't see any signs of normal life: no lights, no cars, no toys on the porches, no washing lines, no trees. He peered into the darkness and realised the mansions were in ruins, their walls crumbling down.

"This is a ghost town!" he blurted. "What are we doing here?"

"Don't panic, kids," said Susan, relaxing back into her seat. "There was a fire here years ago, that's all. We're almost there. Dave, just keep going straight for the next few minutes, then we'll make a turn."

The car rolled past several moonlit ruins, and Ben and Tia pressed their faces up against the car windows on each side. It may have just been the dark night, but Ben felt a cold chill in his body that hadn't been there before.

He was peering at the houses slipping by when one caught his eye: a mansion that didn't have any visible damage like the others. It was grander than the houses on each side, and as it flashed by, he caught a glimpse of someone sitting on the porch, hastily pulling a hood over their head – but then the car had passed and the figure was gone.

He glanced at his father, who was on the same side of the car, but David was focused on the road, carefully steering around potholes and debris. It looked like he hadn't noticed anything out of place.

Ben twisted around and gazed through the back window, but the house had disappeared. What had he seen back there? Had he really spotted a person on that porch?

The car made a left turn and after a few minutes, he was distracted by lights outside the car. They were in what seemed like normal suburbia, with average-sized houses that had lights visible through the windows and driveways illuminated by floodlights. Ben wound his window down for a better look. There were cars parked outside and he could hear snatches of music playing. Warmth stole back through his body at the familiar sounds.

It was hard to believe that a moment ago they were surrounded old burned-down houses that looked abandoned and left to crumble. Although... maybe not completely abandoned. Ben replayed the scene slowly in his mind. A figure on the porch of an old house, pulling their hood over their face. Over their young face. *Her* young face.

What was a young woman doing sitting on a porch in a

village full of old ruined mansions?

~

Ben gazed out the window of the living room as his family bustled around behind him. According to his mother, there was a lot of cleaning to be done, and the fact that it was past midnight wasn't going to deter her. Since her Uncle Arthur had moved to Germany a few years ago the dust had thickened to provide writing pads on every surface, and Tia was using her finger to doodle vaguely on the dining table.

"What's that, honey?" Ben heard his mother ask.

Ben started to reply then realised she was talking to Tia. "That's Earth," his little sister said. "And that's me, holding it. I guess I'm an astronaut or something."

"That makes a change from last week, when you wanted to be a fireman," said Susan, coming up behind Ben, armed with a cloth and some detergent she'd found dormant under the kitchen sink. "Ben love, help your dad with the stuff from the car," she said. "And have a hunt for a broom when you're done, okay? Arthur must have owned one at some point."

Ben sighed under his breath. For the fourth time since he'd arrived in the unfamiliar house, he pulled out his mobile phone and checked the signal. The reception was flickering between one bar and none. He waved the phone above his head, watching the little scale, but it didn't move up any more notches.

"Ben?" A note of irritation had crept into Susan's voice.

"Yeah?"

"Are you just going to stand there, or give us a hand?"

He turned to see his mother staring at him and biting her lip. "Sure," he replied, trying to sound a bit kinder.

David dropped a few bags behind Ben. "Everything's in," he said. "Thanks for your help, champ. Just for that, you'll be making breakfast tomorrow."

"Sorry, Dad," he said, looking around and noticing his father had brought his luggage inside already. "I didn't realise."

David dropped into one of the armchairs that faced the window and leaned back in relief. "I know we've been sitting down all day, but I'm ready to hit the sack," he said, starting to yawn.

"Yeah, five hours in a plane and two hours in a car is a bit much," said Ben, plopping down on the other armchair. He glanced over and saw that his father really was about to drift off. "Look, Dad, before you go to sleep there, will you check this out?"

David opened his eyes sleepily and Ben gestured out of the window. The high vantage point of their house revealed the town of Carmenton spread out in a large semicircle in the valley before them, all twinkling lights and a few moving sets of headlights. But towards the east, the lights were interrupted by an abrupt patch of darkness.

His father leaned forward to look. "We passed through that dark patch on the way," he said.

"Yeah, those weird ruined places," said Ben. "What happened there?"

David shrugged. "Didn't your mother say that there was a fire? Ask around tomorrow. Your cousins will probably know more about it."

He stood up and stretched. "I'm going to bed. Might want to hit the hay yourself soon."

"Right. Night, Dad."

Ben stared out of the window towards the dark spot and felt an urge to call up his cousins right then to find out what had happened in that strange place. But his mother was coming back into the room with a wet cloth and her eyes swivelling around to peer at every visible dusty surface, so he dragged himself out of the chair reluctantly and started his hunt for a broom.

## - CHAPTER TWO -

# Breakfast Duty

Ben woke up with his body scrunched into an awkward position and one arm lifeless and cold. The morning light was streaming through the windows. He looked around blearily, wondering where he was, then realised he'd fallen asleep in the armchair.

He unfurled his limbs, massaged his arm to regain circulation, and gazed sleepily out of the window at the valley below. The small town was bathed in sunlight, with activity going on in most streets; cars starting and tiny figures moving around as people began going about their day. Ben's eyes darted to the place where the dark area has existed the previous night, and although he could hardly make out the details of the houses from this distance, he could see the area was still and lifeless. It was a bleak brown patch compared to the town's vibrant hues and the misty haze of the Blue Mountains surrounding the valley. Although the occupied part of Carmenton curved slightly around the blackened area, there was a gap between the two that looked like trees and wasteland.

Susan wandered into the room nursing the same cloth and bottle of detergent from the night before. "Ben! Did you sleep in here last night?"

"Uh, yeah," he replied. "I'm not sure how that happened." He looked at the cloth and bottle, bemused. "Have you been holding those all night?"

She laughed. "No, just taking care of any spots I missed. Your father says you're making breakfast this morning."

"Right, okay," he said, standing up reluctantly. Although he didn't like cooking, he didn't have the energy to protest. "What do we have?"

"I'll do a grocery shop today and pick up cereal and milk, and some bread," Susan decided. "But for now, just see what's in there. Jonathan said he dropped off some supplies last week when he freshened the place up for us, so have a scout around the cupboards." She glanced around the room she'd had to scrub the night before, looking unimpressed with her older brother's interpretation of 'freshening up'.

After changing his clothes and brushing his teeth, Ben went to the kitchen. His mother's cleaning marathon had made every surface shine, but the green benches had an aged yellow tinge and some of the brown and orange chequered tiles on the walls had large cracks in them. It looked like Uncle Arthur had built the kitchen in the early 1970s and hadn't touched it since.

The fridge and freezer were empty, but the pantry held a lifetime's supply of baked bean tins, some vinegar and vegetable oil, and six new-looking plastic containers full of various white and beige powders. Ben lined the containers up on the bench and gazed at them dubiously. They weren't labelled.

He tugged the lid off the first one and leaned down to sniff it. No scent. With a self-sacrificing sigh, he dipped the tip of his finger in and touched it to the end of his tongue. No taste. Fantastic, it was probably poison and he was about to die. Or maybe Uncle Arthur used to run a drug lab and he'd skipped

14

the country, leaving a pile of cocaine to be found by visiting relatives. Ben  hoped not. He had no desire to have his first drug-related experience in front of his parents.

"Mum!" he called in the direction of the living room, and a few seconds later his mother walked in.

"Don't shout from room to room, Ben," she said automatically. "What is it?"

"That's the problem," he said, motioning towards the containers. "I have no idea."

Susan picked up each container in turn, pulling the lid off each one then shaking it and peering in. She rattled off names as she went.

"Baking soda. Flour. Corn flour. Sugar – Ben, don't you know what sugar looks like? Milk powder. White rice – come on, if you're going to move out you'd better learn what rice is. You're making me question my skills as a mother right now."

Ben snatched the container from her. "Of course I know what rice is," he said irritably.

She spread her hands and shrugged, backing towards the door. "Okay, expert," she said. "I'll leave it up to you. Breakfast on the table in about twenty minutes, please."

Trying to remember which container was which, Ben surveyed his options. He could just heat up some beans, but after his mother's crack about moving out, he wanted to show her that he could make better use of the resources at hand. He could probably make bread from some flour and water and… what other ingredients went into bread? It was starting to sound complicated. Well, maybe he could make pancakes.

He stirred flour, sugar, milk powder and water together in a bowl, then found an old electric mixer in a top cupboard and braced himself as he plugged it into the wall. No electric shock – so far, so good. He plugged in the whisks and fired them up, pushing down into the mixture. It swirled into a thick consistency so he added some water until it seemed similar to the pancake batters he could remember helping his mother make when he was small.

The rings on the chipped white stove still worked, though he almost burnt his fingers with the match as he lit the gas. He poured some oil into the frying pan then spooned four blobs of batter in over it.

"What are you doing, Ben?" asked Tia, appearing at his elbow as he was flipping the pancakes. "Do you need me to do anything?"

She seemed to be in a helping mood so Ben transferred pancake flipping duties over to her so he could clean up. "Careful of the pan, it's hot," he warned her, positioning a chair next to the stove so she could stand on it. He showed her how to transfer the cooked pancakes to a plate and spoon more batter into the pan, then he put the containers back in the cupboard and found a cloth to wipe down the bench.

"Look at me, Ben!" called Tia, and as he turned back to her, he realised she'd moved the pan aside and was slowly waving her fingers through the ring of blue flames underneath.

"Tia!" he shouted, dashing across the kitchen and grabbing her off the chair and away from the stove. Holding her small body with one arm, he grasped her fingers and looked at them anxiously. He twisted around to turn on the cold tap and held her hand underneath it. "Mum!" he yelled.

"I'm fine," Tia said, trying to wriggle out of his grasp. "I'm okay! Let me go!"

Their mother bounded into the room. "What? What is it?" she asked quickly.

She ran over to her two children and Ben passed Tia over to her so he could hold his sister's hand under the water with both of his. "She burned her hand," he told his mother.

"No, I didn't!" said Tia, sounding close to tears. "See? I'm okay!" She pulled her wet hand away from Ben's and wriggled her fingers in front of her mother's face. Susan placed her daughter on the floor and knelt next to her, examining her hand while Ben hovered nervously.

"Are you sure, honey?" Susan asked, then looked up at Ben. "What happened?"

"I don't know," he said, cursing himself for letting his sister near the stove. "I thought she put her hand in the flame. That's what it looked like." Remembering that the gas ring was still on, he strode over and turned it off.

"I'm fine, honestly," Tia told her mother. "Nothing happened!"

Susan examined Tia's hand one more time then gave her a quick hug. "I think you're okay," she said, standing back up. "Go help Dad unpack, will you? And tell me straightaway if your hand starts hurting."

As soon as Tia had run from the room, Susan turned to her son. "How did Tia get the chance to get near a flame?" she asked quietly.

"I'm really sorry," he said unhappily, wishing he'd never agreed to make breakfast in the first place. "I turned away for two seconds to clean up and... I'm sorry."

His mother opened her mouth to say something then paused. "Just be careful with her, okay? She's not invincible," she said finally. She crossed to look at the frying pan which sat askew on the stove. "Finish these up," she told him abruptly, then left the kitchen.

Ben lit the stove again and finished making the pancakes in silence. He still felt shaky, thinking about Tia with her hand in the flame. And now his mother thought he'd been irresponsible.

He dragged some plates from a top cupboard and gave them a quick rinse, then found some cutlery and took it all out to the table. The rest of his family was out on the balcony, standing at the rails. The sliding glass door was closed. David was holding Tia, and Susan had her arm wrapped protectively around them both. Tia was pointing towards the mountains in the distance and Ben could see her talking animatedly.

He finished setting the table and dumped the plate of misshapen pancakes in the middle. They didn't look like pancakes, more like lumps of wet bread that had been flash-fried. In the kitchen before Tia's incident with the flame, he'd thought they'd looked like they had character. Now they just looked stupid. He didn't even have any butter or spreads to put on them.

His father slid the door open and walked in. "Good morning!" he said cheerfully. "Breakfast of champions, I see!"

"Uh, yeah, thanks," Ben muttered. "Look, I'm not really hungry. I might go take a look around."

"Are you okay?" his father asked, but Ben was already halfway out the door. He clattered down the flight of stairs, then plopped down on the last step.

He gazed up at the house behind him. The two-storey dwelling was old and made of weatherboard, painted white but slowly peeling, perched on the side of the mountain with many more identical houses spread out below it. Only the upper storey was habitable – the lower one was just a frame lined with boards on three sides. Between the unevenly-placed planks he could see the gleam of the hire car parked inside.

Ben leaned back against the steps and looked down the hill. The house next door blocked his view of the darkened part of town with all the ruined houses, but he could see a good part of the rest of the town. It looked like a typical Australian country town where nothing interesting ever happened.

He couldn't believe he'd be stuck here for a whole month! When their family home in Perth was flooded in a summer storm and needed to be left for a few weeks, Ben volunteered to stay at a friend's place, but his mother insisted that he join them for one last holiday before he went to university. She'd decided it was vitally important that they all spend some quality time together before her son moved away. His parents reviewed their budget and decided that instead of a beach resort or trip overseas, flying across the country to stay at Uncle Arthur's house in the middle of nowhere would be the best option. His mother had instantly warmed to the idea as her family had lived in the Blue Mountains for generations and there were still a few of her relatives scattered around. "I think it's important that we visit them," she had said, with a defensive expression born of guilt from not visiting sooner.

Ben picked up a piece of gravel and examined it before tossing it down the hill. He knew he couldn't hang around on the steps all day but he didn't want to go back upstairs. He wondered if any of his cousins were in town. His little cousin Oliver was around Tia's age, but Sean and Jay were only a year or two older than him. He hadn't seen them since last Christmas in Perth, when the three of them skipped out on the family get-together to shoot some pool at a pub down the road. His mother would have killed him if she'd known. She thought they were upstairs playing video games, not drinking beers at the local dive.

He resigned himself to going upstairs and asking his mother if they were in town, when he heard shouts from down the road and saw two grinning teenagers running up the hill.

"Ben!" one of the boys shouted. "Hey, Ben!"

He stood up and waved, his mouth open in a grin. Speak of the devil!

The two brothers stopped in front of the house, both bent at the waist and panting heavily.

"I won," Sean wheezed.

"Whatever," Jay muttered at his older brother, peering up through his long hair. "I didn't even know it was a race."

He stood up and flicked his hair out of his eyes. "Hi Ben," he said. "What's with the open mouth? Waiting for your servant girl to fill your mouth with grapes or something?"

Sean wiped the sweat from his forehead with the corner of his shirt and straightened up, grinning. "Yeah, nice look, man."

Ben grinned back happily – finally, some like-minded people! "Hey! I was wondering if you guys were around."

Jay breathed out one last wheeze. "How are you? And where's Aunty Sue and Uncle Dave?"

"Inside, eating breakfast."

Sean straightened his clothes and darted up the stairs, still mopping sweat from his face with his hands.

"Mum wants them to come round when they're done," said Jay, flopping down on the step that Ben had just vacated.

"Yeah, they'll love that," said Ben. "Catching up and all that stuff."

"Fair enough though. It's been yonks."

Ben eyed his cousin. "Yonks?"

Jay grimaced. "This is what this place does to you. A week back here and I'm talking like Dad already."

"I haven't seen your dad for ages. Not since you guys came over for Christmas."

"Have you ever been out here?"

"No. Even my mum hasn't been back since she was little. It's pretty far."

"Especially when you could just stay in Sydney, and not drive all the way up here," Jay sighed regretfully. "But Dad's been going on about how great it is that you guys are finally visiting."

Sean emerged from the house, trotted down the stairs and sat down on the step behind his younger brother. He waved a pancake in front of Jay's face. "Ben, what did you use in these?" he asked. "They're falling apart."

Jay inspected the pancake and Ben crossed his arms. "My resources were limited, okay?" he said. "We got in too late to go to the shops last night so I had to use the stuff from the pantry."

"They taste really bad," Sean mumbled with his mouth full, munching away and swallowing nonetheless.

"Like you could do any better," Jay said, biting into his and making a face. "Ugh! Actually, I think you probably could. These really are disgusting," he informed Ben.

"Yeah, yeah." Ben rolled his eyes. "Stop it with the stupid pancakes. Tell me what there is to do around here."

Jay examined the rest of his pancake thoughtfully then laid it on the step next to him.

"Precisely nothing," he replied. "We've been back for a week – not counting going to Sydney for New Year's Eve – and I'm so bored. It's nice to see the parents and all, but I'd rather be at uni than here."

"You'd rather be at uni than on holidays?" Ben asked, surprised.

"Yeah, during the last exam week I never thought I'd say this," Jay admitted. "But seriously, this is the town that nothing ever happens in. Sean and I are going to give it until the end of the week before we pack it in and go back to Melbourne."

"You live together now?" asked Ben.

"When I decided to go to Monash Uni with Sean, he moved out of campus housing and we got a place together nearby," said Jay. "It's awesome! We have parties, barbecues, poker nights, everything."

"That must be really cool," said Ben enviously. "I can't wait to move out. You guys get to do your own thing all the time!"

"We do study too, you know," Sean interrupted, grinning at his younger brother. "We're only social, oh, about ninety per cent of our lives."

"Which university did you end up going for?" Jay asked Ben. "Your mum said you got high marks. Congratulations and all that. Where are you going to go?"

"Well," Ben started, but was cut off by a door slamming upstairs.

"Hi, boys," his mother's voice floated down, and she walked down the steps. She leaned over to give Jay a kiss on top of his head, but recoiled at the last minute.

"You're all sweaty," she frowned at him, and he laughed.

"Hi, Aunty Sue," he said, standing up to give her a peck on the cheek instead.

She smiled at him. "We're all adults now, you know," she said. "You don't have to call me 'aunty' if you don't want to."

"Years of habit," he replied with a shrug.

"How was your Christmas?" she asked. "I'm sorry we missed it. If we could have come a week sooner, we would have."

"It was fine," said Jay. "The usual. Mum made turkey."

"That sounds nice," said Susan, glancing around at Ben.

He wasn't sure if it was his imagination, but her expression seemed to harden up a tiny bit.

"I know you've been dying to get away from us all," she said with a laugh, and Ben heard a slight edge to the sound.

"So you can skedaddle with Jay and Sean if you want. Just keep your phone on you so I can let you know when to come back for dinner."

She smiled at her nephews, and walked back up the stairs.

"You can come back to our place if you want," Jay told Ben. "We can play some video games or something."

"No, listen," Sean cut in, "We promised Uncle Thomas that you'd visit him."

"Uncle Thomas?" Ben asked. "I have an Uncle Thomas? Who's he?"

"Grandad's older brother," said Sean, peeling some white paint off the wall absently. "He's about one hundred and five. He wants to see who's carrying on the new generation of Diamants."

"We've already been subjected to an hour of his questions and instant coffee," added Jay. "So we figure you should get it over with and just go there now."

Ben frowned. "Do I have to? It's not like my name is even Diamant. I'm not carrying on any new generations for him."

"Come on, he's really old," said Sean. "He's probably going to die in about five minutes anyway. Give him a break."

Ben sighed resignedly. "Are you guys coming with me?"

Jay and Sean spoke together. "No!"

"Aw, come on!" Ben pleaded. "You dropped me into this! I don't even know him. I'm not going to just wander in and hang out with some old guy I've never met."

Sean looked at his younger brother. "We could go for a while," he conceded.

Jay frowned. "No way. My stomach lining will never be the same after Tuesday."

"Get over yourself," said Sean. "No one's forcing you to drink his coffee. Come on."

# CHAPTER THREE

# The Fire

Ben sat in a frayed armchair, clutching a cup of instant coffee while his old, gnarled Great-Uncle Thomas peered at him from the couch opposite. A small fire burned in the grate despite the summer heat outside, but otherwise Thomas's house was dim and slightly musty. Ben wondered why old people didn't seem to have the same access to light bulbs as other people. He shifted slightly in his seat, wishing he'd had a shower before he'd left.

Jay and Sean were seated at the nearby table, just out of Uncle Thomas's eye line. Jay inspected the ceiling while Sean gazed at a painting of a fruit bowl on the wall. They'd already gone past the introductions and how-are-yous, and now Uncle Thomas seemed intent on staring at Ben for a while.

"Well gosh, is that the time?" Jay boomed suddenly, looking at his bare wrist. "Come on, Sean. Time to help Dad with... with that thing at that place."

"Oh, yeah!" said Sean loudly. "Thanks for reminding me."

The two stood up from the table. "Bye," they chorused.

The old man nodded in their direction and Ben watched desperately as his so-called allies escaped. The front door closed behind them, closing off the brief flash of sunlight and fresh air.

He stared into his coffee, wondering what to say now that he didn't have his cousins as a buffer. He moved the cup in circles, watching the watery liquid swish around.

Suddenly Uncle Thomas broke the silence in a surprisingly strong voice. "You look like your father David. Not much like our side of the family."

"Uh, yeah," Ben shifted uncomfortably on the scratchy armchair. "Everyone says that."

"Course they bloody do!" barked Uncle Thomas. "You're half his genes. I'd be suspicious of young Susan if you looked like your postman."

Ben hesitated before answering. "Um, our postman's actually a woman."

"Even more suspicious then!" said Uncle Thomas. "What with modern technology and all those new jing jangs."

Ben looked around a little desperately as the silence settled in again.

"So, uh, you live here long?" he asked, searching for something to say to break the silence.

"I was born in Carmenton," replied Uncle Thomas. "In the new hospital."

Ben was confused. "What? Is it new now?" he asked.

His uncle eyed him. "Of course not, son," he said. "It's long gone. It was new when I was born there. Other one burnt down."

Ben's eyes lit up, remembering the ruins of the houses he'd seen the night before.

"In a fire?" he asked curiously.

Uncle Thomas looked at him as if Ben was slightly lacking his faculties.

"You're a quick young man," he said. "Of course it was

burnt down in a fire; it wasn't burnt down in a bloody snow storm."

"No, no," Ben said, glad he finally had something to talk about with the old man. "I meant was it the same fire that burnt down all those houses?"

The ancient creature opposite him stroked his chin thoughtfully like a grandfather from a fairy story. "Yes," he intoned. "Happened ten years before I was born."

"So what went down?" asked Ben. "How did it start? And why are the houses still there?"

Uncle Thomas sensed a potentially captive audience and settled back in his chair. "It's a long story…"

Ben fidgeted with his cup for a second. He didn't really want to be stuck in this musty old house for too much longer, but…

"I've got a while," he said determinedly.

"Do you want the long version, or the short one?"

Ben hesitated, not sure what he was getting himself into. "The medium one?" he asked hopefully.

The old man assented with a wave of his hand, and started to speak.

"Back about two hundred years ago, Carmenton wasn't really a town – it was a collection of houses owned by people who didn't want to live in society. Hermits, really. Mostly ex-convicts who had made some money and came up here to get away from their pasts. Some of them were stonemasons and carpenters and they built beautiful, big houses, all close together. They farmed the land. They had children. Some moved away and some stayed. They had a shop, a hospital. There were about four hundred people here. And they lived in peace and harmony, young man. There wasn't any of this pointless bickering like you get nowadays. They got on with the job at hand."

The old man stared into the fire, then looked up at Ben suddenly.

"My parents, your grandfather's parents – Benjamin and Beatrice Diamant, may they rest in peace – were the children of the children of those convicts. It was a good, strong family, ours, all boys, all strapping young lads, just like those cousins of yours who just snuck out of here with that flimsy excuse about 'that thing in that place'."

Ben suppressed a smile. His great-uncle was sharper than he'd thought.

The old man continued his tale. "One night, must have been about a hundred years ago now, back before I was born, a fire started in one of the houses, and it spread. There was enough time to get most of the people out before they got caught in the flames, but there was no fire station so the fire raged on for days and days. This was before modern things, young man, before you could turn on big hydraulics to stop the flames. The houses were built so well that the walls didn't burn as much as they could have, but everything inside was lost."

Uncle Thomas looked sadly into the fire as if he could remember the tragedy that happened a decade before he was born.

"Everyone gathered together and watched the fire as it finally smouldered down into embers, until they had to accept that some people just weren't coming out of there. And in that time of tragedy, they found that they wanted to talk to one another, and maybe they weren't as hermit-like as their parent's parents were."

The old man sat up straighter in his chair as he concluded his story.

"When they decided to rebuild the town, there was too

much grief associated with the old houses, and so they started fresh and rebuilt the town a few miles west of the original town site. The government gave them some land, which was generous as the people hadn't actually owned the land they built on originally. The town spread, people moved here, and now," he concluded, with a hint of irony in his voice, "it even has its own tourist bureau, as empty as that place may be."

Uncle Thomas looked at Ben, who sat transfixed by the tale.

"And that's the sad story of the fire, son," the old man said. "Only one house remained standing."

Ben immediately thought of the intact house he'd seen the previous night.

"Does anyone live there?" he asked.

Uncle Thomas stroked his chin again and gazed into the dying embers of the fire.

"Maybe, maybe not. Apparently people see an old lady walking in and out of there sometimes." He shrugged his thin shoulders. "I never have. Probably just a ghost story to keep the local kids out of the houses."

Ben looked at his great-uncle. "Uh, yeah, probably."

"To see that house, you'd think that the fire never touched it," Uncle Thomas said.

In Ben's mind, logic overrode any spooky flights of fancy. "Well, it probably didn't then," he said.

"But that's the strange thing," the old man continued mysteriously.

"What?"

"Apparently that's the house where the whole fire started."

## - CHAPTER FOUR -
# A Really Big Graveyard

Ben walked slowly along the deserted road with his skateboard under one arm, staring at the ruined houses that lined the street. There were no driveways and the road was cobbled, not paved. He felt a little invasive. From the stillness around him, it looked like the locals left the area well alone.

He thought about where his great-uncle had said the fire started. It sounded impossible. Uncle Thomas had to be pushing at least ninety. He probably liked making up mysterious stories, or maybe they just made themselves up in his head.

Ben studied what was left of the houses as he slowly passed. Most of them looked like they had once been two storeys tall. Some had the remains of a short flight of steps leading up to a big porch. The walls and roofs had fancy edging and there were some crumbling turrets still standing.

Seeing the ruined houses gave him a strange feeling. He could see scorch marks all over them, and many had whole walls and roofs missing. Piles of black rubble lay on the ground, almost leaking into the ground with age. There wasn't a trace of greenery or foliage anywhere, and the yards were all grey, lifeless dirt with a few patches of long, dead grass. He couldn't see a single house that didn't have major damage until he slowed to a halt before the house he'd seen the night before.

His uncle had been right about one thing. In stark contrast to the buildings around it, the old grey mansion seemed untouched by fire, and there weren't any obvious repair marks. Ben dropped his skateboard and rolled it back and forward underneath his foot as he stared up at the house.

In the light of day, the house looked less like a haunted mansion and more like a past testament to faded grandeur. Suddenly his ideas about seeing a person sitting on the porch seemed silly. Last night had been spooky, yes, but he was a logical person who didn't believe in any ghost nonsense. He certainly didn't believe those stories about seeing transparent people in the mirror and objects flying around of their own accord, so he should really get a grip on himself.

Well, there was one way of finding out if someone lived there or not. Without even thinking about what he would say to the occupant, he marched up the porch steps and knocked on the door. The noise echoed around the silent neighbourhood and Ben cringed, but the house remained silent. After a minute of waiting he knocked again, a little quieter this time, but there was still no response. Ben shrugged to himself, determined not read anything mysterious into it.

Obviously whoever lived there – if there was anyone – wasn't into house calls. Besides, he thought, what would he say to the person who answered the door? It wasn't as if he could voice what was really on his mind: "Hi, just wanted to make sure you're not a ghost." Or, "Hey, how come this house didn't burn down like the others?"

He turned, walked down the steps, and scooped his skateboard from the road. Just as he straightened, he had a strange feeling he was being watched, and he snapped his head around towards the mansion. There, in an upstairs window, the outline of a person looked down at him. It stayed at the window for only a few seconds while Ben stared, then it disappeared.

He stood gazing up at the window. So somebody did live there. He ran back up the steps and knocked again. "Hello?" he called through the door. "Hi, is anyone there?"

Perhaps the house's inhabitant had just stepped out of the shower and was getting dressed. Perhaps they'd just woken from a nap and hadn't realised someone was at the door. Perhaps neighbourhood kids knocked on the door all the time, and the resident had gotten tired of answering the door to find no one there. Or perhaps, Ben conceded after waiting for a few minutes, whoever it was simply had no interest in talking to him at all. He walked back down the steps, turned, and headed in the direction of home.

Fifteen minutes later, he snuck up the steps to his house. If he was lucky, he could get inside, have a quick shower and be gone again before his parents spotted him.

"Ben!"

Damn.

His mother stood up from the couch. "What are you doing this afternoon?"

"I'm going over to Jay and Sean's place to hang out."

"Well," she said, exchanging a look with her husband. "When you get back, perhaps you could start looking over those university brochures."

"Yes, Mother," Ben replied, staring at the ceiling.

"I know you think I'm going on about it," she said. "But it's time you took this seriously. If you hadn't missed the application deadline, we wouldn't be having this conversation."

"I know," he said, a little guiltily.

"You're practically an adult now," she continued. "It's time you proved it."

"I know," he repeated, his voice starting to rise. "And I'm sorry. But it's just not that easy!"

His father spoke. "Ben, calm down. Your mother's right. This has gone on for too long now."

"I know, I know," he groaned.

"I don't want to get into it now," Susan said. "But I'm serious. Read the brochures. Visit the websites. Call up and speak to the academics if you have to. If you want to defer university, or not go at all, you know we'll support you. But you have to decide something soon, before it's too late."

"Yes. Okay," Ben said, inching towards his bedroom. "Can I please be excused now?"

"Of course," his mother said, biting her lip.

Ben stood under the spray of the shower and thought about the backpack full of leaflets that he'd thrown in the corner of his room the day before. In that bag was his future. Well, the educational and social side of it anyway. But no matter what he did or how many pieces of paper he pawed through, he couldn't muster enthusiasm for any of it.

He grabbed a towel and dried himself off, then threw it over the silver railing, which creaked dangerously and shifted another inch out of the wall. He'd get to the brochures later. Maybe tomorrow.

He pulled some clothes on, then slipped out of the house and headed in the direction of his cousins' house.

~

"*Predator. Rocky.* I haven't seen that for years. *Easy Rider. The*

*Shining*."

Sean surveyed the movies in his father's collection as Ben and Jay slumped in armchairs.

"You guys lived here for years, right?" Ben began.

"Don't rub it in," said Jay.

"Doesn't it fascinate you that there's a ghost town in your own backyard?"

Jay laughed.

"Sure," he said. "Up to the age of ten, when our parents were warning us every day about not going in there. Then we turned thirteen, joined a gang, and we explored a couple of the houses. It's no big deal, man. It's just a really big graveyard."

Sean sat on the arm of Jay's chair. "A few people wanted to bulldoze it and put up new houses," he said. "But practically everyone in this town has ancestors who died in the fire so there's too much respect. They want to leave it as it was. It's not like they need the extra land around here."

"Who does the land belong to?" Ben asked. A thought struck him. "Do you know who owns that house that still stands?"

"I'm not sure," said Jay. "They say the people who built the houses were squatters, so they didn't own the land. The government did."

"So the government owns that house," Ben mused.

"Maybe," said Jay. "But I think the land went on sale and the houses were bought by some guy years ago, way before we were born, I think. But he doesn't do anything with them."

"What do you mean?" said Ben. "Why would you buy land you don't use? You'd rent it out, or farm it, or something. Make money from it."

"Not always," said Sean. "Loads of properties and houses just sit vacant – the owners are too old to care, or moved away years ago, or they own so much land that it's just another title deed in their portfolio."

Ben squinted at his cousin. "How do you know that?" he asked.

Sean shrugged. "It's property one-oh-one, Benny boy," he said. "Everyone knows that stuff."

"So either the government owns those houses, or some guy no one's seen for years," Ben summarised, getting back to the point. "What about new squatters? What happens when they move in?"

"Squatters?" Jay cut in incredulously. "You mean like homeless people? Here? In this town? A hundred k's from any other sign of life? It doesn't happen."

"Sam Adamson slept in one that night he ran away, back when I was about twelve," Sean remembered. "We all said he wouldn't last until morning but he did. He said it wasn't a big deal but we all knew he was a bit freaked out by the fact that people died there."

"And those kids got busted for graffiti that time," said Jay. "Their parents were just visiting. They left pretty soon, too, because anyone who'd been able to get their hands on any of the kids would have put the boot in."

"What about the house that someone still lives in?" Ben asked.

"I don't think they spray-painted anything on that one," said Jay.

"No," said Ben. "I mean, what's the deal there? Who on earth would live in a house in the middle of a burned down town?"

The two brothers exchanged glances.

"Someone that can't let go of the past," Sean said. "Look Ben, we went through the theories when we were younger –

maybe that house is a centre for drug trafficking, maybe it's a brothel, whatever. But the fact is, it's just some lady who still feels that same way as the people who built the houses in the first place. She doesn't like society. So everyone just leaves her alone."

"Some people just want to be left to do their own thing," said Jay. "I guess she's one of them."

"Yeah," said Ben. "I guess. But I just think there's more to the story."

"Come on, don't be that guy," said Jay, rolling his eyes.

"What?"

"You know. The caped crusader who storms into town and tries to whip it into shape. It's just some grey-haired lady, Ben. Leave the old bird alone."

## - CHAPTER FIVE -

# A Conversation

The next day Ben walked away from the local skate park, massaging his knee. He'd just stacked it in front of a load of pre-teens who were way better at skateboarding than he was.

He wandered across the oval, glancing around as he went, checking out the skate park, the kid's playground, the lawn bowls area, and the green slope up the hill with the park bench almost hidden in the shadow of the trees. He almost looked past it when he realised the park bench wasn't empty. He shaded the sun from his eyes, and he could just make out a figure in a dark cloak sitting quietly.

Senses on red alert, Ben stared for a minute. Could that be the person he'd seen before, on the porch and in the window of the mansion? Curiosity took over, and he slowly skirted around the oval and up to the bench, where the cloaked figure sat still and silent.

"Hi," he said nervously.

The figure swivelled around quickly, obviously surprised at Ben's approach. Ben gazed at the face looking at him. It belonged to a young woman with dark eyes and long black hair, who looked like she was in her early twenties. Before he had a chance to study her properly, her head turned away from him again, and he fidgeted with his skateboard nervously.

"Hi," he said again. The girl did not move.

"Helloooo," he tried.

Finally the girl spoke. "Hello. It's nice of you to come over but I would rather be left alone to enjoy the view."

He glanced in the direction she was facing. It was an expanse of grass with a road beyond, which wasn't much to look at. He shifted his weight, deciding what to do. He didn't want to leave. He wanted to know about this person, but wasn't sure how to engage her in conversation.

"Um, this'll probably sound like a strange question," he said, plunging in. "But do you live in that house in the burnt area of town? The house that still looks okay?"

"No," said the girl shortly.

"Oh," he said, disappointed. "Uh, are you sure?"

The girl looked up at him. "Yes, I'm sure."

Ben's previous experiences that involved approaching girls gave him the distinct impression she wanted him to get lost. He hesitated, knowing he should leave, but something compelled him to stay for a few moments longer.

"So are you from around here?" he asked.

"I'm just passing through," she said shortly. "Now, if you would be so kind as to excuse me, I must depart."

"Wait," he said as the girl started to rise from the bench. "I thought… I thought I saw you. I mean, someone who looked just like you. In a house, one of the houses over to the east."

"I'm not sure what you're referring to," said the girl shortly, gathering her black cloak around her and pulling the hood tighter around her face.

Ben continued, feeling like he needed to explain himself. "I thought I saw a person when we drove past the house that night. I thought it must have been the same person. And when

I saw you sitting here, well, I guess I thought it was you."

"It wasn't," the girl said in the same clipped tone.

"Well, where are you from then?" he asked, trying to stall her departure. To his surprise, the girl turned to him and with her eyes slightly averted to the trees beyond, she started speaking quickly.

"I'm just passing through this town," she said. "I arrived last week and plan to leave tomorrow. I decided to visit because this district has some interesting things to see. It's been very pleasant to talk to you but I have a lot of things to do. Good day."

"Uh, right," he said, a little stunned at the fast speech.

The girl took a few steps away from him, but didn't turn straight away. She looked at him, her brow slightly furrowed, but didn't say anything else.

"I'm not staying long in this town either," Ben said awkwardly. "Did you want to hang out a bit longer? It'd be good to have someone to talk to."

The girl didn't reply so he kept talking. "This is a weird town, with that fire and all. We drove through the burned bit the other night. Pretty freaky."

He paused, realising he may have sounded rude, and heard the girl say almost to herself, "that was you?"

"Yeah," said Ben, not sure he'd heard her correctly. "What do you mean? Don't people drive through there all the time?"

"No," the girl said softly. "Hardly ever."

The two stood facing each other. "You are the one that lives in that house," he stated.

The girl looked around anxiously then took a step backwards "I really must depart."

"Don't go!" Ben said; he was so close to knowing more of this strange story. "Please tell me. You do live there, don't you?"

The girl's eyes dropped and she stared at Ben's hands as he switched his skateboard nervously from one hand to another.

"Why must you know?" she asked in barely a whisper.

"I don't know," he said truthfully. "I just feel like... this is a little town in the middle of nowhere and there's this crazy story about a fire, and a bunch of burned down houses with one left standing in the middle. Just left there! For a hundred years! The story really fascinates me, but no one else seems to care. It's the one different thing about this town, but everyone else seems totally not interested. It's weird."

The girl seemed to forget her planned exit for a second. "Why do you think no one else is interested?" she asked him.

Ben was surprised at the question. "I guess everyone who grew up here is used to the story," he said. "And my parents have other stuff on their minds. But it's not like everyone already knows all the details. My own cousins lived here for the whole time they were kids, and they don't even know the name of the person who lives there. It's like I'm the only one who cares."

The girl stared at him for a minute. There was curiosity in her eyes.

Ben spoke to cover the awkward silence. "My mother's side of the family came from this town," he said. "But I don't know anything about it. To come here and find out that there's a whole story about a fire that happened so long ago and all this weird history and I never had any idea! Then there's one house that didn't burn down and someone still lives there and here I am speaking to you and you may just be that person... so can you please tell me, are you the one who lives there?"

The girl's straight posture sagged slightly as something seemed to give way inside her, and she dropped to the bench and bowed her head. "Yes," she said in barely a whisper. "I live in the house that didn't burn."

"Look," Ben said a little desperately, "I'd really like to talk to you." He looked appealingly at the girl, whose face softened slightly. Taking this as a sign of encouragement, he sat down.

"So," he started, "how long have you lived there?"

The woman gave a soft but bitter laugh. "A long time."

"Okay, so you're obviously not just passing through then," he said. "What's your name?"

There was a silence as the woman stared at the trees in the distance.

Ben coughed awkwardly. He wasn't very good at this. "Come on, you must have a name."

The woman looked down at her hands. "My name… is Verla."

"Nice to meet you, Verla. I'm Ben." He paused, wondering what to say next. "Verla's a nice name."

"Thank you."

"So… what do you do for a living?"

"For a living?" Verla looked around anxiously and stood up. "I… I… I'm sorry. I have to go."

She gathered her cloak around her and walked off quickly into the trees behind the bench. Ben sighed and stood up too. He bent to scoop up his skateboard, and when he looked in Verla's direction, she'd gone.

## - CHAPTER SIX -

# A Short Note

"Wow, man. I can't believe you met her." Jay looked impressed. "I've lived in this town since forever, and I've never even seen the person who lives there. I take back what I said about the caped crusader. You can be Sherlock Holmes instead."

The three cousins were scattered around the living room while their two sets of parents were out on the balcony, drinking merlot and talking loudly. The boys had come inside when Jonathan had produced his guitar and announced a sing-along. Thankfully their yowling choruses had been short-lived, and they were back to telling each other off for not visiting each other more often.

"You can't tell anyone, okay?" said Ben. "It was hard enough getting it out of her, and I totally got the idea it's not something she'd like me to spread around."

"I thought she was a myth," mused Sean. "Like a story made up to keep kids away from the old town."

Ben stared out the window. "She's not," he said. "She's not a total myth. But it's like she's not one hundred per cent real either."

Sean's eyes became wide. He was two years into a

psychology degree and Ben started to feel a little uncomfortable under his scrutinising stare.

"What do you mean by not real?" Sean asked, leaning forward in his chair.

Ben shrugged. "Listen, I don't believe in fairies or elves or leprechauns, okay?" he said. "Let's just make that clear right now. But if I had to say that anything might have a slightly, well, unearthly quality, it's be her."

Sean looked like he'd like to start writing notes. "Like... like an alien or something?" he asked.

"Yeah. No," Ben faltered. "Look, I've never met an alien, I can't really compare it."

"She's probably just a hermit," Jay declared. "Or really depressed. Or just antisocial."

"No," Ben disagreed. "It was something – different."

"Maybe you don't want to know," Jay suggested. "What if she's one of those girls who totally ignores you, then as soon as you show an interest in them, they start to stalk you? You didn't give her your number, did you? She could be outside the window watching us right now." He gave an exaggerated shiver.

"She really didn't seem like the type," Ben said, wondering why he was so intent on defending her.

Jay changed tack. "You're obviously into her! Just admit it, you tried to ask her out."

"Did you get her number?" Sean broke in.

Ben shook his head. "No, it wasn't like that at all," he said. "I wasn't thinking about that sort of thing. I just wanted to find out who she was and why she looked so sad."

"You only met her once," Sean pointed out. "This two-minute conversation you had really seems to be bugging you."

"Yeah," agreed Ben. "But I just... I feel like I know her.

Like she needs someone to break through to her, and maybe she's never had anyone try to, and there's a reason I met her."

"I think you're reading far too much into one conversation," Jay decided. "You say three words to a girl, and you're convinced she's E.T. or something. You need to get out more."

"I tend to agree," said Sean apologetically. "I think the boredom of being here is starting to affect you."

Ben sighed, feeling foolish. "You're probably right."

"Look, just go back to her house if you want to know more about her," suggested Sean. "It's not like you don't know where she lives."

"Actually, I've already tried that," Ben admitted. "I went there this afternoon after our weird conversation. She wouldn't answer the door."

"Well if she won't answer the door and you don't have her number or email address, go the old-fashioned way," Jay commanded. "Write her a letter. Slip it under her door. And just hope that she knows how to read."

~

Positioned at the shabby old desk in his room later that night, Ben wondered what to write. "Hi, I have an insatiable curiosity about why you live in that big house, if you give me your life's history I'll leave you alone." Well, that was partly true at least, but not exactly something you could tell a person directly. He couldn't even understand himself why he was so intent on prying into this girl's life. He just had a feeling she needed help. This Verla girl looked like she was going through a pretty hard time. A harder time than Ben could really understand.

Finally, after a few drafts, he settled on a short note:

*Dear Verla. I really hope that's how you spell your name. I don't want to pry into your life. But you look so sad and lonely and I really want to find out who you are. So maybe if you would open your door some time maybe we could have a cup of coffee or something and you could tell me about yourself. From Ben.*

~

The next morning, Ben bounded from the house while the rest of his family was still eating breakfast.

"Where are you off to, love?" Susan called as he was starting down the steps.

"Just going for a walk," he said. "Then I'll swing by and see what Jay and Sean are up to."

"Got your phone?"

"Yeah," he shouted over his shoulder, clattering down the wooden steps.

He strode down the street with his skateboard under his arm. After yesterday's fall at the skate park, he didn't want to risk flying down the hill and going through someone's window. Once he was at the bottom of the hill, he stepped onto the skateboard and set off along the footpath towards the oval.

He flipped his skateboard under his arm and walked past the skate park, going a few hundred metres to the slope with the park bench. It was unoccupied, and Ben frowned. He had hoped Verla would be there, and he could forget about his stupid note and talk to her instead.

"Like this was going to be easy," he mumbled, walking past the bench into the cluster of trees that lined the oval. If his calculations were correct, the deserted area of town should be straight ahead.

Ben felt like an intruder as the trees thinned and he found himself behind one of the crumbling mansions. He picked his way through the rubble along the side of the house, looking up at the blackened walls curiously. Windows were spaced at regular intervals, but he couldn't see any glass in them. He glanced through one of them as he passed, and saw a room lit by sunlight that came streaming through the ruined roof and damaged second storey. A few half-burned wooden structures were dotted around the mossy floor, which Ben supposed had once been furniture. He wondered if all the bodies had been found and removed after the fire, and an involuntary shiver went through him. Of course they had, he told himself. There would have been funerals and the bodies buried or cremated a long time ago. People died in houses all the time and they were never just left there.

He reached the cobbled street and tried to get his bearings. If the oval was behind him, the street where he was standing would be parallel to the street that Verla's house was on. He walked across the street and through the yards of two more old ruins, hoping none of the Carmenton locals would see him and think he was a vandal. He was pretty sure the next street was the right one, so he set off, gazing left and right at the strange houses he passed.

Finally he reached the dark mansion. It wasn't as foreboding now that he'd met the occupant and she seemed remarkably harmless, if a bit vague and reclusive. Ben climbed the steps and knocked on the door.

He didn't expect an answer, and none came. He took the crumpled note out of his pocket and slid it under the solid wooden door.

Walking away from the house, he allowed himself a

backward glance. He wondered if Verla was watching from the windows. He turned left at a corner with a mansion with two half-destroyed turrets poking mournfully out the top, and was soon walking down a tree-lined road back onto the suburban street his family had driven along the first night they came to town.

The phone in his pocket beeped loudly as he walked, and Ben took it out to check. Two missed calls from his mother – how had he not heard them come through? And a text from Jay, inviting him to come over to watch some movies. Ben walked along the street until his phone showed two bars of reception, then after calling his mother to reassure her that he was still alive, he phoned Jay's number.

"We dug through Dad's collection to get some real gems for you," Jay told him, static crackling down the line. "How's this for a brilliant movie marathon? Drum roll, please! And we have: *House on Haunted Hill*, *The Amityville Horror*, and *The Haunting*."

"You are just… annoying," Ben grumbled, but he had to laugh. "Does he actually own those? Or are you just making it up?"

"I'm not kidding!" Jay protested. "They're all originals as well; Dad's a purist when it comes to horror movies. We're actually looking forward to it. Sean and I haven't had a horror marathon in ages, and Dad's up for it too – he's going to make popcorn, old-school style. Mum said she'd rather watch *Sleepless in Seattle* in her room." Jay sighed, sounding disgusted. "How stereotypical! So are you in?"

"Yep, okay," Ben decided. "May as well enjoy the incredibly believable plots and realism."

"You say that now, but I bet you don't sleep a wink tonight," Jay predicted. "What are you doing now?"

"Just going for a walk."

"Oh yeah? Does that happen to involve walking back and forward in front of a big old house?"

"I walked past once," Ben said defensively.

"Yeah right, stalker," Jay laughed. "If you're done harassing that poor girl, come over now. That house isn't going to look so appealing after three rounds of bloodbath movies."

Ben picked up his pace. "Yeah yeah, okay. I'm on my way now. See you soon."

~

Ben walked slowly through the streets of Carmenton on his way home from his cousins' house. The streetlights illuminated the fences and cars lining the road in a soft glow, but otherwise the streets were dark and shadowy. He shivered involuntarily as the warm breeze rustled through the bushes, then jumped violently as a small black silhouette darted across the street in front of him. Just a cat, he told himself. Just a cat.

The impact of five hours of non-stop horror movies had been lessened by a rowdy dinner afterwards with his uncle, aunt and cousins, but Ben couldn't completely shake a feeling of nervousness as he made his way along the dark sidewalk. He was glad when he started up the slope and finally reached the old weatherboard house. Inside, his parents were sitting around the table talking while Tia sat in front of the old television, watching a cartoon.

"Hi, hon," said his mother, looking up as he walked in. "Did you have a good time?"

"Yeah," said Ben. "Although I think I'm done with horror movies for a while."

"Jonathan's always loved them," said Susan. "He made me

watch Dracula when I was only five. I think I've had a fear of coffins ever since."

"Yeah, well. I'm not surprised."

"We're going to Katoomba tomorrow morning. Want to come?"

"What time?"

"Leaving about nine."

"Yeah, okay." They'd passed through the town of Katoomba on the way to Carmenton, and it didn't look too bad.

"Ben," said a high-pitched voice, and he looked down to see his sister standing at his elbow. "Do you want to watch a cartoon with me?"

"Uh, no thanks, sorry," Ben said. "I think I'll just go relax for a while," he told his parents, while Tia walked away despondently and plopped back down in front of the television.

Ben went to his room and lay back on his bed. He took out his phone and tried to check his email and social media feeds, but there wasn't enough reception for them to load. He threw the phone on the bedside table, picked a book at random out of his bag, and lay back to read.

## - CHAPTER SEVEN -

# The Photograph

The next day Ben woke up early. After a quick shower he sat on the balcony watching the town below him come to life. He could see glimpses of cars starting and heading towards the highway to the east. He wondered idly where they were going, and what their occupants did for a living.

Seven-thirty. Over an hour to go before the Katoomba trip. He got up, scribbled a note to his parents and quickly walked out of the house and through the streets towards the burned village. Despite the horror movies of the day before, the old houses didn't give him a sense of dread, just sadness.

To his surprise, as he neared the mansion, he saw a small figure perched on a chair on the porch, dressed in a long black skirt and a plain black long-sleeved top.

"Hi!" he called, waving.

"I thought you might visit," Verla said softly when Ben was near enough to hear her. She placed a book down next to her chair.

"Did you?" he said, surprised at the almost-warm reception. "Oh. I hope you don't think I'm stalking you or anything."

"Stalking?" asked Verla, looking curious.

"But I'm not," he hurried on. "I just thought I'd come by to see how you're doing, see if you wanted to have a chat. It was nice to meet you yesterday."

"It was nice to meet you too," she said. "Ben is your name, yes? I'm sorry if I lacked manners yesterday. It's just that I haven't talked to anyone for longer than a few minutes in a long, long time."

"Why not?" he asked, sitting down on the porch step.

She hesitated before answering. "People tend to… leave me alone," she said. "Aside from the last Mormon that knocked on my door a few years ago, and a couple of people that have approached me in the park like you did… it's been a while."

He nodded. "Yeah, I guess it'd seem like a long time if you live alone like this."

"Yes," said Verla, then she paused. "Yes. Ben. I appreciate the conversation… but you said you want to help me. I'm fine. Everything is how it has to be."

"What do you mean?" he asked.

"I mean that my situation is exactly what it is meant to be."

"Sorry," he said, confused. "I still don't understand."

"I mean… there's nothing anyone can do to change the way things are," said Verla. "I know you are curious about why I live here. But you must be content with my answer: that I live here because I have to. There is no other reason."

Ben was about to ask further but suddenly sensed that it was quite a big deal for Verla to be talking about this at all – and it really was none of his business anyway.

"Well," he said slowly. "Verla. Even if there's nothing I can do to help you, I'd still like to be your friend."

She looked very surprised, as if she had never heard such a strange proposition before.

"Oh!" she said, looking at him as if she was a dermatologist and he was sporting a particularly fascinating skin disease. He began to feel uncomfortable. Finally she said cautiously: "Do you feel well?"

Ben figured friends of Verla's must be more formal than his mates from school, but he decided to respond in kind. "Thank you, Verla, I'm fine, um, how are you?"

She was still staring at him closely. "Are you sure?" she asked. "You don't feel… unwell or distressed at all?"

"I'm starting to feel a little twitchy with you staring at me like that," he said. "Otherwise, I'm all good."

She still looked confused, but nodded slowly. "In that case, Ben," she said. "Perhaps we will be able to be friends."

Ben glanced at his watch. Eight-thirty.

"I have to go, but can I drop by tomorrow?" he asked.

She looked up at him, again letting a long pause settle into the conversation before she spoke. "I will be here."

~

Ben and Verla sat quietly on the front porch of her house, and Ben looked sideways at his new friend. Their conversations so far seemed to consist of him asking questions, then lengthy pauses before she'd answer monosyllabically. So far he'd found out that no, she'd never tried skateboarding, yes, she lived alone, and no, she didn't have a car.

Still, it was nice to talk to someone who wasn't his parents or little sister, especially as he'd been stuck trailing them around arty little shops the day before. Jay and Sean had gone camping for a few days and invited him along, but Ben had declined the invitation. He'd rather be stuck in this town than sleep in a tent, battling snakes and mosquitoes all night.

"Tell me about your family, Ben," invited Verla, surprising him with a question of her own.

He shrugged. "There's not much to tell," he said. "There's my dad, who's pretty typical as dads go. You know, tells terrible jokes, wears shirts with unfunny slogans on them – the usual. I mean, I guess he's not bad. He does publicity for writers. He's on a break from work right now, which is why we're staying here for a few weeks."

"And your mother?" Verla asked.

"She's pretty okay, actually," he admitted. "She can be a little strange sometimes, a bit too fond of cleaning I reckon, but she's strong. Knows what she wants. When I was young it really annoyed me but I guess as you get older you appreciate this stuff. She stands up for herself, and other people if she cares about them. She hasn't been too happy with me lately. She reckons I'm not putting enough thought into my future so she's been giving me a hard time about it."

"Do you have brothers or sisters?" Verla queried.

Ben looked at her and laughed. "Wow, you really want to know about my family!" he said.

She looked embarrassed. "I am so sorry," she said quickly. "I did not mean to pry."

"Oh, no it's okay," he hastened to reassure her. "I have a sister, and she's a bit of a brat. A lot of the time she's okay but sometimes she'll do things just to annoy me."

"How old is she?" Verla asked.

"Only seven. I was ten when she was born, but my parents really wanted another kid. My mother went through a few rounds of IVF before it worked, and I know she was pretty chuffed when she found out it was a girl. She has two brothers and my cousins are all boys so she was happy to have a bit more balance in the family."

"What is IVF?" Verla asked.

"It's when women can't seem to get pregnant for whatever reason, so the doctors make the embryo all ready to start growing before they plant it in the womb," he told her.

Verla looked uncomfortable. "You are very open about such matters," she observed.

"Oh, don't worry, my mother doesn't mind," he said. "She started a support group for other parents and everything. She even went on television once to be interviewed about it."

Verla stared off into the distance for a moment before speaking again.

"I only had males in my family, too," she said. "All men! My mother and I were very close because of that."

"Where is your family, Verla?" asked Ben, seizing the opportunity to find out why she lived alone.

But Verla had placed her hand over her mouth.

"I did not mean to say that," she whispered.

"It's okay," he said awkwardly, not knowing how to respond. Verla looked so panicked, and all she'd said was that she was close to her mother. "Uh, want to hear about my uncles? They both play football. They think I'm strange because I don't play."

Verla sat back as Ben told her the story about the time he'd been made to play at a family barbecue and had ended up with concussion from a football to the head.

She laughed quietly at all the funny bits, but Ben sensed she was not getting much joy out of anything he said. And although he was glad he'd talked to her, there was still an expression behind her eyes that indicated something was very, very wrong.

~

That night, Ben lay fully-clothed on his bed, thinking. No one else seemed fascinated with Verla and her big house, and he felt a little foolish about his persistence with finding out what her story was. But he had a sense of curiosity, not just about the house but Verla herself, and he had a strange but distinct feeling that whatever was going on in her life, he could help her.

But she hadn't been particularly forthcoming about her circumstances, and everyone else was showing a frustrating lack of interest. What did people do when they were in this situation?

In the movies they trotted down to their local library, found a large dingy room with pools of sunlight dropping through the windows, and searched through huge, dusty tomes until they found the answer. But Ben didn't know what he was looking for in the first place. Maybe finding out more about the town's history would be a good start.

"Mum?" he called, jumping up from his bed. "Do you know if there's a library around here? Would it be open now? I need to look something up!"

"It's ten o'clock at night," his mother's voice floated back to him. "Can't you just Google it?"

Right, of course. Ben rolled his eyes at himself.

His phone still wouldn't connect to the internet, so he settled himself in front of his father's laptop in the lounge and brought up a search page. Feeling more than a bit like a stalker, he typed in 'Verla' and 'Carmenton'.

No results.

Like it was going to be that easy, he told himself – did he expect that she'd have a personal website with her full story detailed?

He searched for 'Carmenton fire' and scrolled through the results. Swimming carnivals from 1950 onwards. The official website for the bottle cap museum. After he'd clicked on a few dead ends, the website for the Carmenton Historical Society flashed up in front of him.

There was a page dedicated to the fire, with a few black and white photos of burned houses and a list of everyone who had died. Ben scanned through the names and felt a small pang when he saw the name 'Diamant' appearing a number of times. He'd had no idea his mother's ancestors had been so involved in this little town and its big tragedy.

The photo gallery contained sepia images of large, imposing houses: the mansions before the fires ruined their grandeur. Even though the pictures were faded and marked, he could see how beautiful the town must have been. There were groups of people posing stiffly in front of the houses, with the formal faces that usually appeared in the photographs of that time.

He scrolled through a whole page of these photos, and sighed to himself. It hadn't told him anything he didn't know already. He'd just have to go back and pester Verla again. At least she'd said they could be friends. He closed the lid of the laptop and with nothing better to do, went to bed to read his book for a while before going to sleep.

Hours later, Ben woke with a start, and lay in bed listening to the silence of the night. Something was sitting at the back of his mind, something was trying to tell him something…

He leapt out of bed, into the lounge room and back to the laptop. He hunted through the browser history to find the historical society's website, and clicked on the photo gallery. After scrolling past several images, he finally came to the one he was looking for. A picture of a man and a woman with three little boys and a teenage girl. Ben stared at the picture, then zoomed in impatiently. The girl's face stared at him, unsmiling and formal. She was dressed in a high-collared dress with a long flared skirt, which reminded him of some pictures he'd seen of Amish people. He looked from her clothes to her face, the dark eyes, the black hair and the now-familiar sombre expression.

"Oh no," Ben whispered. "Verla."

## - CHAPTER EIGHT -

# The Carmenton Historical Society

Ben stared at the clock on the wall of the dining room. It was one minute to nine in the morning. He rubbed his tired eyes, wishing he'd had more sleep.

The clock's ticked over to nine, and he snatched his phone up and dialled the contact number from the Carmenton Historical Society's website.

"Hello, Carmenton Hardware Supplies, how can I help you?" a female voice answered.

"Oh, sorry," said Ben, surprised. "I thought this was the number for the Historical Society,"

"It is, dear," said the voice. "My name's Glenys and I'm the secretary of the Society. What can I do for you?"

"My name's Ben," he told her. "I was looking at your website and I have some questions about the photographs there."

"Hold on a second," said Glenys, and Ben heard in the background, "Ed! Can you hold the fort for a minute?"

Glenys came back on the line. "Fire away, Ben."

"Those photographs of the people standing in front of the houses – are they real?"

"Real photos, you mean?" she said. "Yes, they're from the

collection of Gertie Beagle."

"Who was that?" he asked.

"Gertie and her husband Fred lived in Carmenton before the big fire," she told him. "Fred was the local photographer. He died in the fire, but Gertie managed to save a box of his photographs from the flames. She donated them to the society sometime in the fifties, just before she died."

"That was nice of her," he said. "Are all of the photos on that webpage from Gertie's collection?"

"All of them," Glenys confirmed.

"Have any of them been modified?"

"No, I don't think so," said Glenys. "My son scanned the originals straight into the computer then put them on the website. We thought about trying to restore them, but I think it's more authentic to leave the creases and blotches as-is. Keeps them real."

"So they are real," he said, a crease in his brow. "No modern ones managed to slip onto that page? Ones that may have looked similar but were taken recently?"

"Heavens, no," she said indignantly. "We take our roles very seriously at the Historical Society, and we make sure everything we put up there is the true history of our town. Every one of those photos was from Gertie's collection."

"Okay, thanks," he said, then decided to ask one more question. "It's just that I've been looking into the history of the town, especially the part about the fire. Do you know anything about that house that still stands?"

"Yes, for some reason it didn't catch fire properly, though some witnesses said they saw flames in that house first," said Glenys knowledgably. "Of course, that's quite implausible."

Ben took the plunge. "Do you know who lived there?"

"I'm not sure, dear. The problem with that fire is that

almost all the town burned – including the shire office where all the records and documents were kept. That doesn't make the Historical Society's job very easy! And with the land belonging to the government, no one had any deeds. I'd have to check the Society's accounts, but as I recall, it's believed that family all perished in the fire."

"There's a picture of that house on the website," said Ben slowly. "With a family standing in front."

"That could well be the family," said Glenys. "Terribly sad, I know."

Ben's throat started to constrict. "Who lives there now?" he croaked.

"I really don't know, dear. That house isn't really high on our agenda, when there are so many more interesting historical aspects of this town."

"Can you tell me anything else about it?" he asked.

"Not really, dear," she replied. "I don't think anyone's ever asked about it before."

There were voices in the background and Gladys said, "I have to run now, Ben, I have some customers."

"Okay," he said, reluctant to end the conversation. "Thanks for all your help."

"Anytime, dear," she said. "It's nice to know people are still interested in the history of our wonderful old town."

~

"What do you want from me?"

Verla stood framed by her doorway, staring at Ben standing on her porch. Sunlight lit the street behind him, illuminating the printout of the photo in his hand. A few tears leaked out of Verla's eyes as she glanced at the family in the picture, then back up at him.

After his conversation with Glenys that morning, Ben had convinced himself that the girl in the picture was not the same woman living in the house. It was probably her grandmother. Or more logically, given the timing, her great-grandmother. He wasn't sure if likeness was that hereditary through so many generations, but maybe there weren't that many people to go around, and there were more genes shared in this town than he'd like to think. He spared a thought for the fact that some of his ancestors had settled in this area, and hoped there hadn't been too much concentration of the gene pool in his own line.

Now, looking from the picture in his hand to the small woman standing in front of him in the doorway, he had no doubts. Unless Verla and her great granny were also twin sisters – which wasn't possible, no matter how undiluted her gene pool may have been – the girl in the picture and the woman staring at him were the same person, give or take a few years. It felt like something out of a dream.

"What do you want?" Verla repeated, almost hissing.

Ben hesitated. "I just want to know the truth about you."

"Why?" she looked on the verge of tears.

"I just feel like I have to find out," he said. "Why do you live in this big house alone? Why are you so sad? Why is this house still standing, if it's true that the fire started here? And why did I find a picture of you that must be about a hundred years old, and yet here you stand, looking like you're still in your twenties?"

Verla looked away from him, but he continued on. "Maybe this picture is from some fancy dress party you went to. Maybe this house belongs to your grandparents. Maybe you have a job and you're just like everyone else in this town. I don't know, maybe I'm imagining all of that. But I do know you're not happy. And I know I want to help you."

Verla sat down suddenly on the porch rocker, her head in her hands. Her long hair slid over her shoulders and the back of her neck was bare for a second. Ben spotted a small tattoo – a weird symbol above a row of numbers – but before he could make it out properly, she looked up at him, dashing her tears away with the back of her wrist.

"Verla," Ben said determinedly, "Who are you?"

She stood up and marched back into the house, slamming the door behind her.

Ben slumped onto the rocker that Verla had just vacated. He should leave. He should go back to his family and finish out this holiday hanging out with Jay and Sean. Spend some time with his folks before he moved away to university and they became mere names in his phone's contact list. He leaned forward and rested his arms on the railing of the porch. He should go.

Ten minutes later, he heard the door open and close behind him. Verla moved into his view and rested a small china cup full of water on the railing in front of him.

"I'm sorry, I don't have a range of beverages that I can offer you," she said. "I still have a well though, out at the back of the house, and the water has always been clean and clear."

He was surprised to see her again, and even more surprised to be offered a drink. Verla pulled the other rocker up next to his and settled into it, smoothing her long skirt neatly over her legs.

"The water tastes fine," he ventured.

She looked at him suddenly. "How much do you know about this town?" she asked.

"I know some of the history," he replied. "The settlers, the fire, how they rebuilt the town. The original town – the one that burnt down – it sounds like it must have been pretty cool."

Verla laughed softly. "It was… like you say… pretty cool," she murmured. She gazed out at the house across the street, a crumbling mansion with almost the entire west wall complete, but the rest falling in on itself. There was a moment of complete silence, then she bit her lip, looked at Ben, and spoke.

"It was a long time ago… there was my mother, my father, my three little brothers. We moved to this house when I was young, and we had quiet lives together. I went to the local school, and although my parents were quite introverted, I made some friends around town. Eventually I planned to go to the University of Sydney."

Verla stared down at her hands. "My parents often went out, up through the hills to see the stars. My father loved astronomy, and he knew all the names of the constellations. Sometimes I went with them, and we would lie there looking at the stars – I always felt such a connection to the stars and the sky, almost like they were my friends. One night my parents took my little brothers out to see the stars. I was home by myself. And that night, a strange thing happened – something that would change everything."

## - CHAPTER NINE -

# Wealth Beyond Measure

*Verla sat quietly in a chair in front of a large fireplace. The light from the flames sparkled onto the furnishings of the large room around her – chairs and tables upholstered in crimson red fabric, a large ornate rug, and several imposing portraits of sad faces on the walls.*

*She winced as her embroidery needle pricked the tip of her thumb. The sooner this pattern was finished, the better – it had been a silly choice to create a picture of her whole family in embroidery; it would have been much better to use her paints. A painted picture would have taken a lot less time to finish and would have looked more lifelike as well.*

*A spark flew out of the fire and landed on Verla's bare arm, and she flicked it off absently. Her parents would be home soon, and before they'd left they had asked her to think about entertaining the affections of William Ellis, who lived a few streets away. They were eager for Verla to find a husband, as the rest of her school friends were married and some had several children already. William had just returned from university and was setting up a medical practice in town, as Verla's mother had informed her at least six times. And apparently he was interested in her.*

*She had no qualms about getting to know William better – she had been friends with him in school – but before any sort of courtship commenced, she wanted to gauge his feelings about her application to university. Some of the men in the town were outraged that women had*

68

started getting the same education as men. She felt fortunate that her own father had no such feelings.

Verla's thoughts were interrupted by a knock at the door. She placed her embroidery hoop next to her chair, wondering who would be calling. She hoped it wasn't William; she didn't feel like having an in-depth discussion about women's rights at this hour.

A tall man wearing a top hat and morning coat looked up as Verla slowly opened the door. He appeared to be in his mid-forties, with a thin, arrogant face.

The man spoke in a smooth, low voice. "Good evening, my dear."

"Good evening, sir," Verla said politely. "I do apologise, but my parents are unable to receive visitors right now."

The tall gentleman swept past Verla into the room before she could stop him.

"It's you that I came to see, my dear," he said.

"I beg your pardon?" she said, alarmed. "I'm sorry, sir, but I do not know you."

The gentleman seated himself on one of the chairs by the fire and rested his top hat on his knees.

"My name is Mr Duncan. I have important business in this town tonight and I wished to see you while I was here."

"And why is that, sir?" she asked nervously. She glanced toward the open front door and wondered if she should seek refuge in a neighbour's home until her parents returned.

The man smiled. "I wish to ask for your hand in marriage."

Verla was astonished at this unexpected announcement. Someone she knew asking her to consider a courtship was one thing, but who was this tall stranger who swept in and made marriage proposals while her parents were not even home?

"I'm sorry, sir, but – "

The man interrupted her. "And there will be dire consequences if you do not agree."

*Verla overcame her shock quickly and drew herself up to her full five feet and two inches, glaring at the man. "Sir, I must ask you to leave this house."*

*"I think it would be in your best interests if we discussed this," Mr Duncan told her, not moving. "I'm not sure that you understand what you are denying yourself and your family."*

*"Sir," she repeated, her voice rising, "I ask you to leave this house now!"*

*Mr Duncan smiled smoothly. "My dear, if you do not agree to marry me, you will die… tonight."*

*Verla coloured with anger at the audacity of his strange words.*

*"Oh!" she said. "Sir, leave immediately, for I will not have your cheap and immoral fortune telling in this house!"*

*The man stood and repositioned his top hat on his head.*

*"I think you should rethink your decision, my dear," he said. "I can offer you everything you've ever dreamed, everything you've ever wanted… if you will say yes."*

*"No! Please leave immediately," she ordered.*

*"You will not permit me to explain my proposal, explain how I can make you rich beyond measure?" the man asked.*

*"No," she hissed.*

*"I understand that you, with your limited capacity, may need some time to process what I have just told you," Mr Duncan conceded. "I will give you exactly one hour, upon which you will meet me in the town square. I will have an automobile waiting to take you to your new life of wealth and wonder. And need I remind you, my dear, that if you are not there on the appointed hour, your fate — and that of your family — will be an unpleasant one."*

*Verla was incensed. The idea that someone could enter her house, inform her that she would die if she did not marry him, then offer her riches — was this a jest? A ploy to scare her? Perhaps a cheap trick by some circus performers to promote their soothsaying?*

*Shaking with rage, she pointed at the door, and the man started towards it, turning slightly before the threshold to let his last sentence float back to Verla:*

*"If you are not there in one hour, you will die tonight..."*

*Verla pushed the door closed, locked it, and leaned against it, trembling. She would not believe such nonsense, she wouldn't. There had been something terribly frightening about the way the man had so glibly informed her of her impending death – but it was just some cheap trick, a horrible, cruel thing for someone to derive their own pleasure from.*

*A key turned in the lock as Verla leaned against the door, and she jumped back, frightened – was the man back again so soon?*

*"My dear daughter, what on earth are you doing?" her father asked, opening the door.*

*Verla's heartbeat slowed and she looked at her family as they entered the room.*

*"Didn't you see, a man, he just left?" she asked.*

*Her mother spoke sharply. "You had a man here?" she asked.*

*"No!" Verla said. "A man just came here, and he said such strange, horrible things! Didn't you see him? He was just outside the door a minute ago!"*

*"What did he say?" asked her father.*

*"He said that I had to marry him, or I would die tonight!" Verla's words sounded strange even to her own ears.*

*Verla's mother looked at her disapprovingly.*

*"One of those horrible, cheap fortune tellers from that circus that came to town!" she said. "Our fathers came here to get away, and lo and behold, a circus follows..."*

*Verla stared at the door the man had exited through. "But he seemed... so serious."*

*Her father patted her hand reassuringly, then settled down in front of the fire.*

*"Your mother is right, it's simply a quest to garner interest in the*

*circus acts," he said. "But if it will make you feel better, we will double check all the locks and windows tonight."*

*Verla picked up her needlework meekly and settled onto the floor in front of the flames. Her parents were right. All the local houses had probably been visited by that strange man tonight. People would love it, too – they would relish the thrill of excitement that came with danger. Verla had no such thrill. She wished she'd never seen the man. There was something strange, something different about him, something that didn't belong in this town, in her life.*

*But still. There was no point making small things large. She would never see the man again.*

*"Yes," she smiled up at her father. "Thank you. That would be good."*

Huddled in her chair on the dreary porch of her house surrounded by ruined mansions, Verla looked at Ben and spoke softly.

"That same night, some embers must have flown out of the fire and caught the rug in my bedroom," she said. "The flames spread, they engulfed the house, and the other houses caught fire too. The whole town went up."

Ben stared at Verla, his eyes huge.

"What about you? Did you get out okay?" he whispered.

Verla looked back at him, her eyes large and clear, devoid of tears.

"That was the night I was sent to Hell."

# - CHAPTER TEN -

# The Sentenced

Ben stared at Verla. "What?" he asked, not understanding.

"I climbed out of the window to avoid the flames," said Verla. "I slipped and fell, and hit my head. When I awoke, I was no longer... no longer living."

"What... how..."

"The rest of my family died in the fire," she continued. "My parents, my three little brothers. All the uncles and aunts and cousins I knew."

Ben's heart started to pound as he sensed he was in a situation where he had to choose his words carefully. "Verla," he said, trying to keep his voice calm. "I don't understand what you're trying to tell me. I don't know what happened to your family. It's obviously something pretty bad. But you're still alive now."

Verla sighed. "I knew you wouldn't believe me."

"Because it's not true!"

"You wanted to know, Ben. You're the one who has been asking me about my story for the past week."

"I didn't mean for you to make up something like that!"

A look of pain flitted across Verla's face. "I'm not making it up."

Ben leaned forward and stared at Verla. "It's not true, Verla. You didn't die. That would mean you're a ghost. There's no such thing as ghosts!"

"I'm not a ghost." She hesitated slightly, then plunged ahead. "I'm one of what's known as the Sentenced. When I died that night, they didn't send me to St Peter at the Pearly Gates to be judged like everyone else. I didn't get a chance to go to Heaven. They sent me straight to the gates of Hell."

Ben clutched the railings of the porch until his knuckles turned white. "The gates of Hell?" he croaked.

She continued as if he hadn't spoken.

"And it was there that I saw who Mr Duncan really was, not a man of this world, but an employee of the Devil," she said quietly. "He asked me one more time if I would agree to marry him. I asked him if he would restore the lives of my family if I accepted, and he said it was too late for them, but not for me. I asked him why he was so intent on having my hand, but he would not give me an answer. When I refused his proposal that final time, he sent me straight to Hell."

Ben stared at Verla. "You're kidding, right?" he asked hesitatingly.

"No, I'm not," she said, staring straight back at him. "Ben, this is the truth." The look in her eyes was deadly serious.

He shook himself and stood up straighter.

"No, that's not true!" he said loudly, reeling at the impact of Verla's strange words. "You're a real person! Why do you think you're a… a Sentenced or whatever you said? You're real, you're sitting right there, I'm looking at you! Why are you trying to make me believe this… other thing?"

"Ben, I am real," she said. "And this…" – she waved a hand behind her – "this, the house where I caused the death of my family… this is my Hell."

Ben's head started to spin as he tried to take in Verla's strange story, and the way she told in such an earnest tone. He tried to piece together what he knew in his mind. She lived all alone in this big strange house... every other house was ruined... this was the house where the fire supposedly started. For a split second, part of his mind that he hadn't known existed whispered to him: *what if she really is telling the truth?*

"I'm trapped here," she said in a low voice. "In this house, in this village. In Hell. Forever."

Ben turned and stared up at the house. It was a real house, it was solid, he had touched it, he was standing on the porch, and there sat Verla on the chair, solid as anything, not wispy, completely real, certainly not in Hell, neither of them were in Hell, they were on a dingy porch in a ruined town on a sunny day...

"I'm sorry, Verla, but it's just not true," he said, his voice strained. "We're in the real world right now, and you can leave the house; I've seen you. I saw you in the park the other day!"

"The park is within the boundaries of the original town site. But the further I stray from this house, I can't..." She lifted her hand and let it drop. "So here I stay, my body sustained but not really living. Day after day, year after year." She hesitated. "Decade after decade."

"No you're not, Verla!" Ben heard his voice rising, but couldn't stop it. "You're not in Hell, you're real, this is all real!"

He backed away from her and came up against the porch railing, his body jolting as the wood pressed against his shirt. He calmed his breathing and looked her in the eye. "I don't know why you're lying to me like this," he said in a quieter voice. "I just wanted to help you – why are you making all this stuff up about Hell?"

"It's not -" she began, but he shook his head. He felt tired and confused, and suddenly wanted to be far away from the big old mansion.

"I have to go, okay?" he said. "I'm going home."

He grabbed his skateboard, clattered down the steps, and ran down the street. Verla watched him go, her eyes stricken and her face pale.

## - CHAPTER ELEVEN -

# In the Library

Ben let a few days slip past, not knowing what to do. The strange tale that Verla had told him simply could not be real. She was obviously just a girl who lived alone, and that solitude had played with her mind so much that she now viewed her life as being in a form of hell. Plenty of people felt that way about their lives, after all. His uncle Nelson had gone through some terrible times after his wife had died of cancer, and Ben's father had been scared his brother would never lift himself out of his grief. And Sarah, that girl from high school, had had anorexia so badly that she probably considered her life a type of hell too.

Ben sat at his desk, tapping a pencil loudly against the wood. He was momentarily angry that Verla had been allowed to be on her own for so long that she was starting to believe in crazy things like St Peter and some employee of the Devil called Mr Duncan. And she thought she belonged to some group of people – the Sentenced? What was that all about? Where was her family, why weren't they looking after her? Why hadn't someone called a doctor? What about the government departments responsible for the wellbeing of local people?

He flopped down on his bed and stared at the wall. Yep, Verla was definitely suffering from delusions. There was absolutely nothing, not one shred of evidence, to back up her bizarre story.

His eyes wandered around the room and focused on the old notice board where he had tacked the picture of the old-fashioned family clustered in front of their mansion. The picture of Verla that was taken almost one hundred years ago. Standing in front of a house that was now the only intact mansion in a sea of ruins.

Well, maybe there was that. That was a little… strange.

Ben's reverie was interrupted when his father poked his head in the door.

"Are you okay?" he asked. "You've hardly been out of your room for two days. Jay and Sean are back. I thought you'd jump at the chance to get out of the house and see them."

"I'm fine."

"I'm going to drive down to Sydney now. Your mother's not happy but I have to go into work for a few hours to meet some authors who are in the city. I know it's a bit of a drive, but would you like to come?"

"Would I have to stay in your office all day?"

His father laughed. "You're an adult now," he said. "You can do whatever you want."

Ben and his father packed up a few bits and pieces and settled into the car for the drive. They headed out of town on the correct road this time, and Ben realised that if he was to drive into town using the main road, there was no way he'd be able to see the cluster of burned out houses on the east of the town. It was hidden away behind a line of trees.

After half an hour they turned onto the Great Western Highway, which wound down the mountains towards the distant city.

Ben didn't share Verla's strange tale with his father. He was afraid he would immediately send a posse to quickly commit Verla to the nearest mental ward. Plus – and now Ben realised that maybe he didn't think Verla was completely insane – he had a feeling that there was just a bit more to the story. Although he wasn't jumping on the bandwagon for the Sentenced and all the other things she'd said, maybe there was *something* there. He just couldn't put his finger on it.

David glanced at his son as they drove along Parramatta Road towards the tall buildings at Sydney's centre. "Do you want me to drop you off somewhere?" he asked.

Ben didn't hesitate; he now knew where he wanted to go. "The state library," he said. His internet searches hadn't turned up anything helpful aside from the photograph, and all the theological websites he'd seen were so overrun with emotional debates that it was hard to figure out what the real content was. It was time to check out some solid, dependable reference books. He opened a map on his phone and directed his father right into the centre of the city to a building next to the Botanic Gardens.

The state's largest collection of books was fronted by a massive portico with tall, ornate columns. Ben stared up at them as he walked up the steps and into the foyer. He glanced around and found the information desk.

"Excuse me," he asked the lady behind the counter. "I'm looking for your section on religion. Specifically, stuff to do with Hell."

The lady looked at him, a little surprised at his request.

"You'll find theology in the state reference library, up through the corridor then to the left. Let's see." She tapped a few letters into her keyboard. "Stacks 45C through to 47H."

Ben followed the lady's directions to the theology section. The large room filled with massive shelves wasn't as bright and airy as the foyer – instead it was dim, quiet, seemed to be decorated completely in monochrome, and *exactly* like the foreboding libraries where hardworking movie heroes find themselves searching large, dusty tomes for vital clues towards the villain's murderous motive.

Despite himself, he chuckled. "Well, here I go."

He strode to the nearest shelf, ran his finger along the titles, selected one, opened it at random and began to read.

"…so Hephaestus returned to his forge, and said to Cyclopes, 'Who has been here, I sense the presence of a visitor just left'. And Cyclopes replied that there had been no one present but himself in the hours of Hephaestus's leave."

Ben frowned. He returned the book and picked out another one.

"…but what of love, she said to me? What of the beauty and grace and the passion? What of the joy that the deepest of all emotions can produce? What of the giving of oneself…"

Ben put the book back and selected another, flipping the book to the middle and choosing a paragraph.

"…and when Mother Earth saw the humans who now walked her green and fertile land, she took human form, lay with a young and handsome man, and his seed impregnated her to create a child that was human, but could bend the laws of the Motherland itself. And the child had children of its own, whose humanity combined with nature's protection like no other, the deep and lasting result of Mother Earth's one joyful copulation…."

Ew, thought Ben. How unsexy. Next book.

"…as mentioned in Hesiod's Theogony, where it is said Aphrodite was born when Cronus cut off Ouranos's testicles and threw them into the sea, and the testicles caused foam to form and rise, creating the seductive shape of a woman...."

Ugh, even worse! Ben realised that the right book was obviously not just going to jump into his hands. Were there any books that just focused on stories about Hell? He wandered along the shelves searching for a more promising-looking section.

An hour later, Ben had flipped through a mountain of large, dusty books, but nothing that related to Verla's story had caught his eye. There were several books that described Hell, even more that discounted its existence, and even a few, more suited to the self-help section, that explained that Hell is only in people's minds and presented therapeutic methods to banish this feeling.

He selected a few more relevant-looking books from the shelves and began to flip through the first one, which looked almost brand-new. He scanned his eyes across a couple of pages about different mythical interpretations of Hell – some weird symbols – some more stuff about Hell – Ben stopped. He flipped back to the symbols. That strange curly one – hadn't he seen it before?

He couldn't be one hundred per cent certain, because he'd only had a glimpse of it a few days previously, but it looked a lot like the symbol he's seen tattooed onto the back of Verla's neck.

Ben stared at the symbol for a few moments, then looked at the front cover. "*A Lake Of Fire: Myth or Fact?* by Professor Terrence Brightman," he read aloud.

He flipped through the book again, this time examining each page a bit more closely, but he couldn't find anything that talked about the symbol aside from the caption directly below the illustration, which stated 'marked on humans'. Finally he turned to the publishing details in the front of the book. There was no reference to when the book was first published, only that this version had been released only three years ago by some outfit called Veritas Reprints. Ben drummed his fingers on the wooden table, then scooped up the book and headed for the corridor.

He found himself in a reading room, so he settled in front of a computer monitor and did an online search for the reprinting company. Their website offered nothing except for some flowery prose about the brilliance of Veritas Reprints as well as an address and phone number. There was no information or contact details for any authors.

Ben jumped as his pocket vibrated and a sixties rock tune started belting out of it, causing several people scattered around the room to look up and frown.

"Sorry!" he mouthed, and grabbed his phone from his pocket. It was his mother calling.

"Hi, love," she said after he'd answered. "I can't get hold of your father. Can you please ask him to bring some groceries home?"

Ben hunted around his workstation for a writing instrument and found a grubby pencil on the floor. He dutifully wrote the shopping list onto a piece of paper rescued from the recycle bin next to the printer.

"Is that everything?" he whispered.

"That's it, hon," she said warmly. "See you at home later. Take care."

Ben turned his phone to silent in case it rang again, then sat idly in front of the computer for a while. He gazed at the website for Veritas Reprints, sitting there with the phone number displayed on the screen. Then he looked down at the phone in his hand.

He *could* just call them. All he wanted was to find out how to get in touch with one of their authors. It was a perfectly legitimate enquiry.

He swallowed and started to dial.

"Terrence Brightman?" the voice that picked up drawled in response to Ben's question.

Ben heard the sound of a keyboard being tapped and the voice eventually came back with, "yeah, he's in the system."

"Can I get his contact details, please?"

"Why?" the voice replied flatly.

"I'd like to get in touch with him," Ben said, a little taken aback.

"Yeah, I got that," said the voice. "Why?"

Ben cast his mind around for a reason other than the truth. Perhaps if he pretended he was a journalist? He cleared his throat and tried to sound professional.

"I'm writing a, um, review of one of his books and I'd like to interview him."

"I don't think he's written anything new," the voice said, sounding surprised. "Some of his books were reprinted a few years back, but they first got published ages ago, decades probably."

"Wasn't there any publicity for the reprints?" Ben asked, grasping for any terminology he'd heard his father use.

"Nope," was the reply. "Only five were printed."

"Only five? Why? Wouldn't there have been more than that? I mean, what's the point, otherwise?"

"Don't ask me," sighed the voice, sounding like he wished Ben would go away. "There were a few old books we did really small print runs for that year. They were all pushed through by one of the guys here."

"Well, would you mind putting me through to him, then?"

Ben asked impatiently.

"No can do," drawled the voice. "He was only here for a few weeks last year, then he quit. Enough time for us to reprint a bunch of books no one wanted to buy, anyway. We had to give them away to local libraries."

"Look, I'd really like to call Terrence Brightman," said Ben. "Do you have any contact details for him at all?"

"No," said the voice shortly. "There's nothing for him in this system. But I do have a suggestion for you that may help you find him."

"Yes?" Ben asked eagerly.

"Ever heard of Google?" the voice drawled back.

Ben rolled his eyes at himself as he turned back to the computer. So much for detective work. He'd seen that movie *All the President's Men*, and he'd felt sorry for the two reporters who had to make a load of phone calls, scour libraries, knock on doors and meet strange people in underground car parks, all in the name of research. And here he was, trying to do the same thing, when he could just look it up.

Fifteen seconds later, he was looking at the official website for Professor Terrence Brightman, lecturer in religion studies at the University of Sydney. Ben almost laughed. This was almost too easy.

## - CHAPTER TWELVE -

# Jamie

Ben had never imagined himself as the type of person who would front up at someone's office, waving a book and preparing a speech about possible inhabitants of a worldly Hell. But this whole Verla business had sucked him right in, and now, to find that his one clue was penned by someone who could in the same city as he was right now – wasn't it worth doing something a little out of the ordinary?

After two different buses, a conversation about pottery with a street artist and the donation of most of his change to a homeless lady, he finally found himself standing outside the main entrance of the university, which sprawled hundreds of metres in both directions.

It didn't take too long to find Professor Brightman's office. Some sort of summer school must have been in session, because there were lots of students walking around. After only two wrong turns and an embarrassing exit from a gynaecology lecture, a girl with black eye makeup and platform boots four inches high kindly pointed him towards a red brick building.

He walked up the steps and was directed to the third floor by the motherly-looking lady in reception. He found himself outside a door with the professor's nameplate, and knocked.

There was silence for a few seconds, then he heard a crashing noise from behind the door. Ben heard a voice muttering, "oh sod it, you can just stay there then," before it called, a little louder, "coming, coming!"

The door opened, and a middle-aged man with dark hair and sharp eyes stared down at Ben. "Can I help you?" he asked.

"Hi," said Ben nervously. "Professor Brightman?"

The man nodded, glancing down the corridor a little twitchily.

"I'd like to talk to you about a book you wrote," began Ben. "The lake of fire one."

The professor pursed his lips and stared at him. "Have you seen a copy of the book?" he asked sharply.

"They had one in the State Library," said Ben, and the professor's shoulders relaxed.

"Ah, yes," he said. "A Veritas copy. Well, I'm not sure I can help you much as I didn't actually write that book. My grandfather did." The man paused. "He was a professor too."

"Oh, I didn't realise," said Ben, disappointed. The book must be older than he'd thought.

The professor must have noticed Ben's downcast expression because he said kindly, "I do know quite a bit about it though, so you're welcome to come in. Perhaps I can try to answer any questions you have."

Professor Brightman's office was cluttered and messy, with stacks of books on every surface and every wall space crammed with notices, papers and newspaper clippings. There was a pile of books scattered on the floor in the corner next to an overflowing bookshelf. Ben guessed that it was what had made the crashing noise before. The professor himself wasn't ancient like Ben expected every professor to be – instead he looked quite fit and capable, and probably only in his forties.

Brightman looked around briefly, then picked up a stack of papers from a chair and examined them. "Here, hold these for a second," he said, thrusting them at Ben, who reached out his hands to take them. The professor stared at Ben's hands for a second, then motioned for him to sit down. He took the papers back, throwing them onto the top of an already-overflowing filing cabinet.

He introduced himself rather belatedly, and explained that he was researching the concept of Hell.

"It's a big topic," the professor said cautiously. "What area are you interested in? Greek or Roman mythology? Eastern philosophy? Christianity? Representation in pop culture? That's certainly a fascinating one."

Ben pulled out of his pocket the photocopy of the page that he had made before he left the library. He unfolded it and showed it to the professor.

"This symbol was in your grandfather's book," he said, thinking that he may as well dive right in. "It says here that it's marked on humans, and it's got to be something to do with Hell."

The professor nodded and started fussing with books and papers on his desk.

"Are you doing a research assignment on Hell?" he asked, shifting a dried-up apple core retrieve some documents below. "I have a lot of material you might be interested in."

Ben hesitated. "I'm asking for a friend," he said.

The professor stopped flurrying through the papers and turned curiously to face Ben.

"A friend?" he asked. "Really?"

Ben nodded cautiously.

"And what kind of friend is this, may I ask?" the professor

continued.

"Uh," Ben faltered. "Just this person I know. They... asked about it."

"Asked about it, did they?" Professor Brightman eyed Ben shrewdly. "And what did they ask?"

Ben squirmed under the professor's intense gaze. "Just what it was. What it means."

"And how did they know about it? Where did they see it?"

"Just..." Ben's voice trailed off. What should he tell the professor? He weighed up his options. What was the harm in telling the professor the truth?

"It was a tattoo," he said. "Someone had it tattooed on their skin."

"Where? Where was the tattoo on their body?"

Ben paused. "Their neck. The back of their neck."

The professor stared at him with piercing blue eyes. If Ben had thought his gaze had been intense before, it was nothing compared to now. After a full minute, the professor finally broke eye contact, his eyes flicking back down to Ben's hands, then back up again.

"Now... Ben, was it?" he said slowly. "Ben... what my grandfather wrote in that book could be myth, it could be fact... speculation, you could say."

The Professor leaned forward to stare at the symbol on the paper Ben was holding.

"Humans have thought up many different versions of Hell," he said. "It's my job, it's always been my job to study these representations... and what you're holding there is part of just another one that may or not be true, okay?"

"Um, okay."

"In one of these versions – which is just one of many – some believe that this symbol is placed upon the damned," he said quietly. "The ones who bypass the judgment, and are condemned to an eternity in Hell. It's not the classic lake of fire concept at all; in this version of events, the lake of fire is the myth. This concept of Hell is more of an extension of a hellish scenario from real life – one that continues forever."

He paused, then continued: "And there's a number. A number is placed with the symbol, to mark that person's place in Hell."

Some sort of emotion was building inside Ben, but he had no idea what it was. His mind replayed the scene of Verla's hair sliding across her neck, obscuring a tattoo – and a tiny row of figures that could have been numbers.

"Is it true?" he asked. "Could someone actually be marked with that for real? Not just a normal tattoo?"

"In real life?" the professor said, rubbing his neck absently. "As I said before, some believe it to be so…"

They both stared at the symbol on the piece of paper. Ben's thoughts were racing. Did Verla know what it was that was tattooed on the back of her neck? Did she have it done on purpose as part of her delusions? Or was there something else going on here, something deeper and more sinister than Ben ever imagined… something that maybe made what Verla had told him to be… possibly true?

There was a knock on the door and a man poked his head in.

"Terry, hi, sorry to interrupt, we have to get going to the seminar," he said.

"Right, I'll be with you in a sec."

The professor started to get up, but Ben stopped him beseechingly.

"But sir… is it true?" he repeated. "Can someone in real life actually have the symbol on them?"

"Ben… I said it might be true," said Professor Brightman, being irritatingly vague. "We're moving out of normal territory here; this is stuff that I'm not sure you understand the scope of." He sighed. "Sitting here in my office, surrounded by solid, earthly things, it's hard to believe that any of the stories of theology are true. And yet, billions of people in the world believe in things that don't seem solid and earthly."

He glanced at his watch and continued quickly. "I have to go now, but please feel free to come back and see me any time. But call first," he added hastily. He handed over a business card. "I'm quite interested to hear your," he paused, "point of view."

The professor must have picked up on the disappointed look on Ben's face, because he continued kindly. "There's someone else you could talk to, someone who knows a lot more about these things."

He flipped through a stack of business cards, found one, and copied the number onto a sticky note.

"Here, call him, he'll help you," the professor said, ushering Ben back out the door and locking it behind them. "Thanks for coming by."

Ben watched the man march down the corridor, then slowly walked to the lift. Well, that hadn't been terribly helpful. But the professor knew about the symbol, at least. And about the numbers below it. Obviously Verla wasn't the first person to have one.

Outside in the sunshine, he quickly called his father to let him know where he was, then looked at the sticky note the professor had given him. The name Jamie Portman was scrawled next to a phone number. Well, Ben thought, hopefully this Jamie Portman would be a little more forthcoming than the Professor.

Ben sat down on a bench under some shade and watched students walk down the pathways between the buildings. This would be him next year, at some university somewhere, doing some course he hadn't even chosen yet. His eyes rested on a group of girls walking by with books and papers under their arms. Maybe he'd meet a nice girl there. Aside from a few short 'relationships' in year nine and ten that consisted of holding hands during lunchtime and not much else, he hadn't ever really dated anyone.

There had been a month-long fling, if you could call it that, last summer with a girl called Elise, but she'd only been in Perth to visit her father for a while and although they'd swapped numbers, they hadn't stayed in contact. Ben was glad it had happened at all though; at least it made him feel like he wasn't completely out of touch with females. He'd always been paranoid that no girl would ever be attracted to him, especially as he'd once overheard a girl in his class refer to him as 'mediocre'. He didn't know what she was referring to – his looks, his personality, his sporting ability? – but it popped into his mind and put him off whenever he tried to strike up a conversation with a girl he might like.

A man sat down on the other end of the bench and Ben's mind was drawn back to the present. He gazed down at the sticky note he was still holding in his hand, and wondered why the professor had recommended he call this Jamie person. Perhaps he wrote books too, like that one from the library. Either way, Ben would be glad to talk to anyone who could provide more information.

He finally got up the courage to dial the number. It rang a few times before a voice answered, "Hello?"

"Um, hi," Ben said haltingly. "My name's Ben Fletcher. I was wanting to speak to Jamie Portman?"

"This is Jamie."

"Well, uh, hi. I've just been to see Professor Brightman at the University of Sydney, but he had to go, so he said I should give you a call. It's about a book."

"Yeah?"

"Um, Lake of Fire by Terrence Brightman. I asked the professor about a symbol in there, one that said it could be marked on humans. The professor said it marked the, er, damned. And he told me to call you."

There was a long pause from the other end of the line and Ben was about to venture a "hello?" when Jamie finally replied.

"Where are you calling from, Ben?"

"I just left the professor's office. At the University of Sydney."

"That's not what I meant. Which… company are you calling from?"

"I'm not calling from a company. I'm, well, just a student, I guess. I'm on a break from study though."

"Are you one of Brightman's students?"

"No," said Ben, getting distracted. "I'm not actually enrolled anywhere right now, but I think I'm still classed as a student. Anyway," he said, trying to get back on track, "I went to see the professor because I found a symbol in his grandfather's book that I need to know about, and since he had to go, he said to call you and you'd be able to help me a bit more."

"Ah, right," said Jamie. "Well, if we're going to talk about it, I'd rather do it in person. Do you want to arrange a time to meet up? Perhaps tomorrow? Or next week?"

"Are you based in Sydney?" asked Ben. "Because I'm only really here today."

There was a pause in the conversation, then Jamie spoke.

"Well, Ben, I'm free right now," he said. "Are you still at the university? I can meet you at Freddie's Café across from the main entrance, the one near the swimming pool. Say, twenty minutes from now."

"Yeah, that sounds good, if I'm not putting you out too much."

"What do you look like?" asked Jamie.

"Um," said Ben, looking down at himself. "Jeans. Green T-shirt. Brown hair." He caught himself before he said 'mediocre'.

"Right," said Jamie. "See you in twenty. Bye."

Ben said goodbye and hung up. Staring at the phone, he asked himself why he was doing all this for a girl who obviously wanted to be left alone, and seemed a bit whacko anyway. He wondered if he was perhaps developing feelings for her, but when he really thought about it he was almost surprised to realise that no, he wasn't interested in Verla like that. Sure, they were getting on really well and he was starting to enjoy hanging out with her, but he didn't have any romantic notions towards her. She was a nice girl though. Pity about the whole delusional thing – she really seemed to believe that her house was her own little hell.

Ben thought about what Professor Brightman had said, about all the people who believed there was more to life than what you could see and hear. Ben certainly hadn't discounted any theories – who was he to really know if there was a supreme being or not? Maybe there was something out there, but not exactly what everyone assumed to it to be.

He asked a passerby for directions to Freddie's Café. Once there, he bought a coffee at the long formica counter and chose a booth. He sat nervously tapping a spoon against the cup, wondering if this Jamie guy would show. After about fifteen minutes of tapping and watching his coffee go cold, someone slid into the booth opposite him, and Ben looked up.

Jamie Portman looked – Ben's mind lingered on the cliché – larger than life. His black hair seemed blacker than everyone else's, his dark brown skin practically glowed, and when he grinned and shook hands, Ben felt as if he'd just had a battery recharge. Who on earth was this guy? Ben, unaccustomed to being impressed by any males other than actors and sports stars, clutched his cup and stared at Jamie. This guy looked to be only around his late twenties, so how did he seem so comfortable in his own skin? Ben knew it would be decades before he lost his own insecurities about practically everything.

"Can I get you a coffee?" Ben asked.

"Sure, that'd be great," said Jamie. He had a slight American accent that Ben hadn't noticed on the phone.

Ben went to the counter to order the coffee, handing over his last five dollar note. After all the bus trips he'd paid for that day, he'd need to withdraw some more cash soon. He was glad he'd saved some of the money from his supermarket job during his final year of high school. Hopefully it was enough to tide him over until he found somewhere to work part-time during his first year of university. Wherever he ended up going.

The waitress placed the coffees in front of him and he took them back to the table.

"Thanks," said Jamie. He stirred in a spoonful of sugar and leaned back to survey Ben. "So, the professor put you on to me, did he?"

Jamie was wearing dark trousers and a plain white shirt. Ben wondered how anyone kept white shirts clean.

"Yeah," he said. "I don't know why. I was asking him about this symbol, and he started to talk about things that frankly I didn't understand, then he upped and left."

KATY SCOTT

He handed over the photocopied piece of paper, and Jamie took it paper and nodded thoughtfully.

"Uh huh," he said. He placed the piece of paper on the table, then looked at Ben closely. "So what do you do, Ben?"

"What do you mean?" Ben asked, confused.

"What do you do for a living? I know you said you were a student on the phone. But you're not one of Brightman's crew. Are you an author? Is that why you're looking into this stuff?"

"No," said Ben, feeling insignificant. "I just finished high school. I haven't even started university yet."

"Okay," said Jamie, looking a bit confused himself.

"If you don't mind me asking," ventured Ben, fiddling with his spoon, "are you a professor too?"

"No," replied Jamie, studying Ben's twitching hands. "But I have done some work with Brightman before."

"Cool," said Ben. "So – can you tell me about the symbol?"

"Well…" said Jamie. "If you're not a researcher, then I have to assume the Professor asked you to come speak to me because you asked him if this symbol could actually be on someone who walks this earth."

It was an unusual turn of phrase and Ben looked up curiously.

"And that means," Jamie continued, sounding cautious, "that you may even know someone who has this mark on their skin."

Ben paused. "I don't know," he said finally, not sure how much he could trust this Jamie person. "I'm just curious, that's all. I just want to know about it."

Jamie's eyes found Ben's and held them for quite a few seconds.

"Right," he said. "And what do you know already?"

Ben glanced around to make sure no one was in earshot.

Feeling a little foolish, he quickly outlined the scraps of information Verla had shared about the possibility that someone could bypass St Peter's gates and be sent to a Hell based somewhere on Earth.

"That's all I know, really," he said, embarrassed. "And you don't have to tell me it sounds completely crazy – I know already. But I really, really need to know if it's possible."

Jamie leaned back in his chair and stared directly at Ben. At first, Ben held his gaze, but eventually could stand it no longer and dropped his eyes to the salt shaker. An ant was slowly making its way up the side. After a few minutes had passed, Ben's eyes flicked upwards again and Jamie spoke.

"It's possible," he said quietly.

Ben looked at him, a little shocked. To have someone say it out loud, so say with such certainty that something so strange was true, was just plain weird.

Jamie saw his expression and chuckled. "Ben, preachers and prophets get up in front of thousands and say very improbable things that are immediately accepted as the truth. Something has to be true, and why not this?"

"I guess," Ben mumbled.

"And this symbol," Jamie tapped the photocopy on the table between them. "What do you know about this?"

"The Professor told me that it's put on the, um, the Damned, and they get a number as well, and they go to Hell forever," said Ben haltingly.

"That pretty much sums it up, yeah," said Jamie thoughtfully. "They usually place it – "

"On the back of the neck," concluded Ben.

Jamie looked at him sharply.

"I mean, so I've heard," he said lamely.

"Let's go for a walk," Jamie said abruptly, standing up and

walking towards the door, abandoning his coffee on the table.

Ben scrambled up, grabbed the photocopy and ran after him. It wasn't until they'd started walking along the pavement in the bright afternoon sun that Jamie took up the conversation where it had left off.

"The mark," said Jamie. "On the back of the neck. It's a sorting system. Easier to keep track of people using numbers."

"But Jamie," said Ben, deciding to suspend his disbelief for a while for the sake of the conversation. "Why would they need to put a real tattoo on these people? We're not talking about solid beings here. This is, like, another dimension."

"Why?" asked Jamie. "Because you've been told that? These people aren't wisps of smoke that slide through walls, Ben. You're thinking of ghosts, poltergeists, demons – you're thinking of what the religious texts tell you. These are solid people, physical beings with hearts that beat and lungs that breathe. The only difference between the Sentenced and the living is that the Sentenced get their mortality suspended until further notice. And the other difference, of course, is that they're forever plagued by memories, terrible memories, the worst feelings imaginable, that make every day their own personal Hell."

"But what about the other, er, people?" asked Ben. "Like, the Devil and God and all that?"

"Solid too, but immortal – they'll never die," said Jamie. "Look, you're thinking of this the wrong way. It is much, much easier for these beings to exist on a solid level than to be all wispy and fly through walls and things. That would be completely impractical, and seems a little unlikely to me anyway." Jamie looked a little amused.

Yeah right, thought Ben. You've just told me the Devil's a solid guy who will live forever, and now you think flying through walls is unlikely.

"So if this was all true, where do God and the Devil live, if they have bodies like us?" asked Ben. "Would they have their own houses and things?" Despite himself, he glanced around, half expecting to see a red man with horns and a forked tail strolling down the sidewalk.

"Where would you imagine the Devil to live?" replied Jamie seriously, stopping at a park bench overlooking a park and plopping down.

Ben thought for a moment as he slowly sat. "Um. Maybe he would have a big white Columbian cocaine plantation. Or perhaps a guest bedroom in… in some evil dictator's house. Or maybe a tropical island in… in the Bermuda triangle?"

Jamie looked impressed. "You're good. He does actually have one of those, and a whole lot more places to stay, all over the world. Offices in practically every major city as well. And – this may only be a rumour, because apparently the Hell folk have their own global transport – but I've heard he sometimes catches commercial flights, but only ever in first class."

Ben wasn't sure if he was serious or not.

"Look, Ben," said Jamie. "You're just conditioned to think that if there is a God or Devil, they are invisible and omnipresent. But what proof do you have of that? Why shouldn't they be a little different to what seems to be culturally set in stone?"

Ben sat staring across the park to the pond in the distance. It was all so much to take in. He had come here to find out if Verla could be telling the truth, and he was being told way more than he'd bargained for.

"What about the thing where people are made to live in their own Hell on Earth?" he asked, steering the conversation back to something he'd had more time to comprehend. "Does everyone who goes to Hell actually stay somewhere on Earth? The world would get too crowded, surely."

"No, not everyone," said Jamie. "Only the ones the Devil and his cronies are really angry with. And there are a few around, trust me. The ones he never wants to see again, he gets rid of."

"Gets rid of?"

"You know. Gone. Snuffed out, cease to exist, no continuance of soul, et cetera, et cetera," said Jamie. "The thing is, it wasn't always that way. Everyone always thought souls were immortal, that whether you became a drone in the Devil's organisation, went to Heaven or whatever else happened to you after your time was up, you'd keep on going, somewhere, somehow. It was how God designed it. But the Devil found a way." Jamie stared at the grass. "I don't know what it is or how he does it, and I expect it's not just a case of tapping a fairy wand on someone's head. But he can end souls now."

Jamie leaned towards Ben confidentially. "God was *pissed off*."

Ben sat back on the bench and exhaled slowly. "Jamie," he said, feeling completely overwhelmed. "The whole system seems quite, er, structured."

"Oh well yeah, it has to be," said Jamie blithely. "God has about ten personal assistants, you know, just to manage his travel and diary and accommodation and everything. There has to be systems in place, meeting held, negotiations between parties, just to get things done."

Ben frowned. "Why have I never heard any of this before? I've heard of all different theories, but nothing quite like this," he said. "Is it some big secret?"

Jamie studied him. "I wouldn't call it a secret, per se. But it's certainly not common knowledge."

"Then why are you telling me?"

Jamie smiled slightly. "It does seem strange, right? That I met you about five seconds ago and now you're hearing all of this."

"But why?"

"Because you already know a bit about it, Ben," said Jamie. "When you asked me about the symbol, about it being on a real person… what if I'd have just told you that it meant nothing and you should forget about it?"

Ben knew the answer. "I'd have kept hassling you," he said slowly. "Then I would have gone back to the professor and harassed him. Then I would have gone back to the library and searched through the books again. Then I would have looked online until I found something that helped. I guess I would have found out eventually."

"When you finally uncovered the truth, would you have believed it?" Jamie asked.

Ben thought about that. "I don't know," he admitted. "I guess originally I was only interested in the Sentenced stuff. I don't know how I'd have felt if I'd found out about all that stuff you just told me… the stuff about God and the Devil."

"Would you rather have not known?"

"No," said Ben determinedly. "If I have to know about a bit of it, I want to know the whole story. I don't know if I believe any of it, but I still want to know."

"Good," said Jamie, smiling slightly again. "And how do you feel now?"

"Overwhelmed," Ben admitted. "I mean," he gestured out to the lush park spread before them, "look at that, it's so… so normal."

"Yeah, the other stuff is a lot to take in," Jamie conceded.

"So," Ben felt as if he had ventured so far beyond normality, he may as well ask, "is there any way of, er, rescuing someone who's become one of those Sentenced people? Getting them out of their Hell place?"

Jamie studied Ben for a moment before speaking. "Yeah, I think so," he said. "I think I've heard somewhere that every hundred years you get a review. The panel decides if you should stay, be redistributed, get your mortality ticking again, or become a drone. Used to be a different number of years but when the Roman calendar kicked in around two thousand years ago, the Panel decided one hundred was a nice round number."

Ben sat up. A review? This could be exactly what could save Verla! His mind started working quickly. His Great-Uncle Thomas was ninety. According to his story the other day, he was born, what, ten years after the town had burned. Which meant that – could it be – the town was burned down exactly one hundred years ago. Which meant, if what Jamie had told him was true, It might just mean…

"Verla's year is this year," he said.

Jamie looked up. "Who's Verla?"

## - CHAPTER THIRTEEN -

# The Contract

The next day, Ben waited nervously by his window until Jamie pulled up in a car outside the white weatherboard house. A late-model silver Aston Martin Vanquish – very nice. Ben still didn't know what Jamie did for a living, but it must pay well. He made a mental note to ask him later.

"Hi," said Ben, jumping into the car and casting a quick admiring glance around the interior. He directed Jamie through the streets and out onto the main road, then they made the same turn that Ben's father had accidentally taken the first night they'd arrived in town. The car rolled along until it entered the old ruined town site.

"Must have been a big fire," Jamie said, squinting up at the ruins.

"Yeah, I heard it was," said Ben. "Keep going to that one up there, the one that still looks pretty decent," he directed, pointing ahead. "Don't park right outside, though. I don't want to scare her."

Leaving Jamie in the car, Ben trotted up the steps to Verla's door and knocked. When Verla answered, he was suddenly embarrassed. Last time he'd seen her, he's informed her she was lying, shouted at her, and run out on her without even saying goodbye.

"Hi," he mumbled.

"Hello, Ben," said Verla, looking so happy to see him that he felt a lot more at ease.

"Listen, I'm sorry about the other day," he said. "It was pretty rude of me to get all weird and run off like that. It just seemed, like, you know…"

"I know it must have been a shock to you," she said. "Have you changed your mind about… what I said?"

"You mean, do I believe you?" he asked, and she nodded cautiously.

He hesitated. "Look, I'm still wrapping my head around all of this," he said honestly. "So, can we just go with… that I'm open to the possibility?"

"The possibility of what?" she asked, pressing the point.

He laughed nervously. "Wow, you really want me to say it," he said. "The possibility that you might be…" He swallowed. "In Hell."

She nodded affirmatively.

"It's a lot for me to take in," he admitted. "I've kind of had to change my whole way of thinking about things… and my brain's still catching up. You'll have to bear with me."

Suddenly Verla's eyes picked out the sports car and its occupant, and she shrank back a little. "I see you have bought a guest."

"Uh, yeah, I would have called ahead, but you know – "

"I know – I don't have a telephone."

"Yeah." Ben fidgeted. "Anyway his name is Jamie. I met him yesterday when I went to Sydney to do some research on your… situation. He already knows all of that stuff, Verla, all about the Hell thing and everything – and I think he can help you."

"Who does he work for?"

"I'm not sure," he said, realising he'd never asked Jamie. "But I'm pretty sure he's one of the good guys."

"Does he work for Heaven?"

"What? I don't know."

"Ben, do you know anything about this man?" she asked, confused.

"Well, yes," he said, feeling a bit foolish. "He's a friend of a university professor, and he knows the ins and outs of situations like yours."

"I'm not sure I'm ready to receive anyone else. Especially someone we know nothing about."

"Well, how about this," said Ben, thinking quickly. "Just meet him. For five minutes. Then after five minutes, if you don't want him to stay, make an excuse to go inside. I'll wrap things up here and he and I will leave, no harm done. You can come back outside to say goodbye if you want, but if you don't come out after a minute or so, we'll just go."

Verla's brow furrowed as she listened to him, then a tiny smile broke onto her face.

"That sounds like it could be suitable," she said. "You may invite him up."

Ben beckoned Jamie from the car. Jamie climbed out and looked hesitantly up at Ben and Verla before walking forward and slowly ascending the steps. Just before his foot made contact with the porch, Verla spoke.

"Your wrists."

Jamie held out his wrists, palms facing up, and Verla crossed the porch to examine them.

"All drones and workers of Hell have their union symbol burned into one of their wrists," Jamie explained quietly to Ben. "Membership is compulsory. The mark is not something they can disguise."

Ben's eyes widened. Hell workers had a union now? Right. Well, at least it explained everyone's preoccupation with staring at his hands when they met him.

Satisfied that Jamie didn't seem to be in Lucifer's employ, Verla indicated a seat for Jamie while Ben perched on the railing. After the necessary introductions, Jamie leaned towards Verla.

"I think I may be able to help you," he said.

~

Ben and Jamie sat on the porch after nightfall, sipping takeaway coffee from the only coffee shop in town, which celebrated its monopoly by serving weak and strange-tasting java to unsuspecting visitors. Verla was inside the house, searching for the contract she'd been given the night she was Sentenced.

"So if they resumed her mortality," Jamie was explaining to Ben, "she'd actually rejoin the human race."

"She isn't human now?" Ben was confused.

"Yeah, she's definitely human. She's just not in the race."

"Right," said Ben. He thought he got it. "But she wouldn't go back in time to when she first became Sentenced, with her family and stuff."

"No, it definitely doesn't work like that," replied Jamie, staring sadly out into the night sky. "Once a time has passed, it's passed. She would rejoin now. There would be a lot about the current time she'd have to get used to."

"Well, I know she lives in this house, but why hasn't she been able to keep up with modern times?" asked Ben logically. "Watch TV, see movies, read the newspaper and everything?"

"I think she does read the newspaper," said Jamie, nodding towards a collection of dailies stacked neatly under Verla's chair next to a pile of old books; Ben had never noticed them. "She probably knows a lot more than you think."

"It's got something to do with the Hell thing, then," said Ben.

"Yeah," said Jamie. "You think that Duncan bloke would have sent her here if he thought she could go to the cinemas and eat popcorn every day?"

"I don't think she can leave the original town site," said Ben, remembering something Verla had told him. "She said the further away she gets from the house, the worse it gets."

"It'd be the thing they do with the memories, then," said Jamie, tapping his temple. "Makes them so bad she can't leave."

"I wonder what she'd be like if they took that away from her," mused Ben. "I mean, she's nice and all already, how great would she be if she didn't have to be sad all the time?"

"Pretty great, I reckon," said Jamie.

At that moment Verla hurried out onto the porch, and the other two quickly became quiet. Verla looked at them suspiciously, and handed Jamie a large roll of parchment topped at each end with round wooden holders.

"Whoa," said Jamie. "This thing is massive. Have you read all of it, Verla?"

"Well, no. When I was locked up here for all eternity, it wasn't exactly the most desirable reading material."

"Oh ha ha," Jamie rolled his eyes.

"I have read it, in parts here and there," she admitted. "But I've never sat down and read the whole thing in one sitting. I can't imagine it would have done much to cheer me up."

She dragged an old wooden chair onto the porch from

inside the house, and the three of them sat with their heads together to read her contract.

At the top, in ornate copperplate writing, it stated "VERLA 9968514". Ben glanced at the number on the paper then back up at the woman it referred to, and as if reading his mind, she turned her head away slightly, raised her hand, and slid her long dark hair away from her neck. Ben stared at the small patch of skin where the same number was burned underneath the curly symbol that was now familiar to him.

"What does the symbol mean?" he asked quietly as Verla let her curtain of hair fall down her back again.

"What do any of their symbols mean?" she asked with a small shrug. "It's probably just some logo their art department came up with."

"Before we start in on this thing, it would help if we knew why you were Sentenced in the first place," said Jamie, examining the parchment.

"I don't know," said Verla. "Trust me, that's something I've asked myself a lot over the past hundred years."

"Did you annoy this Duncan guy somehow?" asked Ben.

"I'd never set eyes on him before the night I died," she replied. "And I've never been able to figure out any connection he had to me."

"They don't really Sentence people without a good reason," Jamie said cautiously. "Why would Duncan target you?"

"I'm not trying to hide anything," said Verla. "I honestly don't know."

"What do you remember?" Ben asked.

"Duncan offered me money to marry him," she said. "He said he'd make me 'rich beyond measure'. But I didn't wait for him to explain why."

"Weird," Ben declared. "So he drops in, offers to cash you

up, then kills you when you say no."

"That just about sums it up," she agreed. "Jamie, is there anything helpful in the contract?"

"This first part of this thing is pretty clear," said Jamie, skimming over the first few paragraphs of the parchment. "It states that you, Verla nine nine six et cetera, are forever banished to a location of your tormentor's choosing – yep, it actually says tormentor – to live out eternity in a memory-locked abode." Jamie's eyes were skimming down the document now. "Blah blah blah, these are the subjects of your memories, blah blah…" He looked up at Ben and Verla. "All pretty standard stuff, I reckon. What we really want are the clauses."

He and Verla began winding through the parchment, with one of them occasionally stopping to read a paragraph aloud. After a while the legal terms started getting too confusing for Ben and he sat back in his chair to gaze at the stars. How strange that he'd find himself listening to the terms of a legal contract detailing someone's admission to Hell. And yet, it didn't feel that strange anymore. He felt as if over the past week his perception of the world's boundaries had expanded. If someone had sat him down and simply told him everything he now knew, he would have never believed it. But meeting Verla, who was proof that these very strange things could happen to nice people, had made him realise that not everything was black and white.

Exhausted, he eventually fell asleep in the hard wooden chair.

## - CHAPTER FOUTREEN -
# The Past and the Future

When Ben came to, the first light of dawn was creeping over the horizon. The morning was chilly but someone had thrown an old worn quilt over him. Ben wiped his mouth with his sleeve and glanced around. Jamie was awake, leaning back in his chair and clutching the parchment, muttering as he read. Verla had fallen asleep next to him, her head on his upper arm. Jamie looked like he was trying to make minimal movement so as not to wake her.

Jamie looked up at Ben's movement and as he did so, Verla slowly awoke. "Hiii," she said, smiling at them sleepily.

"I didn't know you slept," said Ben.

"I do a lot of things like a normal person," she said rather serenely.

"Do you eat?" he asked.

"No," she said. "I don't need anything to sustain my body – it just keeps in a suspended state by itself. Plus it makes it easier for them, as this way I'm not out scavenging for sustenance. But regardless, food is a pleasure I'm not allowed."

Ben stood and massaged his backside. "Where's the bathroom?" he asked.

"Sorry, no running water. If you're after a wash, you're

104

welcome to climb down the well for a quick splash, of course."

"Er, thanks, but no. I'm might go home for a shower and a change of clothes. I think I need it." Ben looked at Jamie. "What about you?"

"I think I can last a bit longer," Jamie replied. "Need a lift?"

"Thanks, but I'll walk. I need to get my limbs working again."

"I might go find us some coffee, then," said Jamie. "I think we passed a service station somewhere on the highway. It's got to be better than that stuff we drank last night."

Ben and Verla walked Jamie to his car and watched him drive away. Ben turned to Verla.

"So, is it okay that I brought him along?" he asked. "I know it was a bit out of the blue."

"Yes," she replied with a smile. "It is… okay."

As Ben wandered back through the ruined streets, he thought about how much Verla had changed in the past few days since he first met her. She had been so closed in, and yet now she was even cracking the odd joke.

He walked jauntily up the road. It was great to feel like he had made a difference. He was pretty sure that he'd never made any major impact on anyone else's life – aside from his parents' of course.

And about Jamie… Ben had a good feeling about introducing Jamie to Verla. It was sweet, how he'd been trying so hard not to wake her up that morning. Ben realised he'd forgotten to ask Jamie what he did for a living, but he had a suspicious feeling he knew. Jamie had to be a lawyer. Ben couldn't make head nor tail of the contract and Verla had looked pretty confused as well, but Jamie had ploughed through it like a pro. He probably saw that kind of thing all the time.

Ben finally reached his house and marched up the steps. His mother looked up anxiously as he clattered through the front door. "Where have you been?" she exclaimed, standing up from where she'd been lying on the sofa. "You didn't come home last night!"

Ben had been so caught up in Verla's situation that he'd practically forgotten about his parents. "Sorry, Mum," he said awkwardly. "I was at a friend's house and I... I ended up crashing on their couch."

"I tried phoning you a thousand times," said Susan, sounding hysterical. "Why didn't you pick up? I almost called the police, Ben!"

"I'm really sorry," he said, at a loss for what to say. He pulled his phone out of his pocket. The screen informed him that he had nine missed calls.

"David!" Susan shouted, striding down the hall to the bedroom she shared with her husband. "David, he's home!"

Ben's father walked out of the bedroom, dressed in a shirt and trousers despite the early hour. "Hi, Ben," he said calmly. "See, Susan, he's fine."

"Well, I'm not," she snapped. "While you're still living under this roof, Ben Fletcher, you call us if you're not coming home at night."

"I'm really sorry," Ben repeated lamely.

"Just keep your mobile handy next time," said David. "You're an adult now, and we don't mind that you're staying out – just give us a quick call."

He kissed his wife on the cheek, grabbed his briefcase from the table, and headed out the front door. Ben was left facing his irate mother.

"I really am sorry," he said, feeling terrible about how stressed she looked but also wondering how many more times he'd have to apologise before she forgave him. So far it had been at least three. "I was at a friend's place and I just crashed out."

His mother's eyes softened a little. "I'm glad you're making friends," she said, biting her lip. "And I know you're an adult now. But just a call would be nice, okay? I worry."

"I know," he muttered guiltily, walking over and giving his mother an uncharacteristic hug. She gripped him tightly, then finally released him.

"Are you okay?" he asked, peering at her. Her eyes were a little red. "Where did Dad go? It's not even six thirty yet."

"He had to go back into the Sydney office again and he wanted to be there by nine," she said, sitting back down on the sofa. "Our one family holiday, and he has to spend the whole time working!"

"It hasn't been the whole time," said Ben reasonably. "This is the only the second time he's been in."

"And with you out all the time, doing who knows what," his mother continued as if she hadn't heard him. "It's just been me and your sister instead of the family time I wanted us to have."

Ben sat down on the arm of the sofa. He wasn't sure what to say.

Suddenly his mother took a deep breath as if composing herself. After a few seconds she smiled back up at Ben.

"Don't listen to me," she said softly. "Just being here, in this town... it's bringing back so many memories."

"Yeah, I guess I kind of forget you were born here," he admitted. "But do you remember that much about it? I thought your family moved away when you were little."

"Yes, when I was two," Susan said. "I only have a few snatches of real memory, but I guess after that I built a lot of it up in my mind."

Ben swallowed nervously. His mother hardly ever spoke so vulnerably; usually she was the local tower of strength and capability.

"I always thought I'd move back to the mountains for a while after I graduated from university," she murmured, gazing out of the window to the town beyond, lit in slants of orange and yellow from the early morning sun. "But when my father died, I just didn't have it in me. Jonathan was the only one who came back to live in Carmenton. It's a pity really, because your Grandpa Joseph really liked it here."

"Did he?" asked Ben. He hardly ever heard his mother speak about either of her parents. Her own mother had died giving birth, and her father was killed in a car crash on the way to her university graduation. From what Ben's father had told him, she'd never really gotten over her father's death and still blamed herself. "What was he like?"

"He was a great father, despite having to do it all on his own," she said. "He loved this place, but I know he realised its limitations. He really wanted me to do well in school, which I think is one of the reasons why he chose to move us away from here when I was so young. He was so insistent that I got a lot out of my education. There was never any choice about whether or not I was going to university! He wanted me to get the most out of the experience."

"Sounds familiar," Ben mumbled. He still hadn't looked at those university brochures yet.

"Jonathan and Brian didn't go to uni, so it was a big deal for my father that I should get accepted," Susan continued. "We were very close when I was growing up, and he wanted me to have all the opportunities my mother had missed out on."

"Did he talk about her much?" asked Ben hesitantly.

"Not really," Susan sighed. "I think he talked about her a lot with Jonathan and Brian – they were almost teenagers when she died, so they had a lot of memories. Of course it would have hit them hard."

She gazed out of the window and for once Ben's mind wasn't consumed with the situation in the mansion across town.

"For a while, when I was little, I decided my mother's death was my own fault," she said softly. "I must have been about five. It got into my head and I cried for about a week. When my father found out what was wrong, he told me that it could never be my fault, that I was the new life he was given when my mother's was taken away. He said I was his miracle baby."

Susan smiled sadly at her son. "I had almost died too," she said. "He said my heart had stopped too, just as my mother slipped away from us. But there was a doctor there who managed to revive me, against all odds."

Ben had never heard this story before and he sat quietly, listening to the tale.

"My father didn't know what to feel," she continued, staring at her hands. "Brian told me that he sat for days and days staring out the window. The hospital had to send someone to take care of us for a few months – to get me and the boys fed, make all the funeral arrangements, and get the boys off to school every day. It wasn't easy for them either. That doctor who had saved me – he was a godsend. Brian said he stopped by every day to drop off milk for the nurse to feed me, and he brought all brand-new baby clothes and toys and all the things I guess my mother assumed she'd be able to buy after I was born. He visited right up until my father could start looking after us again. A few months later, Dad tried to track down that doctor to say thank you. But he had disappeared. We never saw him again."

She pressed her hands together and gazed down at her fingers.

"So after all that tragedy, and then when your grandfather died on the way to see me graduate, things were never going to be easy," she said. "But you can see why the memories get to me. I almost didn't want to come back here. If the house hadn't been flooded, we'd still be in Perth right now."

She looked up to see her son's worried face, and her expression changed.

"Oh, I'm sorry to put this all on you, hon," she said, standing up and giving him a quick hug. "But do you see why our family is so important to me? It's so vital that we have people who know us, who can get through to us when times are bad, and love us for who we are."

She smoothed back her hair and smiled at Ben. "Now, I'm going to go and wake up your little sister. I've promised her a trip to the local bottle cap museum today."

"Sounds like great fun," said Ben, a little bewildered at his mother's quick change of mood.

"Yes, well, it could be interesting for a seven-year-old," she sighed ruefully. "Now I know you've probably got things to do today, so run along if you have to. But if I could please lock in a date on your social calendar, we're having a family barbecue on Tuesday night."

"Okay," said Ben. He decided that no matter how caught up he was in this Verla business, he would try to be nicer to his mother from now on.

She smiled at him, back to her old self, and he was relieved.

"I've got some plans today," he told her. "But we'll hang out later, okay?"

"Sure, hon, that's fine," she said back almost breezily, heading in the direction of Tia's room while Ben walked to the bathroom for a quick shower.

When he arrived back at Verla's house, he glimpsed the gleam of Jamie's car parked at the back of the house. Verla was curled up in a blanket on the porch, holding the contract and frowning at it.

"Where's Jamie?" Ben asked, taking a seat.

"He's gone for a walk," she said. "He wanted to see the rest of the town. He left you this coffee."

"Ah, yes," Ben said, looking around at the ruined houses and taking a sip from the Styrofoam cup. "It's quite a lot to get your head around."

"Actually, Jamie said he was going to come visit here a few more times over the next few days," Verla said, examining her hands. "So we can sort out the review properly." She glanced around her and shuddered. "Though why anyone would hang around here by choice is something I can't comprehend."

Ben pulled his chair closer to Verla's and they tried to make sense of the first few pages of the contract, but eventually he gave up and leaned back to talk instead. Ben sensed that Verla wasn't daring to put too much hope into her review. He stared at her as she talked. What must it be like inside her head? Her misery must plunge to unfathomable depths.

"I can't understand a word of this thing," she sighed, dangling the parchment. "I could certainly do with a law degree. Do you know what I was planning to study, Ben? Art. Now if I get my time again, I'm going to enrol myself straight into the nearest law school."

"Maybe I should do law," he mused, his thought being dragged back to the decision about university that he still hadn't made.

"Haven't you chosen what you're doing yet?" asked Verla. "You said you've just graduated high school. Where are you going for university?"

"I haven't picked one yet," he replied. "I kind of missed the application deadline. Now I'm not sure what I'll have to do – probably visit the university people personally, and see if they'll accept a late application. But I have no idea where I want to go!" He threw his hands up in the air. "I don't know if I'm interested in any of it."

"Why?" she said curiously, looking like she was glad to forget her contract for a while.

"They spend all your school life teaching you all this stuff you don't even want to learn," Ben burst out, jumping up from his chair and beginning to pace. "Then at the end, they turn around and say to you, 'quick, pick a career! Invest four or five years in it, too bad if you're not even sure what you want to do in the first place!' Then when that finishes, you end up going 'what just happened, why did I just waste all that time and money on a piece of paper that says I can do something I'm not even interested in doing', and then you probably end up just doing it anyway, and hating your life!"

At the end of his little speech, Ben flopped back down in his chair, then looked over at Verla remorsefully. "Sorry," he muttered. "I know that you kind of have the market cornered when it comes to life-hating."

"No, it's fine," she insisted. "So what have you thought about doing, Ben? I mean, what are you really interested in?"

"That's the problem," he muttered. "I have no idea. Last week I wanted to be an architect. Before that I thought I should join the army. Two months ago I wanted to do music and teach guitar lessons for the rest of my life, even though I've never played an instrument."

"What were you good at in school?" she asked gently.

"Nothing," he admitted. "I was Mr Average all the way. I never got into much trouble, but I never really stood out. I didn't win any prizes, but I guess I didn't fail anything either."

"Doesn't that make you the same as ninety five per cent of your class, though?" asked Verla.

"Yeah. Maybe. I don't know," said Ben. "Everyone else seemed to have a calling. Some of my friends have known what they wanted to do since they were about ten."

"What did you want to do when you were ten?"

"I wanted to be a publicist, just like my father. Then I saw how much it stressed him out, and I decided I wanted to do something fun. Problem is, I've never found anything that fits that description."

"What does your mother do?"

"She's a school teacher. But I'm totally not into that stuff. I'd probably murder about ten kids on my first day."

"There has to be something you're interested in," Verla mused thoughtfully. "Maybe you won't find out until you've tried a few different things."

"But that's the problem!" Ben repeated, jumping up to resume his pacing. "I'm going to end up chasing my tail for the rest of my life until I finally settle for something that I'm not that interested in. Then it's going to be work, work, work for the next forty years, broken up with tiny little holidays where I'll do my best to forget my life, but then whoa, suddenly I'll be back at work the next week and back into the whole cycle again. Then when I finally have enough money to retire – probably when I'm at least eighty, I reckon that's the way it'll be then – I'll only have about five years left to live while my body shuts down, then I'll die! And that's assuming I don't drop dead from a heart attack when I'm fifty!"

Ben slumped his elbows down onto the porch railing and gazed, chin in his hands, at the half-ruined house on the other side of the street. "Sorry," he muttered again. "It's just been getting me down."

"You're right, it does not sound ideal," Verla's soft voice sounded from behind him, and she came to stand next to him at the railing. "I suppose you just have to keep looking for that thing you think is enjoyable. Even if it takes ten years to find it, wouldn't it be better to have spent that time looking for it then giving up on ever finding it at all?"

"I guess," Ben mumbled.

"And if you never find it," she continued, "you'll just have to put meaning into your life in other ways."

Ben smiled weakly at her. "Thanks. I know you're right. Hey, maybe you should choose counselling instead of law."

"Well, I know it's not appropriate to revel in another's misfortune, but in a way – thank you."

"What for?"

"It is nice to feel I may be able to help someone else. It's not something I expect after living in this hell for a century. So – thanks."

"Anytime."

The sun was a lot higher in the sky and Ben was eating a burger when Jamie walked back up the street, his shirt wrinkled and untucked. He grabbed a handful of Ben's French fries and perched on the porch railing.

"Nice look," Ben observed, gazing at Jamie's rumpled sleeves and the grass stains on his trousers. It was the first time he'd seen him look anything less than crisply perfect. "Did you have some little adventures on your walk?"

"Far from it," said Jamie, munching on the fries. "I fell asleep on the grass in the park. The locals must have thought I was homeless. They probably wanted to issue me with a move-along order."

"Nah, the locals don't notice much around here," said Ben, motioning towards Verla with his head. "They let all sorts of riff-raff hang around for years."

Verla smacked him on the arm with her rolled-up parchment, and Jamie leaned forward to steal the last of Ben's fries.

"Where did you get that?" he asked, nodding at the burger Ben was eating.

"Local food van," said Ben. "They do breakfast but all the food looked disgusting. The hash browns looked like blocks of lard." He took another bite, chewed, and swallowed. "But I figure you can't go too wrong with a burger and fries."

"I'm going to agree with you, but only because you're eating it right now and I don't want to put you off," said Jamie. "I'm nice like that."

"Are you sure you don't want any?" Ben asked Verla, waving the remains of his burger in front of her face. "I can run down and get some more if you've changed your mind."

"Ugh, no," she said, recoiling. "Even if I did eat, it wouldn't be whatever that thing is."

"What about you, Jamie?" he asked, moving the burger in his direction.

"No thanks," said Jamie. "I think I'm going to be eating a lot of that stuff soon, anyway."

"Verla said you'd come back over the next few days to help us sort this out," said Ben.

"Yeah, it's looking that way," Jamie replied. "This review is going to take more than just a note and a box of chocolates. We'll have to put some decent time into it."

"Do you need to get time off work?" Verla asked.

"I'm on a break right now, so no need," said Jamie. "But I'll have to go back into the city every night to take care of a few things, especially as I don't get any phone reception around here."

"This is really nice of you," said Verla with a smile.

Jamie shrugged, but looked pleased. "It's no trouble," he said. He glanced at his watch. "I have to head back to Sydney now, anyway. Do you two need anything?"

"I'm fine, thanks," Ben said. "I'm going to stick around here and try to become an expert on contracts for people who are sentenced to an eternity in Hell." He paused, reflecting on the statement. "I didn't ever expect myself to say something like that, that's for sure."

Jamie laughed. "Watch out," he warned him. "It's only going to get stranger from here."

~

Ben, Verla and Jamie spent the next three days examining Verla's contract. Jamie arrived from the city every day with books and papers that he and Verla examined and discussed. Ben tried to keep up with the conversation but frequently became lost, and even Verla admitted that she didn't understand a lot of the technicality behind it all.

"I feel bad that I don't know more about this," she confided to Ben while Jamie was doing a coffee run on the fourth morning. "I've had a hundred years to study it – I could have known it inside out by now!"

"You didn't know a review existed," said Ben. "How could you? It's not even written in the contract."

"I know, but think of all the time I've wasted," she said. "Plus," she looked sideways at Ben, "do *not* tell Jamie this, please. But I dislike seeming ignorant in front of him."

She broke off as Jamie appeared, walking down the street and holding two Styrofoam coffee cups. He walked up the porch steps and handed one to Ben.

"Thanks," said Ben, taking a long sip as Verla watched.

"What does it taste like?" she asked.

"Like liquid energy," he said, closing his eyes in exaggerated bliss.

"It's kind of bitter, but the milk makes it creamy. Can you smell it?" asked Jamie, holding his cup near her face.

"No," she said wistfully. "But I'd like to. It's just another thing to add to my wish list, I suppose. Along with avocado and kiwi fruit. And sashimi."

"I'll make a note of it," said Jamie with a smile.

"It's worth it," said Ben, taking a long pull on his drink. "Your life won't be the same until you've had salmon sashimi dipped in soy sauce. Mmmm-mmmm."

"I'd probably need a life to begin with," she said drily, and Ben laughed.

"I need to head back into the city pretty soon," said Jamie, changing the subject. "Want to come along, Ben? I can drop you back in town later on today."

Ben nodded enthusiastically, and they both turned to Verla.

"No, thank you," she said. "I'm a bit stuck here. I'm going to walk down to the park and see if I can find an old newspaper there."

Ben wrinkled his nose. "You go through bins?" he asked.

Verla looked affronted. "No," she said. "The local townsfolk sometimes leave them on the park benches."

"I'm relieved," Ben grinned. "For a minute there I had a vision of you digging through a dumpster, flicking off old banana peels while you searched for the sports section of the paper."

Jamie went to get the car from behind the house, where Verla had requested he park it ("I'd really prefer my eternally-damned house not to become a tourist attraction for car enthusiasts") and Ben jumped in. They waved goodbye to Verla and headed down the mountains towards the city.

"Do you think we should go to see the people in charge of Verla's contract?" Ben asked, loving the fact that he was sitting in an amazing car that was racing down the highway at high speed.

"I was thinking that could be a good idea," Jamie said, glancing at Ben. "What do you think? We're really cutting it down to the wire anyway. I didn't tell Verla this, because I didn't want to panic her – but there's only a week left to lodge the review. We have all the paperwork, we may as well do it now."

"Only a week left?" asked Ben, alarmed.

"Yeah. I don't think she noticed the date on the contract – she probably doesn't even know what month it is, unless she looks at the dates on her newspapers. But next Thursday, she'll have been in Hell for a century."

"Whoa," said Ben, realising what a close call it had been. What if his family had planned their holiday two weeks later?

"So I think we should definitely head in there today," said Jamie.

"Yeah, good idea," said Ben. "Do we have to make an appointment or anything?"

"I reckon we'll be okay."

"Great," said Ben. "But hey, wait! How are we going to lodge it? How do we get to Hell?" He narrowed his eyes suspiciously. "We don't have to die, do we?" Suddenly hurtling along the road in an extremely fast car wasn't so appealing.

"Nope," said Jamie. "Both Heaven and Hell have offices in every major city."

"Oh, of course," Ben said sarcastically. "How could I not have known that? So obvious! And how did you pick up these handy pieces of information?"

"I told you," Jamie shrugged, "I just know a lot about these things."

"Too much, I reckon," Ben said. "You know, Jamie, there are people – many people! – in this world who don't know any of the stuff you've kindly shared with me over the past few days. And they're born, they live, and they die without knowing, and they're happy! Blissfully happy, probably! Lots of 'em out there you know!"

"Probably less than you think," said Jamie dryly. "Just because you're not aware of something, Ben, it doesn't mean the rest of us are too slow to pick up on it too."

"Yeah right," Ben said smugly. "I'm obviously, like, the chosen one."

"Keep telling yourself that, mate."

## - CHAPTER FIFTEEN -

# Mr Strimcrop's Office

After a long drive along the highway, a frustratingly slow negotiation through traffic lights on Parramatta Road and a smooth glide along a pretty café-lined street, the car pulled up next to a modern apartment building that seemed to be made mostly of stainless steel and glass. Glimpses of the sparkling harbour were visible in the spaces between the buildings either side. Ben peered up at the pristine walls and wondered if he'd be able to afford a city apartment instead of university student housing.

"Just got to have a quick change of clothes, be back in a second," said Jamie, disappearing from the car. Only a few minutes later he jumped back in, wearing pale grey trousers and a crisp white shirt unbuttoned at the collar. He threw a similar shirt to Ben, started the car, and navigated his way into the centre of Sydney.

"I think it's along here," he said, squinting up at buildings while Ben buttoned the new shirt over his blue T-shirt. They slowed in front of a tall black building, and Jamie found a parking spot towards the end of the block. They jumped out of the car, and after Jamie had fed some coins to the parking meter and grabbed a folder of papers from the car, they walked back down the street.

The area in front of the building was paved in shiny black and dotted with fountains that sprayed black-coloured water high into the air. Large dark columns framed the massive entranceway, and etched in red letters across the top of the ornate two-storey facade were the words "HADES CORPORATION". Behind the façade, a gleaming black building stretched into the sky, at least ten storeys higher than the other buildings on the block.

"Subtle, isn't it," Jamie muttered, motioning up at the sign. Ben wasn't sure if he was referring to the 'Hades' or the blood-red lettering.

"Isn't Hades a Greek mythology thing?" he hissed back.

"Yeah, but what's a little plagiarism to the Devil?"

They walked through a set of solid stone double doors which were propped open, letting in a stark rectangle of sunlight flood the shiny black tiles. The large black-clad lobby was very glamorous, with subtle up-lighting illuminating the walls and another black fountain bubbling peacefully in the corner. Jamie and Ben, in their crisp white shirts, looked rather conspicuous against the dark décor.

Jamie walked straight up to the long reception desk that ran the length of the far wall, and Ben trailed behind him. The lone receptionist was an extremely beautiful young woman with glossy black hair that cascaded down her back. She smiled seductively at Jamie, her tight red suit hugging her torso tightly as she leaned forward.

"Can I help you, sir?" she asked in a voice like liquid caramel.

"We're here to see a representative of the Sentenced Review Board," Jamie told her with a friendly smile. "It's about a Sentenced whose case is up for review. We don't have an appointment, but I was hoping someone might be free?"

She pursed her lips and clicked her blood-red nails on the keyboard in front of her.

"Do you have some relevant identification?" she asked Jamie, her red lips forming the words lusciously. Ben felt a moment of panic; the only identification he had was his driver's licence, and he wasn't sure that was what the woman was referring to. But Jamie smoothly pulled a white card out of his wallet and showed it to the woman.

Instantly her come-hither eyes hardened into steely plates and she glared at Jamie. "And him?" she asked curtly, nodding at Ben.

"My assistant," Jamie replied smoothly. "Ben Robinson."

She frowned over at Ben, who tried not to let his nerves show. "I'll just see who's available," she said disdainfully, and Ben relaxed.

Jamie and Ben gazed around the lobby as the receptionist murmured into her phone.

"Robinson?" Ben mouthed to Jamie.

Jamie shrugged. "Best to keep you off their radar," he whispered back, then motioned towards the receptionist as she put the phone down.

"We do have someone who will see you," she said. "One of the Review Board associates, Mr Strimcrop, is available right now. I'll show you the way."

She stepped coolly out from behind the counter, and another receptionist with shining auburn hair appeared from a door behind the bench and silently took her colleague's place in front of the computer.

The first receptionist led Ben and Jamie them towards the elevator bank, her hips swaying with each step she took. Trying to be professional, Ben tore his gaze from her pert derriere with some difficulty. Once inside the elevator, she turned back towards them and folded her arms – succeeding in elevating her bust a little more – and said out loud: "Fifty two down."

As the elevator zoomed towards its destination, Ben saw that the massive panel of buttons on the wall indicated that not only did the building rise seventy stories into the air, it also appeared to stretch one hundred stories below the ground. And currently, they were plummeting in a downwards direction.

The elevator stopped smoothly and the doors sprang open to reveal a small, windowless lobby decked out in the same décor as the one upstairs. The receptionist sashayed towards the long black desk, behind which sat another young woman wearing the same outfit and evidently holding the same premium gym membership as her colleague.

"They're here to see Mr Strimcrop," the receptionist told the girl at the desk. "And they're not… one of ours."

"Thanks, Marigold," the girl said, looking at them with a pout. "I'll take it from here."

Marigold re-entered the lift, and Ben and Jamie were left standing awkwardly in the lobby while the new receptionist stared at them, one perfect eyebrow raised.

"You have your identification?" she asked Jamie, and he showed her the same card he'd produced upstairs.

"And him?" she asked, nodding towards Ben.

"With me," Jamie replied.

The receptionist gave a large, long-suffering sigh, her ample bosom heaving.

"I suppose that should be all right," she said. "Mr Strimcrop's office is right through here." She glided from her chair and walked down the hallway like a model down a catwalk, pausing at an unremarkable door. She knocked softly, then opened the door and indicated Ben and Jamie to step through. She closed the door behind them.

Mr Strimcrop's office was a surprise. Ben had expected that someone with the job title 'Review Board Associate' would have a stark grey office with a painting of some dead monarch as the centrepiece of the decorating scheme. Instead, Ben felt as if he'd walked onto the set of a music video. The floor was carpeted in swirly black and white, the bright purple walls hung with leopard-skin drapes, and the desk was a crimson padded velvet monstrosity. Behind the desk, a tall-backed chair faced away from them.

Jamie stepped forward. "Mr Strimcrop," he stated.

The chair swivelled around and with it came a man, hands steepled and chin tilted down, and clad in a sharp black suit that contrasted starkly with the décor around him. He was thin and middle aged but his ebony hair showed no signs of grey. His gaze flicked over Ben and came to rest on Jamie, who held his eyes without blinking.

"Jamie Portman," he said darkly.

Ben saw Jamie's brow furrow ever so slightly. "You know me?" he asked, not averting his stare.

Something passed between the two men and Mr Strimcrop was the first to break eye contact. "No," he admitted. "My receptionist told me."

He waved at the corner at some chairs, and Jamie and Ben dragged some fuchsia fur-upholstered chairs over the carpet.

"I must excuse the décor," said Strimcrop, after Jamie had introduced Ben as his assistant. "I just inherited this office from the Sub-Directory Head of Vice Proliferation. I haven't had a chance to redecorate, and I'm afraid his tastes were not... conservative."

Ben wasn't sure what to say, so he glanced at Jamie.

"Mr Strimcrop," Jamie said, getting down to business. "As your receptionist may have also informed you, we're here to see you about a Sentenced whose case is up for review this year."

"Yes," said the associate, his thin nostrils flaring. He paused, staring at Jamie, then spoke suddenly. "Mr Portman, having gained entrance to these offices you are obviously not just one of the oblivious. In fact, I discern something… else about you."

Jamie made no reply and Strimcrop fluttered his hands. "No matter," he said. "I know whose side you are on. What are the details of the case? I presume you have come prepared?"

"Yes, we have," said Jamie, laying Verla's contract on the table along with a neat stack of papers.

Strimcrop hit a button on his phone. "Jasmine," he ordered, "minutes, please." A few seconds later, a busty young woman who could have been Marigold's sister slinked into the room. She perched her bottom on the edge of Strimcrop's desk and poised a blood-red fountain pen over a pad of paper. Ben was momentarily distracted.

"Begin," Strimcrop commanded, and Jamie picked up the piece of paper at the top of the pile.

"The Sentenced's name is Verla," he said as Jasmine started writing on her notepad.

"Number?" Strimcrop interrupted.

"Oh-nine-six-eight-five-one-four," Jamie read from the sheet, and Strimcrop made a note on his own pad of paper.

"At first glance, this Sentenced's case doesn't seem out of the ordinary," said Jamie quite formally, tapping the thick scroll of paper. "But after examining the contract and the methods in which she was given her fate, it seems this particular verdict needs to be reversed, and indeed should have been reviewed at long before the hundred-year mark."

Pointing to various pieces of paper as he spoke, Jamie explained that Verla's sentence was authorised only by a relatively junior employee, with no senior managers giving their sign-off on the judgment. "The practice of Sentencing is only tolerated by God's organisation because there are so few cases every year," he said. "So why was a junior allowed to not only make this call, but kill dozens of others in the process?"

Strimcrop leaned forward, looking interested.

"If you look here," Jamie said, unfurling the scroll and finding a place he'd marked with an orange sticky note, "You'll see that both the Sentenced and Mr Duncan signed the contract, but the witness section was left blank."

Mr Strimcrop gazed to where Jamie was pointing, while Jasmine scribbled furiously on her pad of paper.

Jamie paused before beginning his next point. "Also, if you'll note these other cases of people being Sentenced." He ruffled around in his stack and extracted a few pieces of paper. "They have all been placed in a situation where they contribute to the Devil's plan of mayhem. In one situation, one George oh-nine-six-nine-two-two-four, previously a blacksmith, was Sentenced in 1932 and sent to live in the local school where he'd been bullied as a child. Once located there, he was assumed to be a beggar, and with his gloomy presence made it impossible for the school to be used. The village of Brookside did not receive funding for a new school for at least fifteen years, and that gap in education contributed to a significant rise in crime in the area in the following years."

Strimcrop looked bored, but Jamie persevered. "In another case, Huong oh-eight-four-nine-oh-one-six was Sentenced in 1781 and located to a temple she associated with bad childhood memories. Obviously once she was there she drove all others from it, and the spiritual purity of her village's residents suffered greatly as a result.

"These are only a few examples," Jamie said to Mr Strimcrop. "Really," he shuffled his stack of papers, "I could go on all day."

Strimcrop eyed the bundle apprehensively, clearly afraid Jamie planned to waste his whole afternoon reading out boring records. "That won't be necessary. Shall we move on?"

"If you like," replied Jamie. "As long as you understand the point I'm trying to make – that Verla's sentencing was purely at the whim of one inconsequential man, and had no contribution towards the Devils' overarching program of destruction and mayhem, as the other examples' verdicts were."

Ben looked at Jamie, impressed. He had no idea Jamie had all those records. While Ben had been looking up things like 'mittimus' and 'non sequitur' in a legal dictionary that Verla had produced from somewhere inside her house, Jamie had evidently been off doing something useful like researching the whole concept of Sentencing.

Jamie spoke for a while about how Verla was clearly a victim of Duncan's sinister agenda, whatever that may be, then wrapped up his argument with a few pointed remarks about the man's poor handling of the whole situation. After finishing with an impassioned plea for the reversal of Verla's sentence, he eased back in his chair, and Ben felt like standing up and applauding.

While Jasmine flexed her fingers in a rather provocative manner, Strimcrop toyed with his fountain pen.

"Mr Portman," he finally said, slowly leaning back in his chair. "I do appreciate your preparation of this appeal; it is refreshing to see someone who is actually willing to put more than a minor amount of effort into these things."

Ben flushed a little guiltily.

Strimcrop continued, eyeing Jamie beadily. "I must ask you, though, if you do realise that all the points you've made, everything you've described … it is simply the nature of the beast."

Ben looked up. He'd heard that phrase a few times now.

"I do realise that," said Jamie. "But there are systems in place, systems that must be adhered to, and the right systems were not used. Even mayhem cannot be achieved without careful planning, and your boss knows that."

"Which boss are you referring to?" asked Strimcrop pompously.

"The Devil, Lucifer, Satan, The Angry Red Bloke with Little Horns, whatever you want to call him," said Jamie impatiently. "He can't have loose cannons like this Duncan character disrupting the order of his chaos."

Strimcrop laughed silkily. "Mr Portman! Whose side are you on?"

Jamie looked Strimcrop in the eye and handed over his stack of papers.

"This woman needs her case to be looked at," he said. "She is permitted a fair review by the Board, as per the Sentencing Guidelines of twelve ninety-one. Can you tell me this will happen?"

Strimcrop looked back at him and the silence lengthened. Eventually he emitted a resigned sigh and placed the papers in front of him. "It will."

## - CHAPTER SIXTEEN -

# Verla's Verdict

"And so, if they've got any kind of justice system going on there, I reckon we've got a pretty good chance of getting you free soon!"

Ben was standing jubilantly in Verla's kitchen. He had never been inside her house before, as nearly all their meetings had taken place on the porch. But the sunny day had turned cloudy during the drive back to Carmenton, and the wind was bringing the pelting rain onto the porch. Without electric lights, Verla's kitchen was dark and gloomy, but Ben could still see the old-fashioned fittings and imagined that nothing had changed in the hundred years she had lived there alone. It was like looking around at a kitchen display in a museum.

Jamie was a bit more cautious. "They promised they'd look at it, anyway," he said, glancing up from his examination of the ancient stove.

Verla leaned back against the kitchen bench and closed her eyes. "Who did you see?" she asked.

"Someone called Strimcrop," said Jamie. "I called a few contacts and asked about him. He's been on the staff for years. One of those bureaucratic types who probably passed the evilness test during his life by giving mountains of boring paperwork to unsuspecting underlings. Still," he shrugged, "hopefully that means he'll be anal enough to actually process the application for review, instead of shoving it under a pile of other papers like some of them do."

Abruptly he straightened up and changed the subject. "I'm going to run over to that burger van and grab some food. Want anything?"

Ben put in an order for onion rings. The rain had died down, so he and Verla dragged the chairs to the rear of the porch where it was least damp and sat back to gaze at the wet street in front of them. Ben stared after the Aston Martin as it turned down the street.

"I think I've figured out what Jamie does," he said to Verla.

"Yes? What do you think?" she asked.

"He's a lawyer for Sentenced people like you," said Ben. "He knew all about it from the start, and you should have seen him in Strimcrop's office today. Knew his stuff. Talked the talk."

"That would explain how he knows a lot about the subject," she said. "I asked him about his background, but I'm not sure that he actually gave me an answer. I think he's rather good at being evasive. He's certainly not a Sentenced, and he told me he was not an employee of God. Yet there is certainly something different. He appears to have no difficulty being in this house."

"What do you mean?" Ben asked.

Verla gazed at him. A slight frown furrowed her brow.

"In all my time here, no one has been able to be in the vicinity of this house for any length of time, without having to leave for some reason," she explained. "Some people are immediately ill, others are immersed in a wave of depression. They leave, and don't come back – yet their interest is not piqued, and they continue with their lives without being curious about this place. It's part of the wards that keep me memory-locked here. My only visitors who have not felt it are employees of Hell. I assume employees of God would have the same resistance."

"But I'm here," said Ben. "I'm not an employee of Hell *or* God. But I feel fine."

"Yes, it is very strange," she mused. "I was thinking perhaps the wards are wearing off."

"That would mean you'd get to have visitors here," he said.

Verla didn't look enthused with the idea. "We will see," she said hesitantly. "At the moment I am quite satisfied with only two visitors! It is probably not the case though. I expect that Jamie is one of those people who work for God, after all. Perhaps they cannot advertise it, and that's why he has been so evasive?"

"Probably," said Ben. "He had this little white card that he pulled out when we were in that office, and wham! They let him right through, and even me because he said I was his assistant. How do you think you get to do a job like that? Do you reckon you have to apply with a resume? He told me God has ten personal assistants, so obviously he has to recruit his staff somehow." Ben chewed his lip for a second then nodded conclusively.

"Yeah," he continued. "He's got to be a lawyer. That's why that professor guy told me to go straight to him. Probably gets a fee for referrals." He chuckled. "I've heard lawyers make heaps of money. That's why he's got that great car and stuff, and I haven't been inside his apartment but the outside looked really expensive, and I think it's in a really good bit of Sydney. Imagine how much he could charge for getting people out of Hell! People would pay *anything!*"

Verla began to look worried and Ben looked sideways at her. "But I wouldn't worry about him charging if I were you," he advised her.

She looked back at him. "What do you mean?" she asked, a hint of suspicion in her voice.

Ben grinned. "Ah, I reckon he's developing a bit of a soft spot for you," he said.

Verla's suspicion turned to a look of confusion. "What does that mean, a soft spot?" she asked.

Ben laughed. He forgot sometimes that Verla was more in tune with the language of a different century.

"It means he might like you, Verla," he said. "You know, like, *like.*"

She glanced away but not before Ben saw that she had some colour in her cheeks for once.

"I don't think you're right," she said. "If you count up the years I am actually an old lady of one hundred and twenty one. Not exactly what a young man wants for a courtship. Not to mention the misery in hell part of my life."

"Well, apart from the fact that you just used the word 'courtship' in a sentence, I don't think there's anything old about you," he told her. "You certainly look like you're young and everything. I reckon some women would agree to be in Hell forever if it meant they could have skin like yours for as long as you have."

"Thank you, that is nice of you to say," she said. She leaned forward, staring thoughtfully up at the sky.

"A hundred years, though," observed Ben. "That's a long time to be stuck in this house. What do you do with your time? If I went to prison for a while I think I'd try to get a couple of university degrees. Then I'd try to do a doctorate or something, a thesis and all that stuff. But I guess that's not really an option for you. You must get so, so bored."

Verla turned back to Ben and gave him her familiar tiny smile. "I don't think I have ever shown you," she said. "Would you like to see what I do with my time?"

She led him through the living room of her house to an ornate wooden door next to a roll top desk. They stepped through the door and Ben's eyes widened.

In front of him was a circular room that stretched to the height of the whole three stories of the house, and up into what Ben assumed was the turret he'd seen from the outside. Light filtered in through long narrow windows to reveal shelves of books – thousands and thousands of them. A spiral staircase led to two levels of galleries, and on the ground floor and at both levels, old-fashioned ladders sat on runners for those books out of reach.

"This is my father's library," she told Ben. "It was his father's, and his father's before that. It has taken many years to collect all these books."

He stared up at the shelves stretching above them. "Have you read all of these?"

"Yes," Verla replied simply. "Most of them at least twice or three times."

"What are they all about?"

"Oh, everything. There are plays and operas and stories and poetry – everything you could think of. I even have old family diaries and histories that date back centuries."

"Didn't they take this away from you when you were, you know, sent back here?" he asked.

"No," she said. "I often wondered why, why they would not take away something that could be a source of such pleasure. I have decided that they must not see it as a pleasure at all. The pursuit of knowledge – it is rather the opposite of the need to destroy everything. They would not see this the way I do."

Verla stared up at the stacks almost lovingly, and Ben finally understood why she had retained her sanity and a spark of her passion for life all of those long, lonely years. She had survived without friendship and love because she had found it in the books before her.

"Verla? Ben?" Jamie's voice rang out from the porch.

"In here!" Ben called back, and a few seconds later Jamie joined them in the library.

"Wow," he said, looking up. "This is amazing."

The three stood staring around at the books for a while. Ben reflected that he'd spent a lot more time in libraries recently than he was used to.

"I can only read during the day, because of the light," said Verla. "Sometimes by moonlight, if it's bright enough, which is why I like to spend so much time out on the porch."

"Do you want me to bring you some lamps or something?" Ben asked, wondering why he hadn't thought of it before.

"Thank you for the thought, but it is not possible," she said. "No electricity or gas functions within this house."

Ben pulled out his phone, ready to prove Verla wrong, but when he pressed a button to illuminate the screen nothing happened. He frowned and stabbed the power button a few times, but it didn't respond.

"It's fine," said Verla, putting her hand on his arm. "I don't mind. I've read by moonlight for a century – I'm rather used to it now."

She smiled at both of them, then looked back up at her books.

"So, is this why you're still... still kind of..." Jamie trailed off.

"Still kind of normal?" Verla said, finishing his sentence for him. "I think so. As normal as a hundred-year-old resident of Hell can be."

~

"Ben? Ben!"

His mother's voice rang out as Ben walked into his bedroom early that evening. He was exhausted. Although it wasn't even seven o'clock yet, he was really hoping to catch some sleep in a comfortable bed.

"Yes?" he called back tiredly.

His mother rounded the corner, dressed in a nice pair of jeans and top.

"Are you ready?" she asked. "We're leaving in about five minutes."

"For what?"

"The barbecue at Jonathan and Anne's!" Susan said with a mixture of affection and exasperation. "You've known about it for days, honey."

Ben stood limply. He was certainly not in the mood to go a barbecue.

His mother must have sensed his lack of enthusiasm. "Come on, hon," she said quietly. "You've hardly spent any time with the family lately."

"Okay," said Ben reluctantly. He waited until she'd left the room before he flopped down on the bed and let out a quiet groan. He knew he should show some more enthusiasm for family time, especially after how much his mother been yearning for it the other day, but all he wanted to do right now was sleep.

After a few minutes of lying down, he slowly got up again.

He unbuttoned Jamie's white shirt, laid it carefully over the back of the desk chair, and went out to join his parents and sister. Tonight, he'd try to forget about what was happening across town, and concentrate on spending time with his family.

They parked next to a black Range Rover outside Jonathan and Anne's house, and Susan's other brother Brian charged out of the house to engulf his sister in a hug.

Ben escaped with just a bone-crunching handshake, and found Jay and Sean on cooking duty in the back yard. He grabbed a soft drink from a nearby esky and leaned over the back of the grill lid, making discouraging comments about the state of the sausages.

"Look at that one, Jay," he said critically. "It's practically bright pink and the other ones are burned to a crisp."

"I disagree," said Sean, loading the steaks onto a plate. "It's not bright pink; it's more of a mauve colour."

Jay tried to relocate the offending sausage to a hotter location.

"Aw, look!" said Ben sadly. "You've snapped the poor thing in half. What are you trying to do?"

Jay laughed and attempted to stab Ben with the barbecue tongs. While Ben was fending him off with a dish towel, Sean deftly transferred the fuchsia sausage onto Ben's plate over at the table.

"How's it going, boys?" asked Susan, walking up to the barbecue. She peered at the steaks on the grill. "They look like they've been cooking on that side for a while. If you're going for well-done, you may have to warn us oldies so we can put our good dentures in."

"Thanks for the mental image, Aunty Sue," said Jay, flipping a steak with the tongs. "They'll be cooked medium, I promise." He picked up a piece of steak but lost his grip, and both the steak and the tongs slipped down the side of the grill into the flames.

"Medium, you reckon?" Ben laughed. "More like incinerated."

Jay started hunting through the utensils for another pair of tongs to use to rescue the steak, but Susan slipped her hand down the side of the grill and quickly fished the piece of meat out through the flames. She put it back on the grill while her nephew stared at her.

"What? I just washed my hands," she said, diving her hand back into the fire to rescue the tongs. "Ouch! This metal's hot."

"She's not exactly 'safety first'," Ben told Jay, shaking his head. "You should see her with our fireplace at home. Practically crawls in between the logs to make sure it's burning properly."

"I do not," said Susan. "But you have to get the wood just right to make sure the fire burns all night." She flipped the remaining steaks and smiled at the boys. "There! Just a few more minutes and they'll be done."

When the steaks finished cooking the boys loaded all the meat onto a platter and brought it over to the table, where their uncle Brian was holding court. Anne had already brought in bowls of salad and bottles of soft drink and wine.

"Thanks a lot," Ben told Jay and Sean, gesturing at the lonely sausage on the plate in front of him. "Not only do I end up with the rubbishy one, but it looks like I didn't wait for everyone else to be served and had to dive in first."

"You would have anyway," Jay pointed out. "We just saved you the trouble, and now you have an excuse to start early."

"Let's dig in," Jonathan declared loudly, and started passing platters of food down the table.

Brian, David and Jonathan were arguing about something to do with motorbikes and Anne and Susan were discussing the share market when Jay leaned down towards Ben.

"So, did you ever crack the case?" he asked with a grin.

"About that house?" Ben asked casually and Jay nodded. Ben hesitated for a second; should he tell his cousins about his latest adventures? He glanced down the table and decided that even if he wanted to, now was not the time. He went for a different tactic instead.

"Yeah," he grinned back, spearing a piece of steak with his fork. "I'm now best buds with the lady living there and we have cups of tea on her porch every day while we discuss philosophy and religion."

Sean laughed. "Ah well," he said "At least you tried, hey? It made things interesting for a while, at least."

Anne started clearing up dishes, and Jay and Sean got up to help her. "No, no," she said, waving them back again. "You boys stay here. This'll only take me a minute."

Susan leaned towards the three boys as she passed some empty salad bowls down the table to Anne. "Isn't this great?" she said. "All you cousins together. Are you being nice to Oliver?"

They looked down the table to where Brian's young son was negotiating a peace treaty between two action figures and Tia's Barbie Doll. Ben noticed Tia looked like she was longing to provide the voice of Barbie and tell the camouflaged soldiers exactly where to go, but she didn't want to look uncool in front of her older cousins.

"Of course we're being nice, Aunty Susan," said Jay. "Aren't we always?"

"You are," she said affectionately. "You know, we should all get together more often. Family is so important, you know."

Uncle Brian overheard this, and interrupted himself in the middle of his spiel about his new boss at work. "That's right, Suze!" he boomed then turned to his nephews, his cheeks looking slightly ruddier than usual.

"Now boys, you don't know how lucky you are, having all of us!" he said. "When Jonathan and I were teenagers and Susan here was just a kid, it was just us and our father, no uncles and aunts and cousins! Not even a mother! None of this big family fun!"

"Um, what about Uncle Thomas?" Ben asked, feeling it was a bit unfair to overlook the frail old man from the family summary.

Brain waved his hand dismissively, nearly knocking an action figure flying. "Thomas was a lot older than our father, and anyway, he was in the army," he said. "He chose a life of service over having kids. And Uncle Arthur's entire life was consumed with researching the history of Bavaria or something – he was hardly ever home and frankly I reckon he was a bit on the barmy side. He's probably got ten illegitimate kids in Europe that we're never going to know about until they show up for their share of the inheritance."

"But still," interrupted Susan hastily, "they're both lovely men and we all enjoy their company. And," she looked sternly at Brian, "I think that when we grew up we had a lot of fun."

"Of course," said her brother, looking slightly humbled. "And if our parents were still around I think they'd be pleased with how we all turned out." He sighed and glanced at his son, who had migrated to the grass with his action figures and was now being bossed around by Tia, whose Barbie Doll had taken over as dictator of the lawn. "It's just a pity some things don't work out in the long run."

Ben averted his gaze awkwardly. His uncle's divorce wasn't

finalised yet and from what he'd heard from his parents, custody of Oliver was being used as the latest bargaining chip.

"Things could have been worse," said Susan gently, putting her arm around Brian. "What if you'd ended up marrying that girl you dated in university, Frida?"

She grinned at the boys, obviously trying to lighten the mood. "Frida seemed to be a nice girl, but they broke up when she went to Europe – "

"And I wouldn't pay for her plane ticket," Uncle Brian interrupted.

Susan laughed. "It wasn't until a few years later that we came across her name in the paper," she said. "Frida had married eight men in quick succession and swindled a few million from them."

Ben was fascinated. "How did they catch her?" he asked.

"She forgot to divorce one of them before she got married again," said Susan. "Of course bigamy's not a huge crime so she was let off pretty lightly, but hey," she nudged Brian, "that could have been you up there saying 'I do'."

"Oh, like you can talk," he told his sister, glancing around to make sure her husband had left the table. His three nephews grinned – this should be good. "What about that guy you saw for a while in high school, Des or Dennis or something? He thought he was a glam rocker or something," he told the boys. "Came over to the house once with his face painted in black and white. Our father nearly had a heart attack – especially when he saw that his daughter was planning to wear a leather mini skirt and leather bra out on their date."

Susan shrugged demurely while Ben pretended to gag. "We all have our phases," she said primly. "And I recall a few glam rock t-shirts in your closet, Brian."

"Well, I was cool back then," he said. "At least I didn't

paint my face." He paused, taking a sip of beer. "And while we're on the subject, young Susan, how about that guy you dated at university? Ernie or something. The one that looked like an undertaker?" He turned to the boys. "I guess she still liked men who wore black because tell you what, this guy was a classic. He only wore black suits and he sent her red roses every single day."

"I didn't like Ernie," Susan said blithely. "He was too old anyway."

"Well, he liked you," Brian told her. "And he did everything he could to make you like him."

"What happened to this guy?" Ben asked his mother. He'd never heard her talk about her past boyfriends – the way she told it, she's been married to his father practically since she was born.

Susan glanced behind her. Her husband had gone inside with Jonathan and they could be seen through the screen door, examining some cables behind the entertainment system in the living room. Brian winked at his nephews and refilled his sister's glass of wine.

"Do not tell your father this – or you two either," she said strictly to her son and nephews, who all nodded enthusiastically and made crossed-heart motions with their hands. "Not that he'd care, but I don't think I've ever mentioned it, and why bring it up now?"

"This better be a good story, now that you've built it up so much," said Sean. "I'll be disappointed if you broke up with him by text or something."

"Uh, dude, text?" said Jay. "Not likely. They hardly even had *telephones* back then. They had to send letters on the backs of donkeys and stuff." The three boys sniggered.

"Anyway," said Susan, rolling her eyes. "He took me out

one night. I'd decided I wasn't interested so I was planning to end things before they went any further – and," she blushed prettily, "your father, Ben, had asked me on a date and I didn't want to do any two-timing. Anyway, he took me to this amazing restaurant and before I could give him my break-up speech, he got down on one knee and proposed."

"What a loser," Jay stated flatly.

"Naturally I was nice about it," Susan continued, flashing a slightly peeved look at Jay, "but after that, we went our separate ways."

"After some serious stalking on his part," Brian put in. "He was one hell of a determined fella. Thought we were going to have to put a restraining order on him at one point. He was a strange one, that Ernie."

"Yes, well, some people take time accepting these things," Susan acknowledged. "Then, Ben, your father and I got married, we had you and Tia, and we all lived happily ever after."

"Boring," Jay declared. "The story would have been way more interesting if Uncle Dave was an army hotshot and you were an undercover spy or something."

"Yeah, it has more of a ring to it, doesn't it?" Ben mused. "I think 'my parents met when my father was leading his troops into Cairo and my mother was there to assassinate the king' sounds a lot better than 'my parents met at university'."

"Well, I'm sorry we're not secret agents or anything," said Susan, looking slightly put out. "But I'm afraid life isn't that thrilling or exciting. Sometimes real life is just plain what you see is what you get."

~

Ben spent the next several days teaching Verla how to play poker, Scrabble and a few other board games. Despite her lack of gaming during the last century, Verla was a sharp player and soon overtook Ben in her ability to hold a poker face.

Jamie joined them most days. He dropped into the Hades Corporation building each morning before he drove to Carmenton, but the receptionists had no word for him regarding the outcome of Verla's application. Deciding that no news was good news, Ben left the house each night confident that soon Verla would receive word of her release.

Verla, too, looked more confident and happy, and her sweet smile was becoming less rare. She and Jamie took frequent walks down to the park and sat on the park bench talking quietly in the spot where she used to sit alone.

One morning Ben clattered up the steps to Verla's porch, dropping his skateboard on the top step. He had a copy of that day's paper and some recently-released books Verla had asked him to buy for her, and he placed them on her chair.

"Verla?" he called. As she wasn't at her usual post on the porch, she must be inside somewhere. He hammered on the door, but she didn't respond.

"Verla!" he shouted through the door. "It's me, Ben!"

A few minutes passed without any movement from within the house, and Ben frowned. He hoped Verla was okay in there. He cautiously tried the door, and found it unlocked.

"Verla?" he called. "I'm coming in. Just yell out if you want me to go back out, okay?"

Verla wasn't in the living room or the library. Ben had another glance around at the shelves and was amazed yet again, but soon backed out of the room. He called for Verla up the stairs, but there was no reply, and he felt it would be intrusive to go up uninvited. Suddenly he had a thought, and ran back out the door and around the house to see if Jamie's car was parked in its usual place around the back.

It wasn't there. Ben sighed and wandered back into the kitchen, and on the bench he saw a crumpled-up piece of paper he hadn't noticed before.

It was from the Review Board.

"Thank you for your application but we are sorry to inform you that the review of your Sentenced status has been… unsuccessful!" Ben breathed, his eyes dashing over the words. "We look forward to receiving your next application one hundred years from now. Signed…" Ben looked at the name and his heart dropped into his shoes. "Hermes Duncan, Head of the Review Board."

"Verla!" Ben shouted, throwing the paper back onto the bench. "Verla, are you up there?"

There was no answering reply, and he was about to break his own little taboo and run up the steps when another thought occurred to him, and he ran out the door, grabbing his skateboard on the fly.

Verla was sitting in exactly the same position as the time she and Ben had first spoken. Bundled up in a black coat, she huddled on the park bench that overlooked the vast expanse of grass.

Ben arrived next to her, panting.

"Verla…"

She looked up at him, tears staining her pale face. Her eyes stood out dark and massive against her white skin as she bit her lip to keep from crying.

"It came this morning," she said. "Some worker with a union stamp on his wrist gave it to me."

"I've seen it," Ben said, his heart almost breaking as he looked down at his friend.

"Then you saw who it was from."

"Yes. I don't know why we didn't realise he could still be around."

A tear slid down Verla's cheek and she whipped around to stare at Ben almost fiercely.

"I want you to leave, Ben," she said. "I want you to forget you ever met me. I will always, always be so appreciative of all the help you gave me, but I really think you should go. This is it for me. I think I told you that the first time we spoke, right here. You can't help me."

She looked at him with a hard look in her eyes.

"Please. It is my last request of you, the only thing that will make me happy, and I know you want me to be happy, so I know you will comply."

Her last word could have been etched in stone.

"Go."

## - CHAPTER SEVENTEEN -

# Some Dirt on Hermes Duncan

Once more, Ben found himself lying on his bed, the light of the moon filtering through the window. An image of Verla's tearstained face that morning was burned into his mind.

Could it have been just two weeks ago that he was in this same position, staring at the ceiling and thinking that Verla had some serious disillusionment? Two weeks and you could learn so much.

Verla didn't seem to want to help herself at all. Granted, she'd been living in that dungeon of misery for a century now, so it probably didn't take a whole lot to set her back. What would happen to her now? Would she just read all the books in her library two or three times more, until her hundred years came around again and Ben was dead and gone?

Ben made a resolution. If that was the case, then he would try and help her. He wouldn't stay away. He'd visit her all the time and be her friend. It would be strange – he would be growing old, but she would stay the same - but they would learn to laugh about it. He would fill her library with new books, give her a century's supply of candles, and maybe figure out a way to get some electricity into the house. Jamie would visit too.

Jamie. Where the hell was Jamie? Ben had tried calling his phone a few times but it rang out, and he wasn't responding to text messages. Using a pair of Uncle Arthur's old binoculars Ben could just make out Verla's house through the living room window, but he couldn't see the silver glint of Jamie's car parked in its usual spot in her backyard or anywhere else around it.

Ben felt frustrated. With Jamie gone and seemingly inaccessible, he wasn't sure who to turn to. There was no way he could talk to his parents about this – he knew for certain they would not believe him. He'd just have to find a car to drive to Jamie's apartment tomorrow, and hope that he was home.

"Ben, are you okay?"

His little sister Tia stood in the doorway, framed by the hall light. "You seem really sad," she said.

Ben sat up slowly and gave his sister a small smile.

"I'm okay, Tee," he replied. "Just thinking about something."

"You never hang around anymore," she accused. "You haven't played Monopoly with me for ages."

"Sorry," he said. "I've just been doing lots of stuff lately."

"I know," she said forgivingly, coming into the room and sitting next to him on the bed. "Want to play a game now?"

"Okay. Yeah. Let's do it."

Playing Monopoly was a nice distraction from what was on his mind. Tia set up the board between the two armchairs in the living room and was on a winning streak from the start. Ben's parents sat at the small table in the kitchen with a glass of wine each, talking quietly. They were pleased to see their son spending some time with his little sister.

Two hours later, all of Ben's properties were mortgaged

and Tia was in the process of buying hotels to put on Mayfair and Park Lane when Ben looked out of the window, taking in the twinkling lights of the town and the dark patch to the east. He looked back down at the board game, then whipped his head back up to look out of the window at that black area again.

Something out there was wrong.

Something was on fire.

Ben jumped up and gave his sister a hasty pat on the head. "I think you've won," he smiled at her.

"You're giving up?" she squealed happily, and he nodded. She ran into the kitchen to inform their parents of her victory, and Ben leaned around the door after her.

"I have to go out," he told his parents urgently. "I'll be back later, but don't wait up."

"Is everything okay?" his mother asked, concerned.

"Yep, I just have to run out to do something. I'll be home late," he said, already halfway out the door.

His mother nodded, confused, and Ben bolted out the door, grabbed his skateboard and clattered down the steps.

On the road outside the house, he couldn't see the fire anymore. The living room window on the second storey was high enough to see the whole town, but the view wasn't as good on the road. Ben looked around at the other houses built on the slope and realised that none of their windows were as high as his had been.

He stopped and debated with himself for a second. Should he call emergency services? Maybe he should let the professionals handle it. But if the fire was at Verla's house, it could be something else…

He made sure his phone was in his pocket ready to dial triple zero, then took off down the road at breakneck speed.

His skateboard wobbled as he rounded a corner and he hoped that there were no unseen obstacles. The moonlight that had illuminated the landscape a few weeks ago was gone, and the night was black and inky.

The streetlights finished at the edge of town and Ben strained his eyes into the darkness as he shot along the familiar road, past the skate park, the oval and a dense corridor of trees. He entered the old town site and flipped up his board, running along the old cobblestone road.

On and on he ran, seeing only the faint outline of the road in front of him and the houses lining the street. He sprinted another fifty metres and could just make out a faint glow in the air around where he thought Verla's house was.

"Verla!" he shouted into the darkness.

There was no fire at the front of the house, but Ben could hear the crackle of burning. He ran down the side of the building, and could see the glow of the fire reflected against the ruined walls of the mansions next door.

In the middle of the back yard, a bonfire raged. Ben looked around frantically, in time to see Verla emerge from the back door of the house, dragging a wooden chair. She threw the chair onto the fire and the flames leapt higher.

"Verla!" Ben screamed.

She looked around, and he had never seen her look so wild. Her eyes were blazing, her hair was tangled and the glow of the flames reflected amber on her usually pale face.

"Ben!" she screamed back. "You're here!"

She glanced at the fire then back at him again.

"Here, help me put this bloody thing out before someone else sees it!"

Verla ran to the side of the fence, motioning for Ben to come with her. There, stacked against the wooden fence, were several kinds of containers – china jugs, flowerpots and vases, plus a collection of old steel buckets – filled with water. She and Ben dashed back and forth carrying containers to the fire to douse the flames.

Finally there was only a slight smouldering of embers making up what appeared to have been two chairs, a wooden bed head, a side table and some books that Verla must have used as kindling. She saw him looking at them just before the last flame died down, and said a little guiltily, "I know – but they were only about the history of crinoline dresses in the eighteenth century, and I'd read them both twice already."

Ben and Verla watched as the last glow disappeared from the embers, then darkness swallowed everything up once more.

They felt their way to the back door of the house. Verla led Ben along her familiar path to the porch, where he groped for a chair and sat down. His heart was still racing from the excitement of the fire, and he could feel a layer of soot on his face.

"Do you think anyone else saw it?" Verla whispered at Ben from her chair.

He stared into the darkness, seeing nothing but the glow of the fire still imprinted slightly on his vision, as if someone had just taken a photo with a flash.

"I don't know," he whispered back. "I only saw it because our window was so high. I don't know if anyone else would have had the same view."

He paused. "Verla, why the hell did you just light a bonfire in your back yard?"

His eyes were starting to adjust to the dark, and he could just make out the outline of Verla's features as she looked back at him, her jaw set.

"I didn't know any other way to get you here," she said.

"I've told you before, I can't leave this area, not unless I'm under guard. I had no way of contacting you. I thought that if this is meant to be, then you will see the fire. And you saw it."

Despite the cool night and the dire circumstances, Ben felt a slight warmth in his chest at her words. It felt good to have someone think he was important enough to go to such trouble for. "Verla… I was going to come visit you again, you know. I wasn't just going to cut off contact completely."

"Ben," she said. "I needed to see you tonight."

He could just make out the slightly wild look he had seen in her eyes earlier at the fire.

"I'm ready to fight," she said. "I've been stuck in this godforsaken place for one hundred years and I have one chance at getting out before I'm stuck here for one hundred more. I've never felt this feeling before, never had the will or the strength to do anything. But meeting you, meeting Jamie…" she paused. "It's cut through the chains of hopelessness they've put on me and it's made me want to live."

She turned away and stared into the darkness of the street.

"You've never felt it, Ben, hardly anyone on this Earth has. To have all hope taken away from you for a hundred years, with no escape, not even death… so how could I not make a real go at the one chance I have?"

"Verla," he said, happiness expanding inside him. "I think it is just so great that we're going to fight this. Just one thing – why the fire? Why tonight?"

"Because I only have tomorrow, Ben!" she said. "I'm not stupid. I know you and Jamie were trying to protect me, but I know what date it is. Hell is all bureaucracy, and if I miss the deadline, there's no way they'll let me try it again until the next review."

"Oh, but surely they'd extend your time, just for a few

days?" he asked reasonably, but she looked back at him desperately.

"You know they won't! It's what they pride themselves on! They'd take more pleasure in denying my application because it was ten minutes past the deadline than they would putting me here in the first place."

"Right. Right," he said, his mind ticking over. "So what's the plan?"

She leaned towards him. "What we need," she said, "is some dirt on Hermes Duncan."

~

Half an hour later, Ben and Verla stood in the house's vast library, staring up at the stacks. About a hundred candles were scattered on every surface, and their light danced over the titles of the books.

"I'm glad you found that stash at your house," said Verla, gazing at the tiny flames. "My collection ran out about ninety-nine years ago."

Ben turned to her for guidance. "So what are we looking for?" he asked.

"We'll start with the theology and mythology section, obviously," she said. "I'll pull out the ones I recall as being possibly relevant while you have a flip through. Look for anything to do with the Devil or his servants. I doubt Duncan would be known by that name, and I'm sure I would recall seeing it somewhere if he had been. Just look for anything that sounds like it could be him. He has to have cropped up somewhere."

"But I thought there weren't any books that talked about what's really going on?" Ben asked. "Isn't it all made up by men who are on the wrong track?"

"Ninety-five per cent of it will be fiction," she said, already pulling out titles and examining them. "We're trying to find the five per cent fact that the fiction is based on."

It was inspiring to see Verla take charge, and Ben obediently grabbed the first book she handed him and took it closer to a candle to start leafing through.

It was a book on Hinduism, and he started reading about the god of death, Yamaraj. He found someone called Chitragupta who sounded like he could fit the bill, but after reading further, there were no real comparisons with Mr Duncan. Ben picked up the next book Verla handed him, and got stuck in.

While the candles slowly burned down, Verla and Ben pored through what seemed like hundreds of books, and finally Ben felt like giving up. He wasn't even sure what he was looking for. What did they need, evidence that Duncan had skimmed some cash from Hell's till or something?

He yawned, put his latest book back, and wandered along the shelves, looking at the titles. At the end he came to a section stuffed with leather-bound books and parchments.

"What's this, Verla?" he asked.

"Those are my family's diaries, notes, drawings, everything really," she said, lowering her eyes sadly. "After they died I gathered everything from the rest of the house and put it all in there."

"May I?" he asked, and she nodded.

He pulled some of the faded papers and books and carried them to the table. He picked up a childish drawing of some horses. Verla looked up from the book she was skimming and saw the picture. She bit her lip then kept reading.

Ben sifted through the information. Most of it was scraps

of paper with lists, drawings, and even a short story about the adventures of some beautiful high-society ladies he suspected may have been penned by Verla during her formative years. Another crumbling piece of parchment depicted a sketch of a woman clothed in leaves and flowers, standing next to a man wearing a tunic, and holding a child between them. Ben admired the detail of the drawing and wondered if it was Verla's work – hadn't she said she was planning to study art? But the parchment looked a lot older than any of the others, so perhaps it wasn't. He carefully placed the paper back onto the stack, and turned to the pile of books instead.

One of the volumes was a leather-bound diary that belonged to someone called Marguerite Grammaire, if the name written in black ink on the first page was anything to go by. Ben carefully turned the yellowed page and almost stopped breathing when he saw the date written in strange, squiggly writing at the top of the page: 1 November 1661.

"Verla!" he hissed across the room. "There's a diary here from the sixteen hundreds!"

"I know, there are some really old items in there," she said. "Be careful with it though – it may fall apart if you breathe on it too hard."

Ben turned the pages carefully. The writing was small and very difficult to read, and the words were jumbled up a lot. He decided that either people from the seventeenth century spoke like Yoda, or English wasn't the author's first language. There also seemed to be an unreasonable amount of Es added after words that really didn't require them. But despite this, he soon found himself absorbed in the diary.

This Marguerite ran an apothecary shop – she spelled it 'apothecarie' – that was apparently very popular with the locals, and they were constantly demanding new solutions to medical problems. Her diary entries were frequently interrupted by scribbled recipes for herbal remedies. She also had plenty of men courting her and couldn't decide who to choose. There was Monsieur Miroir, who owned a business selling fabric but whose clothes were always grubby. (Marguerite used the terms "stainde and markd of dyrt"). There was Monsieur Girard, who had lots of land but Marguerite couldn't ascertain his profession as he would always change the subject when she asked. And there was Monsieur Donnchad, who had no real credentials but talked like a peer and told her that if she married him, he would offer her wealth beyond measure (or "welthe beonde mesur" as Marguerite put it).

Ben put the book down carefully. "Verla?" he asked. "This Marguerite Grammaire, was she a relation of yours?"

Verla looked up, her eyes blurry. "Grammaire, it sounds familiar," she said. "Maybe an ancestor who came over on the ship from England? A lot of those papers have been in the family for a long, long time."

"Mmm, okay," Ben said. This Monsieur Donnchad's proposition sounded familiar. Hadn't Verla told him that Duncan had offered her 'wealth beyond measure' as well? Or was that something every suitor told his potential bride?

Ben continued ploughing through the diary, trying to make out the bizarre handwriting. The candles lowered, and some of them slowly burned out. His thoughts were getting fuzzy and the words blurred together on the page.

Verla had already fallen asleep in her armchair, he registered vaguely. His heavy head was dropping towards the table as sleep closed in on him. His eyes tried desperately to stay open but exhaustion was taking over. He looked down at the diary in his hands and saw the squiggly words blur into nothingness before he fell asleep.

## - CHAPTER EIGHTEEN -
# Jamie's House

"Ben! Wake up!"

Sunlight streamed in through the high windows of the library as Ben slowly opened his eyes. He was slumped forward onto the table with his head cradled uncomfortably on his forearms. Pain shot down his back as he moved slightly.

"Ben?" Verla asked anxiously.

"I'm awake, I'm awake," he replied sleepily. His head ached dully and he could really, really use another few hours sleep. He slowly raised his head and felt his back creak.

Verla was sitting forward in another chair, her foot jiggling, her big eyes looking at his.

"Today's my day," she said.

"We didn't find anything," he said, realising their search for Duncan's weak spot last night had been fruitless.

"I know," she said. "I was so sure we would. But it doesn't matter, we have something else."

"Jamie."

"Yes. Jamie will be able to help."

Verla looked confident but Ben could see a tinge of desperation around her eyes. She knew that this was it, that today was her last chance to have a future – for the next hundred years, at least.

"I know that you've done so much for me over the past few weeks," she said. "No matter how this turns out, I'll be so grateful to you. I have just one more favour to ask, though."

"To go see Jamie."

"Yes," she said. "I would go, but, you know," she gestured around her sadly. "I don't know if he'll be able to do anything, but at least then we'll know that we've tried."

"Okay," said Ben. He had no problem turning this one over to someone who may actually be able to help.

"Thank you," she said with a tiny smile. "For everything."

~

Ben checked his watch as he ran up the rickety white stairs of his family's house. It was just past seven. He eased through the door and snuck quietly into his room.

There were no signs of life within the house yet, so he seized the opportunity for a hasty shower and washed the layer of soot from his skin. When he emerged from his bedroom with his hair wet and a fresh change of clothes on, his mother had surfaced and was filling up the kettle in the kitchen.

"Morning, Ben. You're up early," she said as he walked in.

"Uh, yeah," he said, quickly deciding there was no need to tell her he'd only just come home.

"Was everything okay last night? You left here so fast," she commented, spooning instant coffee into two cups.

He hesitated. He was so tempted to spill the beans and tell her everything that was going on. It would be so nice to hand Verla's problems over to someone else. But the story was just so unbelievable, and he didn't have time to convince her. Besides, what could she do? Call the police?

"No, it was fine," he mumbled. "I just had to get out for a while and clear my head."

She didn't look convinced, so Ben stepped it up a notch.

"I've been thinking a lot about university lately," he ventured. "About which one I want to choose. And what course I want to do. It's been building up in my mind and last night, I decided to go for a walk and I ended up sitting in the park for hours, just thinking."

He stole a quick glance at her, expecting her to look dubious, but she was nodding and looking relieved.

"Oh honey," she said softly. "I understand that it's been getting you down. Did you decide anything?"

"Kind of," he said, feeling bad for deceiving her. "But I've still got some things to think about."

She handed him a coffee and he took a sip. "Okay," she said. "I'm just glad you're finally getting around to it."

"Yeah, I'll let you know how I go," he said. "Also, I was wondering if you could take me to the nearest train station." He knew there was one in Mount Victoria, a town nearby.

"I'm not sure, Ben," she said. "Where are you going? We're having lunch at your Uncle Thomas's house today. Will you be back for that?"

"Probably not." He paused. "I need to go into Sydney."

"Why, honey?"

He hesitated again. It was getting hard to cover things up around his parents. He longed for the future, when he'd be master of his own time.

"I'm helping out a friend," he said, rather lamely.

"A girlfriend?" asked Susan. "I was wondering if you'd met someone here. That's where I thought you'd gone last night. You don't seem to spend much time here anymore."

"No, not a girlfriend, just a friend," he said, getting

impatient. He didn't want to be interrogated right now; he just wanted a lift.

Susan took a sip of her coffee, then smiled at her son. "If it's important, hon, then I guess that's okay," she said. "Your father can drop you off at the station. Give me a call when you're on your way back and one of us will come pick you up."

~

Almost two and a half hours later, the train pulled into Central Station and Ben realised he had no idea how to navigate to where Jamie lived. He tried calling Jamie on his mobile phone but there was still no answer. What the hell was Jamie doing? This was not the time to be ignoring calls.

He tried to remember where Jamie lived, cursing himself for not asking for his address. He picked up his mobile and toyed with it for a minute, then had an idea. He searched for the phone number for the University of Sydney, and called it.

The woman at the switchboard transferred him to Professor Brightman's phone. Ben waited as the phone rang, then he heard the start of the professor's answering message. He frowned and hung up.

He walked into a deli, where he bought a drink and casually asked the cashier where there were apartments right on the harbour.

"You're in Sydney, son," the cashier squinted at him. "Thousands of places are right on the harbour."

"It's a white and silver apartment building, about four storeys tall. It's really nice and modern," Ben described hopefully. "I think you'd have to be really rich to live there."

"Planning a robbery?" asked the man, one eyebrow raised.

"Not exactly," Ben told him with a laugh. "Just trying to

find out where my friend lives."

"And you can't ask him?"

"No, he's not answering his phone, and it's really important I get in touch with him. Today. As soon as I can."

The cashier shrugged then reached over and pulled a map book out of a display. He flipped it open and pointed to a map of Sydney. "Do you know where it is it in relation to the CBD?"

"If you're coming from the Blue Mountains, you haven't reached the CBD yet – but almost," Ben said, trying to remember. "We were going along Parramatta Road for a while, but we turned off before the city. We took a left turn onto – I think it was a highway, but we weren't on it for long. Then... then another left onto a windy street with lots of little cafes and shops and stuff."

"Sounds like Rozelle or Balmain," said the cashier. He trailed his finger along one of the map's roads. "You probably turned off here," he said. "Then went up Balmain Road. Know how far you went?"

"Pretty far down that peninsula thing, I think," said Ben, looking at the map. "I think we went through a roundabout then kept going until you could see the water, then we turned off and went a few hundred metres up a road." He was impressed that he could remember so much.

The cashier jabbed his finger on the very end of the peninsula. "Probably Balmain then."

Ben decided to take the plunge. "Okay. How do I get there?"

"Got a car?"

"No."

"You'll have to take a bus then. Or a train. At least you're in the right place to catch one."

Half an hour later, Ben walked along a street lined with stylish old houses and modern apartment blocks. He could see glimpses of the harbour between them. This was definitely the right area. He tried calling Jamie again, but there was still no answer. The air was starting to get chilly, and he shivered.

It took him another frustrating half hour of walking and peering up at different buildings before he decided he was looking at the one Jamie had stopped by a week ago. He glanced at his watch. Just past ten o'clock. Not too bad, he decided as he walked up to the entrance.

As Ben pressed the buzzer next to Jamie's name, it suddenly occurred to him that he may not be home. He could be off saving other people from Hell or whatever it was he did with his days. Thankfully a voice came over the intercom.

"Hello?"

"Jamie! Is that you?"

"Yes, this is Jamie. Who's this?"

Ben felt relief wash over him at the sound of his friend's voice. "It's Ben. I really need to see you."

"Ben! I was just about to… just give me two seconds and I'll come and get you."

Jamie appeared at the door a few minutes later.

"Hi!" he said. "What are you doing here? How did you find the place? I was just about to call you!"

"I searched," Ben replied, unable to keep the edge out of his voice. "I walked around for an hour looking for this place. And I called about twenty times. Maybe I could have saved a bit of time if you actually answered your phone for once!"

"I'm sorry," said Jamie, tugging at his collar. "I've been… out of phone reception. I only just got home. There have been missed call alerts and texts coming through for the past few minutes."

"Where out of reception?" demanded Ben. "And don't say you've been at Verla's house. I've practically just come from there."

"Verla. How is she?"

Ben suddenly remembered the reason he was standing at Jamie's doorstep. "She got the letter. They said no."

Expressions of disappointment, anger and hopelessness flitted across Jamie's face, before settling on concerned.

"How's she holding up?" he asked, leading Ben to the elevator and punching a button.

"Not too bad, actually," said Ben as the elevator doors closed behind them. "She doesn't want to accept it. She wants to fight it."

Jamie stared thoughtfully up at the digital numbers as the elevator passed a few floors. It made an old-fashioned 'ting' sound and the doors opened. He led the way down a corridor, unlocked a door, and motioned for Ben to step through.

Ben's dream apartment lay before him. The floor was covered in plush white carpet, and massive windows opened up to a panoramic view of the Sydney Harbour Bridge and the city. White couches were grouped at one side of the room and a stainless steel kitchen and a glass dining set occupied the other. In the middle of the long space was a shiny white baby grand piano. There was so much white that he felt like he needed sunglasses.

"Drink?" Jamie asked and Ben nodded. He wandered around the room. Next to the couches was a set of shelves stuffed with books and papers. He couldn't see a television but suspected there was one craftily concealed in the wall or behind a picture.

On one wall was a massive black and white print of a scene from what looked like a jazz club. In the foreground was the silhouette of a woman's face leaning into an old-fashioned microphone. In the background, barely discernible, were tables filled with men and women. Ben spotted a lady wearing a jewelled headband and what looked like a fox fur around her neck. Men sporting trilby hats faded into the back of the shot.

Jamie handed Ben a glass of Coke and they both studied the picture.

"Very cool," Ben assessed.

"Those were the days," Jamie replied.

Ben remembered why he was there and took a seat on one of the couches.

"I'm sorry didn't come by yesterday," Jamie said, sitting down too. "I've been trying to chase some leads."

"I tried calling you a bunch of times," said Ben, feeling a little embarrassed as he said it. He didn't want to sound like a jealous girlfriend. "Why didn't you pick up?"

"I honestly didn't have any phone reception. I only just drove back into the city fifteen minutes ago."

For the first time, Ben noticed the dark circles under Jamie's eyes.

"Have you been up all night?" he asked.

"Yeah."

"Chasing leads?"

"Yeah."

"Well? What leads, and did anything come of them?"

"I'm not sure," said Jamie. "Okay. Listen. Verla's not the only one who's ever been Sentenced. I did some research, called around, and found out the locations of a few other Sentenceds. I drove out to talk to them to see if they knew anything about Duncan, or could tell me anything that might help Verla."

"And?"

"There's one that knew him. A woman called Elizabeth. Sentenced about one hundred and eighty years ago."

"Wow. Was it the same sort of thing as Verla? Did he kill her?"

"No, looks like he didn't have anything to do with her death. She was Sentenced to a room in an abandoned hospital after she died in a smallpox epidemic. She didn't meet Duncan until about ten years after her initial Sentencing."

"What did he want?"

"He showed up with a standard Hell communiqué, but then he stuck around a while longer and questioned her about her heritage. Wanted to know if she was related to some French woman. Maryanne or Marceline or something. Elizabeth couldn't really remember. And he kept asking her about whether or not she'd had a garden when she was alive. He wanted to know all about it."

"Why?" asked Ben, confused.

"I don't know. Either way, Elizabeth said she doesn't have a green thumb and never kept a garden, so she couldn't help him with whatever he wanted to know."

"Strange," Ben mused. "Anything else?"

"Yeah, one thing. Duncan lit a cigar as he was getting up, and he tripped over the chair and grabbed her arm with the hand that was holding the cigar. The cigar got stubbed out on Elizabeth's arm."

"What! Accidentally or on purpose?"

"Elizabeth didn't know. She says she assumed accidentally. Either way, you can't hurt a Sentenced. Their bodies are on hold."

"That's so weird. Did she ever see him again?"

"Yeah, a few times, but he just delivered the messages and left. Then about thirty years later a different Hell guy took over."

"Did Elizabeth say anything that could help us with Verla?"

"I don't think so," said Jamie. "Nothing I could figure out. And I visited five other Sentenceds but none of them had heard of Duncan."

Ben set his drink on a side table and leaned forward. "One of Verla's ancestors was called Marguerite and I think she was French. Maybe Duncan was talking about the same one."

"Do you think so?" Jamie said doubtfully. "I think it was a pretty common name back then."

"How many French women called Marguerite could Duncan be after?" Ben asked. "Maybe he was looking for Verla the whole time."

Jamie frowned. "Why would he? She wasn't even born when he visited Elizabeth."

"Maybe… maybe Marguerite jilted him and he wanted to take revenge on her descendants."

"I don't know, Ben. Seems like a long bow to draw."

"I guess. We're back to square one, then," he sighed.

"So what happened yesterday? When did Verla get the letter?"

Ben quickly filled Jamie in on the developments of the night before.

"We've got today, and today only, she says," he concluded. "She reckons they won't consider any requests beyond today since today's the official cut-off date."

"Yeah, that's the way they work," said Jamie. "But what can we give them that we haven't already? I think if Duncan wasn't so involved, we may have had a chance. I don't know what we were thinking, assuming he wouldn't be around anymore."

Ben stood up and wandered over to the piano, distracted by its shiny surface. "Do you play?" he asked.

"Yeah, I do," said Jamie, his eyes lighting up.

Ben stared at the piano. "Guess you get a lot of time to practice," he said.

"Yeah, I guess so," Jamie replied. "So you guys didn't find anything worthwhile on Duncan, then. But what kind of thing would you be looking for? Fraudulent invoices or something? I don't know. Doesn't really seem like the right track."

Ben laughed. "That's what I thought. But what else are we supposed to do? We've got one day to come up with something."

"Did Verla think of anything else? Any other reason they'd let her go?"

"No, but we searched all night," said Ben, looking at Jamie out of the corner of his eye. "We were kind of hoping you might think of something."

Jamie laughed a little ruefully. "I don't know, man," he said. "They're pretty strict on this stuff. But if there's a way, we'll think of it."

He sat back against the cushions of the sofa, seemingly lost in thought.

Ben's eyes wandered around the room for the umpteenth time. This was a really nice apartment in a good area. It must have cost Jamie a fortune. He wondered how much Jamie usually charged his clients for getting them out of Hell. Probably a lot.

"Maybe we should go to your office," said Ben finally. "Surely you keep stuff there that we could, you know, look through or something – I'd feel more useful if I was at least doing *something*."

Jamie looked up curiously. "My office? I don't have an office."

"Well, where do you work from?" Ben asked reasonably.

"Right here most of the time."

Ben looked around slowly. Maybe Jamie had an office in one of the other rooms? It suddenly dawned on him that Jamie had never actually told him he was a lawyer for the Sentenced. He had just assumed that he was one, and that it was the reason Jamie knew so much about the procedures of Hell. Ben realised that despite the time they'd spent together, he didn't actually know much about his new friend at all.

The plush and modern apartment, the classy location, working from home… the pieces of the puzzle were fitting together in Ben's mind. He looked over and noticed for the first time… Jamie was wearing a white suit.

Everything suddenly slotted into place.

"You're a pimp!" Ben gasped, then realised with horror that he'd said it out loud.

"What?" Jamie looked confused. "A pimp? What? Where did you get that from?"

Ben turned scarlet and wasn't sure what to say. Would Jamie be angry he'd guessed his profession?

But instead of being angry, Jamie began to chuckle. "A pimp, Ben? Do you seriously think I run prostitutes or something?"

Ben looked around again. Maybe he'd gotten it wrong… suddenly the pieces he'd thought slotted into place so conveniently were actually not fitting their holes at all, and he realised how ridiculous his guess had sounded.

"Oh no… I'm sorry," he stammered.

Jamie just looked at him, his shoulders shaking and his mouth twitching. Ben felt the desperate need to turn back time.

"I didn't say that just because you're black, I promise," he said, mortified. "But this place looks so good, and you don't

work at an office like normal people, and you're wearing a...
a...."

Jamie started laughing so much that he buried his head in a couch cushion.

"A white suit?" he gasped, emerging from the fabric.

Despite his embarrassment, Ben was starting to feel a little defensive.

"Well, not everyone wears a white suit," he said, folding his arms.

Jamie just laughed again and wiped some errant tears away with the back of his wrist.

Ben thought he may as well make light of his faux pas. "So if you don't have hookers parading in and out at all hours," he asked, "what is it that you actually do?"

Jamie finally regained his composure and studied Ben thoughtfully. "If I tell you, you'll have to keep it to yourself," he said.

Ben nodded. "Of course."

"I play the piano," Jamie said. He stood up, walked over to the baby grand, and rested his fingers on the keys without making any sound.

After thinking that Jamie was either an underworld lawyer or a pimp, Ben felt the answer was a little anticlimactic.

"Where do you play?" he asked.

"Lots of places," said Jamie. "I do some session music on recordings if they need it. Sometimes I play with symphony orchestras. Any time someone needs a spare concert pianist," he shrugged, "I'm there."

"Wow," said Ben. That actually sounded pretty impressive. "Are you famous?"

"Noooo," said Jamie. "That's something I'm, uh, not allowed to be."

"What do you mean, not allowed?' asked Ben. "Who would stop you?"

Jamie looked as if he'd like to change the subject. "I think keeping a low profile is best, that's all."

"You didn't say keeping a low profile," Ben persisted. "You said you weren't allowed."

"Slip of the tongue," said Jamie, settling back onto the couch. "You know what I meant."

Ben wasn't put off, but changed tack. "Do you make a lot of money?" he asked.

"I do pretty well," said Jamie. "Enough to keep me in white suits."

"Do you have a girlfriend?"

"No."

"A wife? Kids?"

"No and no."

"Ever been married?"

"No."

"You have an American accent. Where are you from?"

Jamie hesitated for a second. "Chicago."

"When did you move here?"

"When I was… younger."

"How old are you now?"

"How old do you think I am?"

Ben considered. "I don't know," he said. "Twenty-eight? Twenty-nine? But you could be older. I mean, I get mistaken for being in my mid-twenties all the time."

"Mid-twenties?" Jamie asked, one eyebrow raised.

"Well, maybe not *mid*-twenties," Ben amended. "But twenty-one, sometimes. It's just that… well, we've been hanging out for the past few weeks and I don't know anything about you. If I played piano at big concert things I'd be telling everyone. But you keep everything to yourself."

"Ben, the past few weeks really haven't been about me," said Jamie. "We've filled every minute working on Verla's case. And somehow I don't think it's appropriate for me to be parading up and down boasting about having a great car and apartment and job while she's looking at another hundred years moping about in that old house."

At the mention of Verla, Ben remembered that time was ticking away on her appeal, but he had a feeling that finding out about Jamie's life was somehow important.

"Jamie," he said with as much firmness as he could muster. "You're still not telling me the whole story. If you just play the piano for a job, how do you know so much about the Sentenced and everything that goes on in that, er, world?"

Jamie looked back at him thoughtfully. "I know a few people," he said.

"Yeah yeah yeah," said Ben, getting annoyed. "You're said that before. But it doesn't tell me anything, it doesn't help at all."

He jumped up from the couch and started walking around the apartment, stopping to stare at each thing he passed – the piano, the view from the windows, the pictures on the walls, the dining set. Jamie watched him, a strange expression on his face.

"You have a great car and place to live and everything," said Ben. "You know far more about the whole God and Devil thing than anyone else seems to. You knew about the Sentenced review thing – not even Verla knew about that, and *she's* one of the Sentenced. You call people on your phone to do a background check on an employee of the Devil. You even get recommended by university professors! What's your story, Jamie?"

When Jamie remained silent, Ben rounded fiercely to stare at him across the top of the piano.

"How do you know about all this?" he demanded, his voice rising. "You have a normal job – well, normal as in you're not a Hell worker or an assistant to God or something that sounds like it's straight out of a Sunday school book. How did you know about the review? How did you know what to say to that guy we saw at the Hell office?"

Ben and Jamie looked at each other. Jamie was quiet, but he still had that strange expression – was it fear? Confusion?

Ben knew he must be on the right track – and then he had a sudden feeling he knew where that track would lead.

"Ohh," he said slowly. "I get it. I get it! You're... you're one of the Sentenced too."

He tore his eyes from Jamie's and looked around wildly at the lavish furnishings. Something didn't make sense. "But you're happy," he said, half to himself. "You live in a nice place, you can go wherever you want... so you're not in Hell anymore. And that means that you used to be in Hell, but you had a review, and it was successful. That's how you know. That's how you knew how to help Verla."

Jamie opened his mouth as if to speak, then paused before making a sound. Ben charged back into the silence.

"What did you do to get out of it, Jamie?" he asked, getting angry. "You found a way, didn't you? You knew something that got you out of Hell, or you found someone to help you. Or you made a deal with the Devil to get out!"

Ben was shouting now, but he didn't care. "You know how to get around it, don't you? You know the magic formula that will make the Devil go away. And yet you won't tell Verla! You pretend to help her, you spend hours going over her contract with her, you buddy up to her, and all the time you already knew how to get out of Hell!"

Thinking about the hope he had seen in Verla's eyes when she met Jamie almost made Ben's heart break. She had trusted them to help her, but the whole time Jamie had a massive ace up his sleeve that he didn't even feel the need to share. Who knows what his motives had been. Befriend a lonely young woman in a big old house, pretend to be her friend, then what?

"You make me sick," he hissed at Jamie, then stood up and made for the door. This was the last day Verla had to appeal, and he wasn't going to waste it sitting around with someone who had already used up too much precious time. He didn't know exactly what he was going to do, but he figured his first stop would be Professor Brightman's office. He should have gone back weeks ago. Maybe this time the professor could refer him to someone who was actually helpful.

Ben had reached the front door by the time Jamie finally spoke. He sounded tired and worn out, like he was ninety years old.

"Ben," he said. "Ben, wait, stop. You've got it wrong, stop."

Ben paused, one hand on the door knob, and looked back at Jamie.

"I'm not a resident of Hell, and I never have been," said Jamie, staring at the floor, then looking up to meet Ben's cold look.

"Well?" Ben asked. "What are you then?"

"I'm a resident of Heaven."

## - CHAPTER NINETEEN -

# Saturday Night at the Emerald Club

*The inside of the club was smoky and dark, but the talk and laughter of people clustered around the small tables, along with the cheerful piano music in the background, lent a warm atmosphere to the room. Handsome men in sharp suits and trilby hats wooed giggling women in feather boas and colourful knee-length dresses. Waitresses navigated between the tables, holding drink trays high above their heads. It was late, and everyone was merry.*

*From his position behind the piano, Jamie could see the local mayor with his arms around two of the showgirls who had just been dancing on the stage. The mayor was one of the most vocal supporters of the alcohol ban, yet on the table in front of him sat a glass of something that was definitely not iced tea. And there was the wife of the city planner, her thick makeup doing nothing to obscure her age, holding onto the lapels of a young man Jamie recognised as the son of the local Presbyterian minister. A politician visiting from the Capital leaned over to light the cigarette of a young starlet who was in town to make a picture, then he turned back to the mob boss to resume their earlier exchange of anecdotes. The local chief of police sent one of his constables to the bar for a round of drinks and tried to engage the starlet in conversation, but she simply looked bored and blew out a cloud of smoke.*

*All in all, it was a typical Saturday night at the Emerald Club.*

*Jamie's fingers picked up the pace as he changed his tune. The saxophone player chimed in with a few wailing notes, and the drummer quickly put down his glass, picked up his sticks and jumped back on his stool. The trio built the music into a crescendo as the people in the club slowed their conversations and turned their faces to the stage expectantly. The owner of the club, a large man named Leo who was approaching sixty, checked his notes and lurched to the microphone at the front of the stage.*

*"Hope everyone's havin' a good time," he rumbled. "Whether you're local or visitin', you're all very good friends of mine so I don't need to remind you to keep this place a secret between friends."*

*There was as cheer from the crowd and Leo smiled. "Now for our final song, we have a lovely young gal who is makin' her debut at the Emerald Club tonight. Ladies and gentlemen, please welcome Miss Penny Johnson!"*

*The crowd cheered as a young black woman dressed in a glittery green dress made her way to the microphone. She glanced back at Jamie nervously and he grinned and nodded encouragingly, but as she turned back to the crowd and started singing huskily into the microphone, his grin disappeared and he cursed himself silently.*

*What the hell was he thinking, letting Penny come here? When their mother found out – and she would, she seemed to find out everything – she was going to murder him. Penny was only nineteen. Practically a kid, really. She shouldn't be here. She had no idea how to handle herself.*

*Jamie's hands were playing the song but his mind wasn't on it. They'd leave straightaway, he decided. Usually he stayed back, had a few drinks, had a good chat with everyone. They liked him, liked his manners and his sense of fun. But not tonight. They'd be going straight home after this.*

*Penny was doing a great job, though. She had a lovely singing voice that suited the jazz song. As she crooned her final note into the microphone, applause erupted from around the room and Jamie allowed himself to relax a bit.*

*Penny glanced around and grinned at him delightedly. They had liked her! He returned her smile as the club's owner blustered up to the microphone to thank her and inform his patrons that the club was now closed. Not that it would do much good – this crowd looked like it would take a long time to move.*

*Jamie threw a cover over the piano then hurried over to his sister. "We'd better get home," he told her. He pulled on his jacket.*

*"Can't we stay?" she asked beseechingly, motioning at the people who looked like they had no intention of putting an end to their merriment. "Everyone's having such a swell time."*

*"No," he said firmly, grabbing her coat from a chair next to the stage and shrugging her into it. "Let's go."*

*He hustled his little sister through the crowd, up the stairs, through a corridor and out onto the street. There were only a few people milling around – evidently everyone was still downstairs drinking, albeit in a music-less room. Leo would be grumbling but his cash would be stacking up, so he wouldn't really mind all that much. He'd be seeing the last punter off at dawn.*

*Penny chattered about her performance as they hurried along the street to where Jamie had parked his Ford. She was describing her initial jitters when he put up his hand to stop her. There were two men coming down the street towards them, and in the dim glow of the streetlights, they didn't look friendly.*

*Against his better judgment, Jamie continued steering his sister towards the car. This was definitely the last time, he told himself. Letting her come here was a mistake. It was just too risky.*

*Jamie and Penny had almost passed the two men when one of them reached out his arm and blocked Jamie's path. Jamie looked at the man. He was big and thuggish with a large pudgy face, and his cheeks and nose were a purplish colour. His companion was of similar appearance but seemed a bit vacant.*

*"You're the piana player," the man rasped into Jamie's face. "Down at the Emra' Club."*

*Jamie nodded cautiously, not sure where the man was going with this. Thug Number Two gazed at Penny, who tightened her grip on Jamie's arm and shifted her body behind his.*

*"The piana player," the man repeated. "Down at the club with all them pollies n' all."*

*He paused and stared at Jamie. "So you think you can walk into a club full-a law-abidin' citizens and reckon you're good as them."*

*Jamie backed away slightly. The man stank of liquor and was clearly looking for trouble. And Jamie was certainly not going to correct his assessment of 'law-abiding' – those drinks the club patrons were knocking back certainly weren't legal and everyone knew it, but this was not the time.*

*As Thug Number One leered in Jamie's face, he knew it would be best to make a quick exit, and he started to steer Penny towards the car again. Suddenly he felt a strong hand on his shoulder jerking his body back. Penny stumbled on the sidewalk and he knew they were in trouble.*

*"Penny –" he started anxiously but Thug Number One cut him off, shouting.*

*"Think you're as good as them, do ya?" he yelled. "Don't know your place, do ya!"*

*The large man shoved Jamie, and caught off-balance, Jamie fell over. The thug kicked him in the side and grabbed his jacket, dragging him into the gap between two of the buildings lining the sidewalk. Jamie regained his footing and caught the man in the side of his head with his fist. The thug grabbed both his arms and Jamie jerked back, but then the thug used his weight to topple straight onto Jamie and force him to the ground. Jamie pushed back against the weight, but his mind was on Penny.*

*"Get back to the club!" he screamed in her direction. "Find Leo!"*

*But it was too late. Thug Number Two, spurned into action by grunted orders from his companion, had run after Penny and now dragged her into the alley.*

*Thug Number One had Jamie around the throat and was hissing into his face, his breath reeking of bourbon.*

*"That your little lady, is it?" he whispered. "Well, boy, for not knowin' your place and punchin' me in the head, I think I'm gonna make you watch as we see how much pain she can handle. And you can tell her that if she doesn't do what we ask, we're going to make her hurt even more."*

*Thug Number Two was staring absently at the wall, but one hand was over Penny's mouth and the other was clamped around her waist. No matter how much she kicked and twisted, she couldn't get free.*

*Fury shot through Jamie like a white-hot sword. He reached up to the thug's hands and scrambled at his vice-like grip, finally grasping the man's little finger. He jerked it backwards and heard a snapping noise, then a yowl of pain as the thug released his grip. Jamie kicked out and the ugly man staggered backwards, his look of pain and surprise quickly being replaced with rage.*

*"I'm going to kill you," he shouted at Jamie. "Right after I kill your little woman." The man lunged towards Penny but Jamie got to her first. His fist slammed into her captor's face and the man reeled back, letting go of her.*

*"Run!" Jamie shouted at his sister.*

*She caught her balance and sprinted for the street, her high heels wobbling in the dirt. Jamie reeled around and saw Thug Number One bearing down on him. The man's body hit him like a tonne of bricks and the two men landed on the dirty ground.*

*The thug's weight pinned him down, and Jamie covered his head with his arms as the man's fists pummelled his head. He managed to grab the man's hand as it landed on his cheek and he squeezed it tightly. The thug yelped in pain at the pressure on his broken finger, and Jamie used the moment to twist the man's torso over. He hooked his elbow around the man's neck into a headlock and was about to apply pressure when he felt someone hoist him up by the shoulders from behind.*

*For a second he thought Leo and his cronies had finally arrived on the scene, but he'd forgotten about Thug Number Two. The large man shoved him up against the wall, pulled a handgun from his belt, and pointed it in Jamie's face. The eyes of the two men met for a split second – Jamie's eyes angry and desperate, the thug's vacant and vague – and the man pulled the trigger.*

## - CHAPTER TWENTY -

# Elysian Links

"My family was absolutely devastated," Jamie told Ben quietly. "It was so hard for them, especially Penny. She blamed herself, although it wasn't her fault at all."

Ben sat back on the couch cushions, his eyes wide.

"How do you know?" he asked. "Did you see your family after you, er, died?"

"No," said Jamie sadly. "I just got to hear about it, that was all. Penny thought it was her fault because she'd wanted to sing at the club that night. But we were just in the wrong place at the wrong time with some drunk guy who took issue with us. It happened to a lot of black folk back then."

"Did they catch the guys that did it?"

"No. My death didn't get much attention, really. Leo got a new pianist at the club, the police made a few half-hearted enquiries, and everyone got on with their lives."

"That's pretty messed up."

"You could say that."

Ben felt angry and frustrated at the events of over ninety years previously, but he could see from Jamie's face that he'd gotten over it a long time ago.

"So if you're a resident of Heaven, why are you living on

Earth with everyone else who's still alive?" Ben asked.

"Ah, that's a good question," Jamie smiled. "And more than anything else I've told you, Ben, this is really one you have to keep to yourself."

Ben nodded. He was getting used to hearing that.

"I'm not supposed to tell anyone any of this," said Jamie, gazing out of the window. Clouds had rolled in and little drops of water were trickling down the glass. "I'm not sure what they'll say when I tell them that you know."

"Who's they?" Ben asked, but Jamie was already continuing.

"When I died, I was pulled up before St Peter," he said. "Most imposing person I've ever met, but at the same time you wouldn't meet anyone nicer. And he told me I was definitely going to Heaven, but I had a choice.

"The circumstances of my death were special, St Peter said. I had died to save someone else, and that meant I had the choice of going to the actual place of Heaven. Or I could choose to stay here and live amongst those who are still running the race, becoming what they call a Caelun."

"So you chose to stay," Ben said.

"Yeah. I just couldn't imagine going somewhere where everything is supposed to be perfect, you know? I know society has its problems, but I'm comfortable with that." He looked pensive. "It's probably a massive character flaw, and I don't want to take away anything from people who have real problems, but the thought of living forever in a place where nothing could ever go wrong – it scares me."

"Um, I kind of feel the same," said Ben, and a look of understanding passed between the two.

"Yeah, well," Jamie shrugged. "I love it here, so as clichéd as it sounds, this is Heaven enough for me."

"Aren't there lots of people who die for others, though?" Ben asked. "Do they get the choice, too?"

"Yeah, some choose to stay, some choose to go straight to Heaven," said Jamie. "Lots of people who end up dying that way haven't had brilliant lives, so going to a perfect place is exactly what they want. But a few choose to stay. The Devil really hates it because it means people who know the full story are out there walking amongst the living, spreading hearts and flowers and whatever. Plus anything that rewards those who die to save others can't be good in his book, you know?"

"I suppose. So did you ever track down the people who killed you?"

"No. It was one of the conditions of returning. And I couldn't contact anyone I'd known from my old life. I had to change my name and live somewhere completely different."

"Really? You couldn't even tell your family you were still around?"

"No, the powers-that-be are very strict about that, but I always kept an eye on my family. Which was really hard at first, relying on word of mouth. But over the past little while, thanks to the internet, it's become extremely easy." Jamie laughed. "Penny died about thirty years ago but she left three kids, seven grandkids and eighteen great-grandkids. Most of them have profiles online, and many are pretty slack with their privacy settings. So I definitely get to keep up with what's happening back home."

"Have you contacted any of them?" Ben asked.

"Oh, no," Jamie said. "I'm really not allowed to."

"Do you ever tell anyone about your... circumstances?"

"No. You're the first person I've ever told."

Ben wasn't sure how he felt about being the only one who knew what sounded like such an important secret. "Why haven't you told anyone else?"

"Well," Jamie began. "Aside from A, no one would believe me and B, what goes on in the so-called afterlife isn't knowledge everyone is privy to, I was forbidden to tell anyone because it could start getting people into difficult situations. If everyone knows that if they die for someone they'll get to live on Earth as an immortal and get massive perks in the process, then you'd have all kinds of people trying to set up situations where they snuff themselves to save someone else. Not good."

"I suppose," Ben repeated.

"So now that you know my dirty little secret, I may as well tell you what I've been thinking," said Jamie briskly, finally getting back to the reason Ben had shown up at his door in the first place. "We've read everything we can get our hands on, we've talked to other Sentenceds, and I think we've left no stone unturned when it comes to researching this thing. So surely it wouldn't hurt to have a chat with a few people I know. I mean, let's not get our hopes up, but you never know what they might say."

Jamie jumped up and went to the phone on the wall next to the kitchen bench. He pulled a book out of a drawer, flipped through it, then punched a number into the phone.

"Hello, it's Jamie Portman," he said. "Yeah, hi Amora… Good, thanks…. Yes, Yes…Oh, you heard it?… That's great, I don't know about the last part though, I think I may have hit a few of the wrong notes right before that bit where the clarinets came in… well thank you. Anyway, I was just wondering who's in the Sydney office today?"

Jamie paused as he listened to Amora's response.

"Oh, he's not?" he said, sounding disappointed. "What about… oh, he's not in either? In London, hey? Fair enough. Okay. Um, Moses? No? How about – yeah, that would be great, I'll hold."

Jamie held his hand over the receiver. "She's just going to look in the calendars and tell me who's around," he whispered, and unclamped his hand as Amora came back on the line.

"Okay, then how about in any of the other offices in the area?" he asked, and there was another pause as Amora did whatever it was she did with calendars.

"Perfect," he said, listening to her. "Perfect. No it's okay, I don't mind the drive. Thanks, Amora. Bye."

He hung up the phone and grinned at Ben. "Good news," he said. "Come on!"

~

The Aston Martin sped through the streets and onto the freeway, dipping down into tunnels every so often. Ben sat in the passenger seat with Jamie's big lug of a phone directory on his lap. Jamie seemed to know his way as they passed the airport and headed south.

Dark clouds were clustered in the sky above them, and droplets of rain started appearing on the windscreen.

"Why don't you get this digitised?" asked Ben, holding up the massive book.

"I keep meaning to, but it's a big job," said Jamie, glancing at the tome.

"You wouldn't have to do it yourself," scoffed Ben. "Just hire someone else to do it. One of those assistant-for-a-day people."

"Yeah right, that would go down well. Have you seen some of the numbers in that book?"

Ben flipped to a random page and read some of the faded handwriting. "Matthew," he read. "Who's Matthew? He doesn't have a surname." He flipped to another section. "Lot? That isn't even a real name."

Jamie shook his head. "Don't worry," he said.

Rain drummed on the roof of the car as it travelled down the highway. How late was it? Ben dug his phone out of his pocket.

"It's noon already," he told Jamie. "Is this place very far away?"

"About an hour," Jamie replied. "But I think it's important we do this in person."

"Yeah, well, Verla hasn't got much time." Ben hadn't meant them to, but the words came out sounding a bit snippy.

"I know that, Ben," said Jamie, a little impatiently. "You think I don't care about her or something? Trust me, I care. I'm doing my best here."

Ben didn't want to fight with Jamie but he couldn't help saying something.

"If you really wanted to do your best, why didn't you tell us about your whole Heaven deal before now?" he muttered at the wing mirror.

Jamie tapped his fingers against the steering wheel and stared grimly at the wet road. "It's not just something I go around telling people, okay?" he said. "I already told you the reasons I can't go blabbing it about the place. The world would be chaos if everyone knew what really goes on. People are much better off believing whatever they get told to believe by their books and religious leaders. It may not seem that way, with all the religious wars and everything, but it's true."

Ben turned back to Jamie. "If you'd have told us earlier, we could have helped Verla earlier," he said accusingly.

"I did everything I could do with the facts I had at the time," Jamie said a little defensively. "I can't just pull a rabbit out of a hat, you know, just because I've got the Heaven thing going on. I'm not an angel or anything. I don't have any powers."

"But *still*," Ben insisted. "If you'd have thought to make some calls to these contacts of yours last week, we'd have a whole week to do stuff. Instead, here we are, with less than ten hours to go before midnight, and a couple of miracles to perform in that time."

"Don't you think I feel guilty enough?" Jamie asked, and Ben heard an edge of desperation in his voice. "Don't you think I feel bad that I didn't do this sooner? This is the first time in so long I've felt this way about someone, but I've probably ruined her life instead because as usual, I thought I knew better."

He gripped the steering wheel tightly and shook his head. "Just because you get given a ticket to Heaven doesn't mean you're any less stupid than you were when you were alive."

"Did you want to tell us?" Ben asked cautiously. He hadn't expected Jamie to show so much emotion.

"Of course I did, but I'm just so used to keeping it to myself that it's second nature not to tell anyone from the start. Then before I knew it, I was in too deep, and I thought hey, it's not important anyway, let's just get Verla out of there and then I'll worry about everything later on."

"Hmmm. Okay."

"In hindsight it probably wasn't a great decision, I know that. But if I can make up for it now," Jamie said determinedly, "I will."

~

The Aston Martin turned off the highway onto a winding

road that dipped in and out of bush-covered hills. After about twenty minutes the car made a left into a long driveway, and Jamie braked in front of a massive set of wrought iron gates. He identified himself to an intercom, and the gates slid open.

The rain had eased to a drizzle and the sun was valiantly trying to reappear from behind the clouds. Glimmers of sunlight reflected off acres of grass that rolled in each direction. At the top of the driveway on a hill, Ben could make out glimpses of a big house behind some trees, and as the car drew closer he realised it was a large modern mansion made of white brick, glass and steel, about four stories high.

"Is this a church?" he asked as Jamie parked the car next to two Bentleys, a Rolls Royce and a yellow Ferrari.

"Kind of close, but no. It's the local offices of God."

"I was expecting it to be… bigger."

"Ben, God doesn't need a seventy storey office with heaps of sexy secretaries to be powerful."

"Aw, why not?"

They both laughed and got out of the car.

"What does everyone else around here think this place is?" asked Ben, thinking of title deeds and local governments and neighbours.

"This bit's a private golf course but the whole area's a national park."

"A golf course in a national park? Is that allowed?"

Jamie shrugged. "It is when you know the right people."

Ben noticed that the acres of lawn were interrupted by the occasional sand trap, small lake and patches of long, wiry grass. Beyond the green was a long sandy beach that led to the ocean.

The rain had finally stopped and the sun filtered through some gaps in the clouds. Ben and Jamie walked up the path to the front of the building, where elegant script over the entrance spelled out 'Elysian Links'. Jamie identified himself to yet another intercom, and when the door opened they walked into the large foyer.

The area was pristine and quiet, with a young woman sitting behind the reception desk, wearing a telephone headset and tapping away into her computer. She had long dark hair and understated makeup, and she was wearing a pale blue suit that showed off only the slightest hint of cleavage. She looked up and smiled as Jamie walked over.

"Hello, my name's Carys," she said warmly. "How can I help you?"

Jamie and Ben introduced themselves. "Ah, yes," Carys said mysteriously. "We've been expecting you."

Ben was a bit spooked until Carys continued, "Amora called me and said you were coming. Now, can I see some identification?"

Jamie pulled out his usual white card and Carys nodded affirmatively, then looked at Ben expectantly.

"Uh, I don't have one of those," he said awkwardly.

"He's with me, Carys," Jamie interrupted smoothly. "He's important to the case I'm here to discuss. I'm sure it'll be okay, but perhaps you want to have a quick word just to check?"

"Give me just a second," she smiled, then swivelled in her chair to murmur into her headset before turning back to them. "That's fine, gentlemen. Now just sign in here while I get you some visitor's passes."

They scribbled their names onto a sheet, and Carys handed over a couple of cards that they obediently pinned onto their shirts.

"Safety pins, how metaphysical," Ben whispered to Jamie, but luckily Carys didn't hear.

"Right, all good! Go right through." She smiled at Jamie.

"You know where to go."

Jamie led Ben through the foyer and up some stairs. They came out at a corridor lit with big windows and scattered with potted plants.

Ben stared at the names on the doors as they passed. Mary Magdalene. Archangel Gabriel. Mother Teresa. John the Baptist. Mahatma Gandhi.

Jamie saw him staring. "They probably won't be in," he said. "They have heaps of offices all over the world. In fact, I've never even heard of Gandhi dropping by here – what would he want with golf?"

They passed a few more nameplates until Jamie stopped and indicated the next door. They looked at each other hesitantly, and Ben noticed that Jamie seemed a bit nervous for once.

"Let's do this," said Ben, and knocked on the door, just below the nameplate that spelled in clear copperplate writing: ST PETER.

## - CHAPTER TWENTY-ONE -

# The Gatekeeper

The door creaked open to reveal a spacious but rather cluttered office. Every surface was bright and free from dirt, but stacked with papers and books, not unlike how Professor Brightman's office had been - give or take a few mouldy sandwiches. Ben noted some squashy armchairs on one side of the office and a table with chairs at the other, before his eyes finally rested on the old man sitting at a massive desk at the far side of the room.

Jamie was already striding forward. "St Peter," he said quietly, bowing his head briefly. "How are you?"

"Good, Jamie, good," said St Peter, standing and grasping Jamie's hand to shake it firmly. Ben inched forward and Jamie introduced him.

"St Peter, this is a friend of mine, Ben Fletcher," he said. St Peter shook hands politely, but Ben noticed him frown slightly at Jamie.

Ben felt intimidated. This was St Peter! Like, the St Peter he'd read about in books and stories and those limericks that mention a profession, and how those people had their share of hell already. He would never have thought he'd actually ever meet him.

St Peter motioned for them to sit down and Ben obliged, still studying the old man across the desk. He'd always imagined St Peter to wear a robe, but he was decked out in what appeared to be golfing attire instead. Of course he'd have a white beard, but Ben thought rather critically that it should at least go all the way down to his waist, not be trimmed neatly with only about two inches worth of growth. His long hair was tucked under a golfing hat, but appeared to be tied back in a loose ponytail. Right.

Ben suddenly realised St Peter was speaking to Jamie rather sternly, and Jamie was staring at the floor.

"It's a contract, Jamie," the old man was saying. "And there's a reason that clause is in there. You can't just go telling people your situation; who knows what domino effect that may have? I don't want to hear about this happening again."

Jamie looked miserable and as Ben caught on to what St Peter was talking about, he felt like sinking through the floor. It was his fault – he'd nagged the truth out of Jamie. He felt St Peter's stern eyes glance in his direction, and he suddenly knew what Jamie had meant when he said St Peter was imposing. This was worse than that time he was twelve and his dad told him off for decapitating Tia's cabbage patch doll. Much worse.

Ben fervently vowed never to do anything bad ever again. He couldn't imagine facing up to St Peter on his judgment day and having all his sins read out. He cringed, picturing being forced to go over the cabbage patch incident with the old man in front of him.

The two sat studying the carpet as St Peter finished his lecture. Ben had a feeling St Peter knew about his part in Jamie's admission – and the guilt trip Ben had taken him on for not admitting it sooner – and had kept him in the room for that reason.

St Peter clapped suddenly and the two men looked up. St Peter had lost the forbidding expression and was now smiling, his eyes all crinkly.

"And I'm sure it won't happen again, won't it?" he asked Jamie.

"No, sir."

"Then onto other things! I know you didn't drop by just for the pleasure of a lecture. Now, Jamie. Did you get my Christmas card?"

Ben was surprised by the quick change of subject but Jamie handled it with ease – he'd obviously dealt with St Peter before.

"Yes, I did," he said. "Did you get mine?"

"Yes, yes of course! I can't believe you found one with me depicted in it; I only seem to get a real look-in during Easter. I'm not sure if the illustrators were right – I was only four when Jesus was born, certainly not a grown man with a big brown beard. The likeness was unmistakable though!"

St Peter laughed heartily and Ben wasn't sure what he was talking about.

"You're lucky you caught me here today," said St Peter. "I wasn't planning on being in Australia at all, but an annoying storm blew up on my way to Argentina and they landed my plane at Sydney Airport. I thought I may as well stay for a few rounds of golf when the weather's clear enough."

St Peter leaned back into his chair and his eyes levelled on Jamie. "Now, Jamie," he said, settling back comfortably. "Everything satisfactory?"

"Yes, everything's great, thanks."

"Friends all well?"

"Yes, everyone's doing fine."

"Found a nice lady to settle down with yet?"

"Uh, not exactly. It's hard to meet anyone when I can't tell them my situation. I think they'd start to wonder why I don't get old."

"What about that lovely girl Evelyn I told you to contact? You know, the Irish woman who drowned when saving her friend last year. She chose to live in Brisbane, don't you remember?"

"Yeah, I did call her and we meet up for coffee whenever I'm up in Queensland, but she's not interested in me – or men at all, really. Her new girlfriend is really nice, though, you'll be happy to hear."

"That is good news! So. Getting enough gigs?"

"Enough to keep me busy, for sure."

"I heard some concert recordings a few weeks back and recognised your style. I liked that improvisation you did before the clarinets came in; it really added some dimension to the piece."

"Thanks, St Peter," Jamie said, looking surprised.

St Peter leaned forward and twiddled a fountain pen around his fingers. "So what can I do for you, boys?"

Ben wasn't sure how he felt about being called a boy, but figured St Peter had to be over two thousand years old – so anyone less than five hundred was probably a baby to him.

"We're here to see you about someone who belongs to the, uh, other camp," said Jamie. Ben was glad they were finally getting to the point.

"Ah," said St Peter simply.

"She's a Sentenced," Jamie continued. "We submitted her review but it was denied, and today is the last day before her next century commences. We were kind of wondering if you could maybe use your influence to get them to take another look."

"I've never really agreed with these reviews," said St Peter seriously. "Gives false hope, I say. In the past few hundred years I think only about three of the Sentenced have had successful reviews. I believe one lives in your city, Jamie. A professor of some sort."

"I know the one," said Jamie, and Ben leaned around to stare at him. "I actually helped him get his review pushed through about twenty years ago."

"I should have known it was you," said St Peter. "What was he in there for in the first place?"

"Writing books they didn't agree with – they were too close to the truth," said Jamie. "One of Hell's workers ran him over with a horse and carriage. They got rid of most of the books, but I think some were reprinted years later and there's one or two still out there."

Ben sat back, surprised. He knew that was true – he happened to have a photocopy of one of the pages stuck to the pin-up board in his room.

"This is a similar case," said Jamie. "It's a woman named Verla. She was Sentenced for refusing to marry a Hell worker, a man called Hermes Duncan."

"Ah, yes, Hermes Duncan," said St Peter. "I remember that young lad. Applied for a job with us, you know. Must have been about four, five hundred years ago? We took a look at him but he wouldn't have fit in."

"Why not, sir?" asked Ben, speaking for the first time in what seemed like ages.

"Very ambitious, but not in a good way," said the old man shortly. "Had a plan about some jezebel who would give him an incredible power. He worded it in a way that made it seem like he'd use that power for good, but I could see through him. The man was evil. Last I heard he'd wormed his way into management over in the other camp."

"Did he tell you anything else about his plan, sir?" Ben asked, hoping to get more leads – maybe it had something to do with Duncan's proposition of Verla.

St Peter looked at him a little sternly. "Not really, son," he said. "Just that there was a French woman who had something special about her. Oldest tale in the book. He was obviously just smitten with her, but I could sense something evil going on with him, and that's why he didn't get the job. It was a long time ago."

The old man sat up straighter. "Now, what's the story with this girl Verla?"

Jamie spoke first. "Her centennial review has come around and I did all the usual things," he said. "Poked holes in the contract, protested the methods used, tried to cast doubt on Duncan's motives and character et cetera. Only problem is," he exhaled slowly. "Duncan's the head of the Review Board now."

St Peter looked impressed at the irony of the situation. "Duncan would have been none too pleased," he said, and Ben and Jamie nodded. The old man leaned back in his chair and resumed his fiddling with his fountain pen.

"It's a bad situation, boys," he said. "You've done everything right, but this Duncan lad obviously has no intention of letting it happen. Head of the Review Board, eh."

St Peter sat thinking for a minute. "Hmm," he said slowly. "An interesting situation indeed. The question is, how far are you willing to go to make this work?"

Ben opened his mouth to say something appropriately brave and selfless but Jamie beat him to it. "All the way," he said.

St Peter leaned back then forward in his seat. He repeated

the action a few times and it took Ben a second to work out that he was actually sitting in a rocking chair. The old man rocked back and forth for a while staring thoughtfully first at Jamie, then at the pen in his own hand.

Ben's leg started jigging and he longed to look at his phone to see the time, but he'd left it in the car. It had to be at least two o'clock now, if not later. They were wasting valuable time sitting here and St Peter seemed more concerned with studying his pen than anything else that was going on.

Ben glanced over at Jamie, expecting to see the same look of impatience he expected was apparent on his own face. Instead, Jamie was assisting with St Peter's visual examination of the pen. There was a strange look on his face as he gazed across the desk at the black and silver writing instrument.

Minutes ticked by and Ben's leg started jerking in a staccato fashion. He didn't want to be the one to interrupt the silence. He only hoped that there was some extremely profound and productive thinking going on in the minds of the other two men.

Finally St Peter looked up from his precious pen and studied Jamie instead.

"I could ask," he said simply. "But Jamie - the price."

Jamie nodded slowly and Ben felt like the last person to arrive at a party and who missed witnessing all the scandalous hook-ups.

"Um," he said, not wanting to sound like the ignorant one. "You mean you can help us, sir?"

St Peter had one of his quick personality changes, and smiled at him warmly. "Yes, I may be able to help, though please don't get your hopes up too much," he said briskly. "I don't know if anyone's told you, son – the religious texts certainly don't – that the system is rather a bureaucratic one."

Ben nodded; he'd heard it a few times now.

"You could ring every single day to get an appointment with someone, but your message might never get past their assistant's assistant," the old man said. "You have to know the right channels, and this, I believe, is where I may be able to help. As it happens, I, as Heaven's Gatekeeper, have the privilege of being able to schedule a meeting with the other camp's Gatekeeper at any time I want. A privilege that he, unfortunately, also has with me – which is very inconvenient sometimes, especially during the cricket season."

"So that means…" Jamie said.

"That's right," said St Peter. "And I'm pretty sure that gatekeeper just happens to be young Duncan's boss. If I know he's in, I can just show up, and he has to see me."

"Are you saying you'll talk to him about this case, sir?" asked Ben.

"I can try," said St Peter. "I can't promise anything of course, but I happen to know he's based in Sydney this week, and it would be such a pity not to take this opportunity to annoy him while I'm in the area too."

~

Ben checked the time on his phone as St Peter's limousine rolled smoothly into the city. Four o'clock. There was still time.

"And so I said to him that if he didn't consider it a sin, then maybe he should double check it with his girlfriend!" St Peter was telling Jamie. "We didn't have much trouble with that lad from then on."

St Peter leaned forward to the chauffeur in the driver's seat. "You probably won't be able to get any parking around here, Len," he said. "Just drop us off at the front and I'll let you know when we're done."

Len let them out at the Hades Corporation building and St Peter led the way inside. He strode through the empty lobby and up to the reception desk, and the curvaceous receptionist looked up, first surprised then delighted when she saw who it was.

"Why, St Peter!" she breathed. "It's been so long! How are you? Can I get you anything? You're looking so, so good!"

St Peter shook her hand cheerfully. "I'm fantastic, thanks Marigold, and may I say you look wonderful yourself. I'm here to see your Gatekeeper, if that's okay."

"Of course it is!" Marigold flirted. "Anything for you. Take the elevator to your left and go down to sub-47 – and I expect you to drop by for a quick chat before you leave."

St Peter thanked her, promised a later rendezvous, and led Jamie and Ben to the elevator bank. Marigold leaned low over the counter to wave to them as they left.

A lift opened in front of them and Ben glanced idly at the man who stepped out. Black suit. Dark hair. Emerald green tie. The man looked at Ben as he passed, and as their eyes briefly met, Ben felt a strange feeling surge through his body like a mild electric shock. He stared at the man as he hurried into the lobby and out of the building's front doors.

"Come on, Ben," said Jamie, who was standing in the lift with St Peter. Ben gave himself a quick shake and stepped in next to them.

"Speak of the devil – well, not the Devil himself," said St Peter, pushing a numbered button on the panel. "That was young Hermes back there."

"That was Mr Duncan?" Ben whipped his head around at the now-closed doors. "What's he doing here?"

"He was probably called to Sydney to sign off on Verla's

review," said St Peter logically. "Or in this case, reject it."

Jamie narrowed his eyes. "Good thing I didn't know it was him," he said. "Or there may have been a bit of a scene."

The lift doors opened, and the lobby before them was decorated in stark black and white tones. The receptionist's shiny black suit strained at the seams as she jumped up to greet the trio.

"Why, St Peter!" she said. "How lovely to see you! Marigold said you were on your way down and do you want to know what I told her?"

The gatekeeper smiled as he clasped her hand. "I'd love to, Rosemary, but right now I need to see your boss," he said.

Rosemary looked slightly crestfallen but rallied with a pout. "Oh, of course!" she said, gesturing to the door behind her. "You know your way."

St Peter, Jamie and Ben went through the door into a luxurious office decorated in wood panelling. At the end of the room, a mild-looking man was eating a sandwich at his desk. St Peter strode up to him.

"Good to see you, good to see you!" he told the man, who looked slightly peeved at the interruption.

"Yes, well, Marigold only just told me you were coming," he said. His accent was vaguely British. "I was having lunch."

St Peter laughed heartily. "Well, that gets you back for that three hour long meeting you needed right during the last innings of that cricket match last season!" he said cheerfully. "Ben, Jamie, come over here, I'd like you to meet the Gatekeeper of Hell. This is Judas Iscariot."

Ben stopped, mid-handshake with the brown-suited man. "Judas Iscariot?" he said, looking back at St Peter and hastily pulling his hand back. "Isn't he – "

"Yes, yes, yes, it was me," Judas interrupted testily. "And

no, I don't regret it, it got me the top job here. Well, not the top job. But close. And don't ask me to retell the story, I get sick of it. And everyone makes fun of the kiss bit."

He sat back down, looking around at his visitors in an irritated manner. "I'm sick of it," he repeated, as if daring them to bring it up again.

"Sorry," said Ben nervously, as they all took seats in front of the desk. Ben looked down at his hand, almost expecting some sort of stigmata to have appeared after touching Judas, but it seemed intact.

"Right!" St Peter hurried on. "Judas, we're here to see you about a young woman."

"Oh, not this Mary Magdalene business again," said Judas, flaring up again. Ben decided he must have a pretty short fuse. "I already told you, I wasn't trying to impress her – "

"No, no," St Peter interrupted calmly. "That's all put to bed now, Judas – "

"'Put to bed?'" Judas mimicked. "What's that supposed to mean?"

"Judas!" St Peter said sternly as Ben and Jamie shared an impatient glance. "We are not going over that again. What happened 2000 years ago is in the past. I and the boys here want to talk about something that's happening *now*."

"It's about a girl called Verla," Ben interrupted, his desire to get things moving overriding his intimidation. "She's a Sentenced up for her centennial review, your Duncan guy rejected it, and today is the last day of appeal."

St Peter nodded approvingly. "Well summed up, young man," he said, then turned back to Judas. "We'd like to get her case looked at again."

Judas sat back in the chair, looking happy to have the upper hand. "And what makes this case different from any other case out there?" he asked. "I don't see all the other Sentenceds having their applications approved willy-nilly."

"Well, it seems your Duncan had more of a personal view on this one," said St Peter. "He proposed to her, and when she rejected him, he killed her and Sentenced her. Purely self-serving, and a bit of an unnecessary tax on your resources, if you don't mind me pointing it out."

"That's still not a good reason for me to reconsider the application," Judas said, nonetheless making a note on a pad of paper.

Jamie took the floor and outlined the finer details of the case, but Judas still didn't look convinced. Ben glanced at the clock on the wall. It was almost five and they didn't seem to have made any progress at all. Verla's time expired at midnight, and knowing how anal they were, the Hades staff would probably kick them out of the building before long.

"I'm sorry, gentlemen," Judas said grandly to the three men before him. "I'm just not seeing why this case should be reconsidered."

"Judas," said St Peter, shaking his head sadly. "All the times we've negotiated and I've made concessions for you? I never expected that you would be so unmovable about something that means so little to you."

"Well, my dear Peter," said Judas. "Maybe you'll remember this next time I need something."

"I sure will," St Peter replied. "I'll remember to treat your cases exactly how you're treating mine now."

"I look forward to it," the other man said haughtily. "But if you don't have anything else – no more, shall we say, bargaining chips – then I'm afraid this will be the end of our discussion."

Jamie spoke out. "We do have one more," he said slowly.

St Peter stood up abruptly. "Jamie, might I have a word with you?" he said quickly, and before Ben could react, the old man grabbed Jamie's arm and steered him through the door. Ben stood up uncertainly, but it didn't look like he was invited to their little tête-à-tête. He sank slowly back into his chair and looked self-consciously at Judas. A few minutes passed by in silence and Ben hoped that Jamie and St Peter wouldn't be long.

Judas sat at his desk sharpening a pencil and staring at Ben. He flicked the shavings into a waste paper basket and silence resumed. A second pencil was selected.

The magnitude of the situation dawned on Ben. He was sitting in an office with Judas Iscariot. Suddenly he longed to be back at home, hearing boring stories about his parents meeting at university and having a normal life that didn't involve being stuck in gloomy offices with the biggest betrayer in history who seemed to be on a power trip and was now starting in on his third pencil.

Ben was beginning to wonder if his companions had forgotten about him and left, when they walked back into the office. Jamie looked determined; St Peter looked resigned. They walked over and sat down while Judas put down his fifth newly-sharpened pencil and eyed the men beadily.

"Do you have anything further for me?" he asked.

"Yes, we do," said Jamie. There was a pause.

"Jamie is a Caelun," St Peter said heavily.

"Ah!" Judas looked at Jamie. "I knew it!" His eyes swivelled to Ben expectantly and he frowned. "This one is not; I can tell. This boy is… something else."

Ben almost felt as if he should apologise for not being particularly special, but Judas was back to staring at Jamie again.

"He bears no mark," he said questioningly.

"You know that we don't mark ours, Judas," St Peter replied quietly. "Jamie came to us in nineteen-twenty-three. He chose to stay here."

Judas stared at Jamie with a greedy look in his eyes. "You just can't help yourself, can you," he said, his eyes flicking over to St Peter. "You keep bringing them back and letting them roam. If there wasn't a system in place you'd have the world overrun with Caelun by now." He turned back to Jamie and Ben saw a glint of loathing in his eyes. "I can't stand your type," he said quietly to Jamie. "Holier-than-thou, treating the place as if it's your playground just because we can't get rid of you. Well, don't get too comfortable. Things won't be this way forever."

Jamie squared up and looked him in the eye. "I'm offering to change it right now," he said.

Judas's eyes shifted between Jamie to St Peter. "I see," he said. "I see. Are you saying that your status as a Caelun will be your bargaining chip?"

"Yes," said Jamie.

"And what are you prepared to give up?"

"All of it," said Jamie. "My status goes. I become mortal again. I rejoin the race."

"And the girl?" asked Judas. "You think I will let Caelun status be bestowed on her? You are dreaming, boy."

"No," said Jamie. "She rejoins too."

Judas stared at him for a few seconds then snapped his head around to look at St Peter. "You realise what this would mean," he breathed triumphantly at his nemesis. "One of your star recruits, back in the race, ready to fall prey to the temptations of the mortal world. And there are plenty of temptations, Peter. Oh, we have *plenty*."

"I understand," cut in Jamie.

"But do you?" asked Judas, now looking a bit puzzled despite himself. "Do you realise everything you will lose? Have your years as a Caelun made you forget the lives of those who run the race?"

"I understand," Jamie repeated.

"Do we have a deal, Judas?" asked St Peter.

"Yes," Judas said slowly. "Yes, we do."

# - CHAPTER TWENTY-TWO -

# An Untimely Stupor

Ben was elated. He couldn't believe that they'd actually been successful in their mission to free Verla. He smiled, giving himself a moment to enjoy the fact that he was behind the wheel of an Aston Martin Vanquish, winding up the mountain road and fulfilling a major car-related fantasy. This was amazing. He changed down a gear to overtake a truck in front of him, and the gearbox made a grinding noise when he lifted his foot off the clutch too early. Whoops.

Jamie stirred slightly at the noise. He was slumped in the passenger seat where Ben and St Peter – who had demonstrated surprising agility – had put him when they picked up the sports car from the country club. He'd be out for another two hours at least, St Peter had said. The anaesthetic would take a while to wear off.

St Peter had suggested taking Jamie back to his apartment for a rest, but Ben had convinced him that going straight to Verla would be the best course of action. And with Jamie out for the count, who was going to drive? Well, Ben, of course! He hoped the two flaps of paper with 'P' scribbled on in red marker would satisfy the police if he was pulled over.

He glanced across at Jamie. He hadn't moved much. In the

dim light Ben could see part of the bandage taped to the back of Jamie's neck, right at the base of his head, where the two different needles had gone in. Ben shuddered. He hated needles. The first one with the anaesthetic hadn't looked too bad, but when a second syringe was produced – a massive one that looked like it should only be used on elephants – Ben had excused himself and stood in the corner of the room, fidgeting and occasionally looking over to the trolley where St Peter, Judas Iscariot, Rosemary and what looked like a mad scientist were fussing over Jamie's prone body.

Ben checked the time on the car's dashboard. 8.28pm. He gave himself a mental cheer. Solved with three and a half hours still on the clock!

He dipped down into the valley and made the same right turn that his father had accidentally made a few weeks previously. It felt like a hundred years ago. As they sped into the dark streets, he glanced up at the burned houses, bathed in moonlight again. They didn't seem forbidding now, just sad. He wondered which ones his ancestors had lived in when they perished.

Verla's now-familiar house loomed up on the right and Ben pulled the car around the side, parking next to the remains of the bonfire. He glanced at Jamie, who was still dead to the world, and debated what to do. He didn't want to waltz into the house and take full credit when Jamie had been the one to give up his mortality and all. On the other hand, he certainly wasn't going to sit in the car while Jamie finished his nanna nap.

He decided to get Verla and bring her out to the car, where she'd be able to see firsthand what Jamie had done. She should be waking up from her anaesthetic about now. Judas had dispatched another mad-scientist type to arrive at her house around the same time Jamie would be receiving his shot, so the exchange would be almost simultaneous.

Ben had wanted to drive back to Verla's house and be there with her when she received it, but there hadn't been time. He hoped she hadn't been too alarmed when Dr Doom showed up at her house unannounced, waving a massive syringe. Ben and Jamie had written a note for the doctor to give to Verla, and hopefully it had set her mind at ease. The note said simply that the appeal had been successful after all. Jamie hadn't wanted to tell her the truth in case she refused to let him complete the deal and give up immortality for her.

Ben gave Jamie a quick poke, but his friend just moaned slightly and turned away, so he figured he'd be out for a while longer. He hoped Verla wouldn't be as sluggish.

He jumped out of the car, trotted around to the front of the house and up the steps, and knocked softly.

"Verla!" he called. "We're back!"

There was no response so he eased open the door and slipped inside. "Verla?" he called. "Verla! It's Ben!"

He quickly checked the rooms downstairs, but they were empty. Verla must be asleep in her room. He slowly walked up the stairs and called her name from the landing, but there was still no response. Where was she? He crept down the unfamiliar corridor, across pools of moonlight spilling through the windows.

She wasn't in any of the rooms.

Judas had assured them she wouldn't have to leave the house to receive her shots, and he'd received a phone call from Dr Doom to say it had been administered successfully. Ben wondered if Judas had been lying. But St Peter had insisted on having a word with the doctor too, and when he hung up he had been confident the deal was complete. Surely he'd have sensed if something was amiss.

Verla must have woken up and gone for a walk. What was she doing out at this hour? If she was out wandering the streets, she could be anywhere. Surely she wouldn't have celebrated her newfound freedom by boarding a bus somewhere. Ben didn't even think buses stopped by Carmenton at this hour.

Perhaps she was at the park. He could drive there and check, then canvas the streets to see if she was wandering around.

He went downstairs again and was almost at the front door when a strange feeling made him turn. He stared up at the room around him, feeling the big, dark house closing around him. Something in him knew that the house was empty, and for a second, a tiny prickle of despair stole through his body. There was something about this house. He'd spent weeks wandering through it and hanging out on the front porch, but without Verla in it there was a feeling of vexation, as if the house sensed its captive had fled.

Almost as if, in Verla's place, the house wanted Ben.

He took a deep breath. He wanted to leave, right now, but something inside him, a feeling linked to that prickle of despair, was propelling him to the ornate wooden door next to the roll top desk. He'd checked before and Verla wasn't in the library, but he needed to go in there again.

It was at the table in the middle of the room that Ben found the note.

"If I cannot have her," he read aloud, tilting the paper into a thin stream of moonlight, "no one shall."

Ben's heart dropped like a rock. He brought the note up closer to his face. He'd seen the writing before, the A's, the N's, the R... he'd seen the same writing before. He'd seen it in the signature of Hermes Duncan.

His body jerked to life and he looked around wildly. Where would Duncan have taken her? She was a Sentenced, she was already damned, surely there was no worse fate that he could give her than she had already…

Ben stopped.

She wasn't a Sentenced anymore. As soon as the chemicals entered her body, she had rejoined the race. She could die like anyone else now. Where would she go for her afterlife? Ben's mind raced over the possibilities quickly. Surely, if Duncan killed her again, St Peter would be quick to step in for a fair judgment? And Duncan would lose. But surely he wouldn't let that happen; his pride was wounded enough. Did he know that Verla wasn't a Sentenced anymore? Was there a memo that went out when people's statuses changed? Was there a bandage on the back of her neck, and would Duncan know what it was from?

Ben's eyes fell on the books on the table. Verla must have been reading them when Duncan came for her. Marguerite Grammaire's diary lay open, and some old parchment was spread in front of it, detailing what looked like a family tree. Ben crumpled Duncan's note in his hand and started for the door, but then stopped, turned, and gathered the books and paper. He ran out the front door to the car and dumped the items onto Jamie's lap.

"Jamie!" he hissed, shaking the man's limp shoulders, but he didn't stir. Ben looked around frantically. What should he do? He needed to find out where Duncan took her. Would Duncan have a car? Maybe he could call the licensing department and find out what cars were registered to Duncan, then call the police and get them tracked? No, that wouldn't work. He couldn't really report Verla as a missing person either. Ben cursed to himself. All the nice normal avenues you take when things go wrong just didn't apply in this new world he had found himself in.

He needed Jamie to wake up, but slapping him and shouting only resulted in Jamie turning over and snuggling up to the books Ben had dumped on his lap. But as Jamie shifted, Ben noticed a much larger book wedged under his feet.

It was the big address book from Jamie's apartment. Ben tugged it out and started flipping through frantically. What should he look for? His mind fell on a mental image of the Hades Corporation building, and he flipped to the H section, grabbed his phone from the centre console, and started dialling.

"Hello, Hades Corporation Sydney office, how may I help you?"

"Um, hi, this is, um," Ben paused, screwing up his face, "this is Lovejoy from St Peter's office. Mr, er, Peter would like to speak to Mr Duncan, is he in?"

"I'm sorry, I'll have to transfer you to his assistant's phone," the voice purred. Ben desperately hoped his assistant would be in at nine at night. Maybe he or she was extremely dedicated to her job.

"Hello, Mr Duncan's office, how can I help you?" A new voice interrupted Ben's thoughts and he zipped back into Lovejoy mode.

"Hello, Lovejoy from St Peter's office here," he said, trying to sound warm and cheerful. "Mr Peter would like to know if Mr Duncan is available to speak to him?"

"He's not here, I'm afraid," the voice said cautiously. "Can I take a message?"

"No, that's okay," said Ben. He paused. "Do you know if Mr Iscariot is available instead?"

"I'm sorry, I think he's left for the day," said the voice.

"Well, thanks anyway," said Ben, dejected. "Have a most lovely evening. Bye."

He flipped through the book again and put in a call to St Peter, but there was no one answering the phone at the office. A quick scan of the other numbers revealed nothing that stood out, and Ben banged his head back against the car seat, frustrated.

Where would Duncan take Verla? Again, Ben's mind went over the possibilities, but this time he paused to examine each one more carefully.

The Hades Corporation building was the obvious spot, but was he only thinking that because he didn't know anywhere else the Hell lot hung out? Ben's mind ticked back to the first conversation he'd ever had with Jamie. What had he said – something about there being an office in every major city. Ben closed his eyes and tried to visualise this part of the world. Was there an office in Melbourne or Canberra? How would Duncan get there? By plane? Helicopter? Hovercraft? Ben tried to remember what Jamie had said about transportation. Did they use cars? Ben couldn't remember discussing it – only that they took commercial flights sometimes. Then he remembered something else Jamie had said: that the Hell lot probably had another way of getting around.

What did that mean? Did they have broomsticks or something? At this rate, he wouldn't be surprised. Ben reached over and grabbed Duncan's note from the pile of papers slipping off Jamie's lap into the car's centre console. *If I cannot have her, no one can,* he read silently. It had to mean that Duncan was taking Verla somewhere to kill her off permanently. Ben squinted. Was that even possible? Now that she was mortal, wouldn't she just die again and get sent to be judged? Even if

Duncan intervened before she got a proper hearing in front of St Peter or Judas, she'd just be in the same familiar boat that she'd occupied for the past 100 years.

Suddenly frustration overwhelmed Ben and he pounded on the steering wheel, yelling out a few choice swear words. Jamie stirred slightly at the noise, and Ben turned to him.

"Wake UP!" he screamed, slapping Jamie around the head. "I don't know what to do! WAKE UP, Jamie!"

Jamie's only response was to snuffle a bit before starting to breathe regularly again. Ben slumped back in his seat, staring unhappily at his unconscious companion. Though his face was relaxed, Jamie seemed to have a few slight lines around his eyes that Ben had never noticed before. He wondered if they'd appeared when Jamie was made mortal again, or if he'd gained them over the past few arduous weeks. Again, Ben thought back to the first time he met Jamie, when they sat on a park bench near the University of Sydney, and Jamie had proceeded to tell him things that would change his life forever.

As Ben visualised that conversation, something slid back into his mind – Jamie talking about the Devil. *"I don't know what it is or how he does it,"* Jamie had told him. *"But he can end souls now."*

The Devil could end souls. So maybe his workers could too. Perhaps it wasn't a spell or an enchantment or anything; all of the logistical elements of this God-Devil world seemed solid and physical, so maybe it was some sort of weapon, like a chemical or a machine.

Maybe that was where Duncan was taking Verla – to the soul-ending thing, whatever that was.

Jamie stirred again and Ben took the opportunity to shout at him a bit more. "I NEED you, Jamie!" he yelled, shaking Jamie's shoulders. "Just bloody wake up! You're the one who knows about this stuff, not me! I don't even know why I'm here, I just stumbled into this mess by accident! WAKE UP!"

When Jamie still didn't stir, Ben suddenly decided that sitting in a car in Verla's back yard wasn't the most productive thing he could be doing. "You SUCK!" he shouted at Jamie, jamming the car into gear. He turned left, and the headlights cut through the darkness of the street.

Ben concentrated all of his frustration into his foot, jamming the accelerator pedal flat to the floor. The sports car responded obediently, almost fishtailing in its haste to obey the driver's command.

The car careened off the side road onto the main highway towards Sydney. Ben had no idea if he was going in the right direction, but that building in Sydney was the only place he knew of that played host to the Devil's little crew.

The car broke every speed limit racing down the highway, but Ben didn't care. He changed up into every gear he could find, and zoomed along the road at a speed he'd never before experienced on land.

He had pulled back into his lane just in time after a harrowing overtake when he noticed something blinking on the dashboard. His first thought turned to the fuel warning and he was about to scream aloud in frustration, but the he realised the light was nowhere near the petrol gauge and seemed to be coming from a phone.

With one hand tightly gripping the steering wheel, Ben ripped the phone out of the car charger and looked at it. Private number. Hopefully it was someone who could help. Ben hit the 'accept' button and wedged the handset between his shoulder and ear, returning both hands to the steering wheel to overtake a semi-trailer in front of him.

"YEAH?" he yelled into the handset.

"Jamie, it's St Peter here."

"ST PETER!" Ben screamed. "We need your help! Duncan took Verla somewhere and I don't know where!"

"Jamie?" came the surprised voice at the end of the phone. "Is that you?"

"It's BEN!" he yelled in reply. "Jamie's still out of it! When we got to the house, Verla was gone and there was a note – "

"I know he took Verla," St Peter interrupted calmly. "That's what I'm calling about."

"WHAT?" shouted Ben. "What's going on?"

If St Peter was annoyed by Ben's lack of volume-control, he kept it to himself. "I just got off the phone from our friend Judas," he said. "Duncan was seen in the lobby of Hades Corporation a few minutes ago, with the female subject of our earlier arrangement. Judas called to tell me that with his great regrets, we would have to reverse the chemical procedures, because one of his staff members had different plans for the girl."

"WHAT?" screamed Ben again. "Just like THAT? He can't just DO that!"

"Judas didn't sound too happy about it," admitted St Peter. "In fact, he sounded a little scared. Whatever Duncan said to him, it shook him up. Usually Judas would never be so frank with me – best to keep the other camp guessing, you see, and even when we were kids we were never the best of friends – but Duncan must have touched a nerve."

"Why, what did Duncan say?" asked Ben frantically.

"Well, don't quote me on this, because you can never take anything they say at face-value," St Peter cautioned. "But it sounded like after he dispensed with the girl, Duncan was going to take the final steps to, er, 'harness the power of the mother herself' – that's what Judas said, anyway. Though what he meant I do not know, because I just confirmed with St Paul that Verla's mother Francine is safe in Heaven, as is her grandmother Constance."

"I don't know either," said Ben, overtaking two cars in a row. "But I'm more concerned about getting Verla out before she's 'dispensed with'. So is that all Judas said, that Duncan and Verla are in the lobby now?"

"They'd just taken the elevator down," said St Peter. "Ben, if you're on the way there now... be careful. This is a different world from the one you're used to."

"Yeah, I'm beginning to realise that," said Ben grimly. "So where would he take her? Jamie told me something about how the Devil can end souls now. How would Duncan get to wherever that is?"

"I'm sorry, I really can't help you there," the Gatekeeper replied sadly. "Our intelligence network hasn't been able to figure that one out yet."

"That's okay," said Ben. "I guess I'll have to find it myself."

"Well, you do that then," said St Peter. "I'll try to get hold of the legal team and see what I can do from over here. Just... please be careful, Ben. Let me know how you go, okay?"

"Okay," he said shortly. "Bye."

The drive to Sydney that usually took two hours had been eaten away in less than ninety minutes. The lights of the city loomed ahead, and Ben directed the car straight to the area with the tallest buildings. He was concentrating on sneaking through one red light after another when he heard a sleepy voice by his side.

"Wha... whass going on?"

Ben's head snapped around and he stared at Jamie, who gazed back at him vaguely. A car horn screeched at them from off to the side, and Ben quickly brought his eyes back to the road.

"You're finally awake," he said, but didn't feel total relief like he expected – instead, there was just a fleeting feeling of gladness that his partner in crime had finally decided to make himself useful, then a snap back to steely determination to find Verla.

"Duncan took her," he said shortly. "Left a note. Said something about how if he couldn't have her, no one else could either. I reckon it means he's going to use that thing that ends souls. St Peter called about ten minutes ago. They were in the Hades Corporation lobby and they took a lift down to somewhere. We should be there in about," he scrutinised the lights of the buildings in front of him, "seven or eight minutes."

"Wha-at?" Jamie said blearily. "He took Verla?" He struggled to sit up straight in his seat, but slumped back down again.

"I don't know what we're going to do there," Ben admitted. "I don't even know where in the building he'd take her. To the roof, maybe. He might have a helicopter waiting there. I doubt this big important soul-killer is actually in this branch of the office."

"He din' taker to th'airport, then," Jamie muttered, holding his head in his hands.

"Yeah, I guess that's something," said Ben. "Or maybe we're about to find out what this special transport method is."

Jamie gazed at Ben, his eyes sliding out of focus. He looked like he was about to fall asleep again, and Ben reached out and gave him a hard shove. "You've got to stay awake, okay?" he commanded. Jamie gave a slight nod, then giggled quietly. Ben looked over in surprise, but Jamie's attention was focused on the neon-lit shops that the car was quickly sliding past.

"ASS-ten Burgers," he smirked quietly to himself. "ASS! Hahaha. An' look. Pants and Socks. Pantsensocksenpants, hahahahaha!"

"JAMIE!" shouted Ben, hoping to shock him out of his doped-up reverie. "Just CONCENTRATE, okay? This is NOT a good time to be funny!"

"You're a funny guy, Benny," mumbled Jamie, his eyes half closed. "You're fun-ny. We've had some GREAT laughs."

"Uh, yeah, we have, Jamie," said Ben, glancing back and forth from the road to Jamie's face, alarmed. "Are you okay?"

"Yup," Jamie whispered, then giggled again. "Yup-yup-yup-yup-yup."

Ben bit his lip, not sure whether to laugh or cry. He was completely unaccustomed to the usually cool-as-a-cucumber Jamie being in a doped-up, stupid mood, but he knew he had to get him alert again before they found Duncan.

"You're COOL!" announced Jamie, with a burst of energy. "Iss like, you're my FRIEND, Benny."

"Uh, yeah, we're friends," said Ben, squinting at the buildings ahead of him.

"Yeah, like, FRIENDS, friends," confirmed Jamie fuzzily, then after a short silence he announced a little mistily, "I think I LOVE you, man."

"Uh," said Ben, not sure what to say, while Jamie's wide eyes stared at him searchingly. "Uh, yeah, me too."

"Coolies," Jamie announced happily, his eyes sliding back out of focus. He started twitching around in his seat, and grabbed the papers that had somehow become wedged into the small of his back. He began pawing through them, his eyes half-closed.

"Look, herezumfunny names," he said, giggling fuzzily and holding up a large piece of parchment. "Constance. Constant.

Constantly."

"Seriously, Jamie," said Ben cautiously. "You've got to snap out of this. We're almost there."

"Hey, lookathis," mumbled Jamie. "Here's your name. Benjamin. Benjamooin. Benjamima!"

This time Ben spoke more sharply. "Jamie, we're almost there, just wake up!"

"Benjamamamamina!"

Ben aimed a slap at the side of Jamie's head, desperately trying to knock him out of his stupid state before they reached the building. Jamie didn't notice, too absorbed in trying to focus on the words on the parchment.

"But this'n't your last name," he muttered, sounding confused. "Who's Benjamin Diamant?"

"I'm not an Diamant because that's my mother's maiden name," Ben explained, irritated. "My last name's Fletcher, after my dad."

"Diamant," Jamie repeated in a singsong voice. "Diamant, diamond, diamonds are a girl's best friend!"

Suddenly losing what energy he had, Jamie dropped the piece of parchment and sunk his head back into his hands. He shook his head groggily and moaned. Ben turned the car left, then left again, and realised that although he could see the Hades Corporation building ahead, it was across a large median strip.

"Sorry about your suspension, Jamie," he said, and clenching his jaw, he jumped the sports car up onto the curb with a loud scrape of the chassis. The car crunched back down onto the damp road on the other side and drifted sideways to face the large, imposing façade of the building. Ben jumped the curb once more, mowed down several shrubs and a small tree, and skidded the car to a stop outside the front doors.

"Jamie!" he shouted, turning to face his companion. Jamie had his face in one hand, with the other hand massaging his temple. Ben distinctly remembered hearing a loud bump as the car had started to drift, and realised it must have been Jamie's head hitting the window. Jamie looked at him, still rubbing his temple. "What?" he asked groggily.

"Are you awake now, Jamie?" Ben asked him urgently. "Are you, uh, ready to go?"

"Ummm," Jamie clenched his eyes shut, then opened them. "Yeah. Yeah. I think I'll be okay. What's... what are we doing?"

Ben felt around in the darkness at Jamie's feet for Duncan's note, but his hand closed around something else instead. Bringing up a bottle of water, he quickly unscrewed the cap and with a feeling of guilt – though not that much, really – he started pouring the water over Jamie's head.

"Hey!" Jamie tried to grab the bottle away, and Ben leaned away quickly. Jamie shook his head and little droplets sprayed onto the dashboard. He gazed at Ben indignantly. "What was that for?"

He definitely looked a lot more awake now, Ben noted. "Come on," he said, opening the door. "Duncan's got Verla in there and," he bit his lip, "it may even be too late."

"What?" Jamie was half out of the car, but his body stopped in shock. "Duncan took Verla?"

"Yes!" Ben shouted, exasperated. "I told you before, you idiot! Duncan took Verla into the elevator, probably about twenty minutes ago now, so God knows what he could have done in that time!"

Jamie sagged slightly, and even though Ben could tell by his bleary eyes that he wasn't fully awake yet, he charged on angrily. "If you hadn't been so obsessed with making ass jokes about shops, and singing songs about my mother's maiden name, we may have been able to work out a plan!"

"Why was I singing songs about your mother's name?" asked Jamie, looking confused and shaking his head as if trying to dash away the last of his fogginess.

"I don't know," Ben shouted, throwing his hands up. "Because you thought you were a singer. Maybe if you'd – "

He stopped abruptly in mid-sentence, then spoke again. "Yeah, why *were* you going on about my mother's name, Jamie?"

They both scrambled for the parchment at the same time. Jamie got there first, despite his weak state, because he was already half-slumped onto the passenger seat. Tilting the parchment up to the streetlights, he stared first at it, then at Ben.

"What did you say your mother's maiden name was?"

"Diamant. Why?"

"Um, Ben... it's got that name written all over it."

## - CHAPTER TWENTY-THREE -

# Through the Stone Doors

Ben and Jamie stood outside the massive double doors of the Hades Corporation building, with the light of the half-moon illuminating their faces. Ben's mind was still reeling about the familiar name that was dotted all over Verla's family tree, and he was still trying to make out what it meant. Unfortunately, more urgent matters were at hand, in the form of the thick, sturdy, solid stone door before them.

"We could call St Peter," suggested Ben, one hand still clutching the parchment.

"Yeah, but what's he going to do?" asked Jamie weakly, holding onto one of the pillars at the side of the entrance. "It's not like he has a set of keys. Despite all the diplomacy that goes on, we're outside enemy territory right now, and the last thing they'd want people like us to do is get in."

"Maybe we could scale a wall?" said Ben, his mind drifting back to the Enid Blyton books he'd read as a kid. He stepped back and appraised the brickwork for a handy creeper he could use to climb up.

"This is probably the most fortified building in Sydney," Jamie whispered. "I don't think they'd have left a window open for us."

Ben kicked one of the massive doors. Why hadn't he thought about this on the way? He glanced at Jamie, irritated. Maybe if his friend hadn't been giggling away about unfunny store signs, he'd have had more time to think about this.

Jamie was still staring up at the doors. "Do you remember anything about them from when we were here earlier?" he asked. "I can't. I think they were open when we walked in."

Ben shook his head. "They were open when we carried you out, as well," he said dejectedly. "No one said a secret code or anything to unlock them." He ran his hands over the smooth surface. "Where's the doorknob? I can't even see a lock!"

He glanced up and down the street, hoping to spot something – anything – that may give him some clues. All he could see were bubbling black fountains and a deserted city street. He sighed, frustrated. "We've got to find a way in!"

Jamie's strength gave out for a second, and he sagged against the pillar and closed his eyes.

"You okay?" Ben asked, a little concerned. He hadn't expected Jamie's anaesthetic to take so long to wear off.

Jamie nodded, his eyes screwed shut. "Yeah," he whispered. "Just a bit groggy. Tell me," he looked up at Ben, "is this how you feel all the time?"

"What, groggy?" asked Ben, leaning his back against the door and pushing against it. "No."

"No, no," said Jamie. "I mean… weak. Heavy. Not strong. A bit, well, not *sad*, but certainly a bit more down than I was yesterday."

"Ah," said Ben, understanding – he'd forgotten that Jamie had just had his Heaven residency revoked, and was back to running the human race like everyone else. "You'll be fine. It won't be that bad once you're used to it." He pushed his back against the doors again, then looked across at Jamie, feeling irritated to see him just standing there. "Feel like giving me a hand here? Maybe we can push them open."

"Unlikely," Jamie said, straightening up and stepping over. "You think they'd just forget to lock them?"

"Well, at least I'm trying!" said Ben, his voice rising. "At least I'm not moping around on the ground. I'm trying to do something to help Verla!"

"Oh, you think I haven't tried to help her?" Jamie retorted, joining Ben at the doors and putting his weight against them. "I just got injected with some of the strongest drugs out there! I just gave up living on Earth forever! And you think I'm not trying to help?"

The duo glared at each other as they pushed against the doors, which still hadn't budged.

"Oh, that one's not going to get old," Ben said sarcastically. "Are you going to pull out that line whenever you get pissy with any of us?" He put on a high, mimicking voice. "Don't try to reason with me, I had to have a big needle! Don't call me on my crap, because I gave up mortality! I don't want to do the dishes, because I just –"

"Cut it out!" Jamie yelled, straining his back against the door. "Of course I'm not going to be like that! I'm just saying that these doors are locked!"

"Thanks, that's very helpful!" Ben shouted back. A roll of thunder grumbled in the distance, and he paused before continuing his rant. "Why don't you suggest something else then, Mr I-Know-Everything-About-Heaven-And-Hell? I could use some help right now! Use your expertise and get us in there!"

Jamie stared up at the doors dejectedly. "I bet if I was still immortal I'd be able to get through these doors somehow," he said. A few droplets of rain landed on his face and he reached up to wipe them off.

"If you were still immortal," Ben said, throwing up his hands. "Verla would have, oh, about two hours before her appeal time was up, and then she'd be back in Hell for another hundred years!" The wind blew some dead leaves against his jeans and he kicked them away angrily.

"Yeah, true," said Jamie, the fight draining out of him. He closed his eyes wearily and slid down the pillar to sit on the step. "Instead, she's in there with a homicidal maniac, who, if he hasn't already, is about to end her life permanently."

At Jamie's words, Ben's heart dropped like a stone. In all the excitement of getting here then figuring out a way through the doors, he hadn't spared a thought for the fact that Verla's life was about to be ended.

*If she wasn't dead already.*

The thought ripped through him and his heart stopped for a second. Verla couldn't be dead. But almost half an hour has lapsed since St Peter had said the girl was seen alive. There had been plenty of time for Mr Duncan to end her existence. In all likelihood… Verla was gone.

Ben started breathing heavily and felt his heart rate speeding up. The anger he had just felt towards Jamie started building into a rage inside him, fuelled by every thought and memory he had of Verla. The parchment in his hands started to tear slightly as he clenched his fists so hard that his knuckles started straining out of their sockets.

As the fury burned brighter and brighter inside him, the wind started picking up, blowing leaves and pieces of garbage through the entranceway. All Ben could think about was one thing: the face of the sad, sweet, dark-haired young woman who was about to be murdered.

Drops of rain began pelting down onto him, but he didn't

notice. He stared at the doors before him, the thick stone doors that stood between him and Verla. The doors that stood between him, and her life.

His heart was racing and his breath came out in short, sharp bursts. Raindrops were hitting his face, but seeming to evaporate instantly as they connected with his white hot skin. The wind was building itself to a gale now, making the small trees that were planted around the entrance bend almost double, but Ben stood firm. All he could think about was Verla.

That Verla was probably dead.

Ben could hear Jamie shouting at him from a thousand miles away over the sound of the wind and rain, but he didn't care. With his whole body trembling and every inch of his skin burning with fury, he walked slowly up the last few steps towards the large wooden barricade, and placed his palms flat on each door.

These doors would not stand in his way.

Ben clenched his eyes shut, his rage bringing his blood to boiling point, and an image flashed into his head: Verla, the sad, wistful but strong woman – the last time she had shared her rare sweet smile with them.

These doors would *not* stand in his way.

Ben took a deep breath, opened his eyes and tensed his hands against the flat surface, and a split second later his world came to a standstill.

His body was hit with a deafening crack and a hot flash of blinding white light. As he flew forward with the force of the blow, something hard and solid fell past his shoulder, hitting the ground with a loud crash. The smell of acrid smoke filled his nostrils and the wind howled past him, bringing smatterings of rain with it. His vision was filled with a white blur, and the only sound he could hear was a long, loud roar from above.

He lay crumpled on the ground, unable to move, with rain falling lightly on his face and the rage slowly ebbing out of him. Suddenly he felt his arm being pulled and his body being dragged over a smooth surface. The wind was pushing less and less against his face and body, but the smell of smoke still hung in the air.

Ben's vision was still edged with milky white but the sound of the wind and rain was starting to recede. As his body came to a standstill, he let all the tension go and lay limply on the ground, his whole body aching. He wondered when, if ever, he'd find the strength to get up.

"Ben!"

The sharp whisper cut through his aches and pains and reminded him that he was here for a reason. Slowly he opened his eyes and looked blurrily at Jamie, who was kneeling over him.

"Ben! Are you okay?"

Ben clambered onto his elbows and looked around him as his vision cleared. Only a few dim lamps lit the vast area where he was lying. Fifty metres away at the far wall, there was a large gap where the large stone doors used to be. He could see one door still hanging onto half its hinges, but sagging dangerously down towards the other door, which he could scarcely make out sticking up from its position on the entranceway steps. Beyond the outline of where the doors used to be, he could see streetlights reflecting against the buildings on the other side of the road, but they were slightly hazy as if rain was still falling outside. Ben blinked, and a few blobs of white light seemed permanently seared onto the insides of his eyelids.

"What happened to the doors?" he croaked. "Are we inside?"

"Wow. Ben. I can't believe you're still alive," said Jamie, sounding shocked.

"Why? What happened to me?"

"Well I'm not completely sure, but I saw what I saw, and I think —"

Ben shook his head impatiently. "Jamie! Just tell me what happened!"

Jamie looked like he couldn't believe his own words as he said, "I think you were struck by lightning."

Ben scrambled into a sitting position and ran his hands all over his body. All his limbs seemed intact. He ran his hands through his hair and realised it was standing on end, with the tips of each strand strangely hard and brittle. He brought his hands back down and could smell the unmistakable scent of burnt hair.

"We have to get out of here," Jamie said, looking around nervously. "Someone's bound to turn up soon and they're not going to be happy."

Ben looked up and saw they were sitting just off the main foyer in the small, short corridor of the elevator bank. He was about to berate Jamie for wanting to leave when he saw him reached up and hit the button for the lift. The light on the down arrow glowed.

"We're going… down?" Ben asked, his breath still coming rapidly.

"Yeah," said Jamie. "We may as well start there."

"St Peter," said Ben thoughtfully. "When I spoke to him on the phone, he said they'd just taken the elevator down."

"Down it is then. Are you sure you're okay?" Jamie asked, helping Ben stand up.

Ben's legs were wobbly and his body still ached, especially his shoulder where the massive stone door had scraped past him.

"I think I'll be okay," he said a bit shakily. "Though if what you said is true, I'm pretty sure I should be burned to a crisp right now."

"It got you straight on," said Jamie quietly as they watched the lit numbers at the top of the lift door slowly count down. "It looked like it went straight through you and hit the door."

"I don't know how I survived if the doors didn't," said Ben, looking back to the silhouetted shapes in the entranceway.

"I don't know either," said Jamie. He paused. "But for some reason, I think the weather's on our side."

Ben was still gazing at the entranceway when he remembered.

"Wait - Jamie! Your car!"

Jamie cursed and said, "Where are my keys?"

Ben dug them out of his pocket. The metal was hot, and he winced as he handed them over.

"Hold the elevator," said Jamie, and dashed back across the lobby.

There was a low chime as the elevator doors opened smoothly in front of Ben, and he stuck his hand between them so they wouldn't close. He looked up at the sign above the lift doors: 'Staff Only'. Well, this wouldn't be the first rule he'd broken today.

A few minutes later Jamie returned, and Ben followed him into the lift, limping. They stood staring at the massive column of buttons and corresponding labels.

"Should we check his office?" Ben asked, starting to regain a feeling for the urgency of the situation. "Where else would he take her?"

"He's not going to take her to his office," said Jamie, running his finger down the list of labels corresponding to the underground floors. "It's got to be somewhere different, somewhere…" His hand stopped right at the bottom of the list, where a small, shiny button was set slightly lower than the rest. Instead of the engraved script of the other labels, a small piece of white paper was taped to the wall next to the button. It said in handwritten black ink: PORTAL.

Without even thinking about it, Ben reached out and pushed the button, and with a jerk, the world dropped out from underneath him.

He screamed.

## - CHAPTER TWENTY-FOUR -

# The Portal

Fifteen seconds later, Ben's lungs ran out of air and his scream weakened to a wheeze. After the initial drop, the elevator had whizzed down so fast that Ben felt practically weightless. But a few minutes later, he started feeling that they should have arrived at their destination long ago.

"It's going faster than last time! We must be going deep down!" he called to Jamie, who was slumped in the corner of the lift where he'd fallen after the elevator first dropped. Ben could see him struggling to get up, so he inched his way around the edges of the falling elevator and helped him to a standing position.

Ben opened his mouth to speak again then paused, realising that the elevator's speed may soon be the least of their worries. As he felt the vessel accelerate, the noise of the lift slowly built up until it became a roar that almost deafened him. He clutched the shiny handles that lined the walls of the silver capsule, but his hands were sweaty and couldn't get a grip. He could feel the air temperature slowly rising as the elevator zoomed downwards.

"Where are we going?" he screamed at Jamie.

Ben could see Jamie's face staring at the walls around them

– not that the interior of t he lift was offering any clues. His brow was furrowed and he looked like he was trying to work something out.

"JAMIE! Where are we going?" Ben screamed again.

Like Ben, Jamie was struggling for a grip on the railings but the heat in the elevator was making him perspire too much to get a proper grip.

"I don't know!" shouted Jamie. "I think – I think we might be – we're going –"

"WHAT?" yelled Ben.

"Down, downwards!" yelled Jamie, his feet slipping under him slightly. "We've gone down so far already, we must already be thousands of metres down… I think it's…"

"WHAT?" Ben yelled again.

"It must be where…" Jamie shook his head and Ben could see him grappling with his thoughts.

"COME ON!" Ben shouted impatiently.

"We know the Devil can destroy souls now, right?" Jamie shouted.

Ben nodded. "Apparently, yeah!"

"Maybe we're going to wherever that is!"

"Where he destroys souls?" Ben yelled, his voice squeaking a little at the end of his question. "What, underneath their Sydney office?"

"No, we've gone way beyond that now… and if we keep dropping so fast, we'll be headed for the centre of the Earth! We might even end up coming out on the other side!"

The heat was rising in the lift and Ben wiped some sweat away from his face. He tugged off his jacket and dropped it next to him. He felt cooler for a few seconds before the heat tightened back around his skin.

"Oh, of course!" he shouted sarcastically. "The centre of

the Earth, why didn't I think of that? Jamie, be serious!"

Jamie glared at him from his corner as the lift plunged deeper and deeper. "Oh, right," he yelled sarcastically over the roar. He slid off his own jacket and threw it over the lift's railing. "All the stuff you've found out in the past few weeks, and you think that it isn't possible too?"

Ben thought about this as the speed of the fall made beads of sweat slide upwards into his hair. He rubbed his forehead with the back of his arm and conceded that Jamie had a point. "So why the centre of the Earth?" he yelled.

"I don't know!" shouted Jamie. "But God's crew couldn't find any evidence of this killing machine on the surface, or anywhere within Earth's atmosphere. It must be well-hidden. So why not deep underground?"

"But how could they make an elevator shaft this deep?"

"I don't know," Jamie shrugged. "Really big drills?"

"We can't get to the centre of the Earth though," Ben reasoned with him. "The Earth's core is made of molten lava or liquid iron or something!"

"I know what you're saying is true," said Jamie, and Ben strained to hear him over the roar of the lift. "But this is different. They would have had to think outside their usual methods to create something that even God can't – or wouldn't – make."

"But how?" Ben called.

"I don't know!" said Jamie, a bit louder. "I don't know everything they do, you know! But it's probably got something to do with Mother Nature!"

"Mother Nature!" Ben screamed. "You mean she's somewhere around here too?"

"No," Jamie boomed. "No one knows for sure if she even exists. I mean, just, you know, Nature! The Earth itself! The force behind everything!"

It was Ben's turn to slump to his corner of the lift. "What do you mean?" he yelled. "Is there someone in charge of nature as well?"

"Who knows?" shouted Jamie. "But there has to be something controlling the laws of the Earth! God and the Devil only affect humans. Someone else is behind the trees and the animals and the weather and everything!"

Ben leaned his head back against the wall, trying to take in what Jamie had just said. His words had triggered a memory. It was something he had seen recently. A book he had read in the State Library, perhaps? Or maybe one of the things from Verla's own collection? Something to do with a woman of nature having a child.

"Is this ever going to stop?" shouted Jamie, interrupting Ben's thoughts.

Ben shook his head. "I don't know."

He wrapped his arms around his knees and tried to ignore the strange feeling of weightlessness that had taken over his body.

The silver capsule hurtled down for what seemed like forever, and Ben started feeling very claustrophobic. The air was hotter than anything he'd ever felt before, and his tongue felt thick and dry. He remembered the water he'd poured over Jamie's head earlier, and the rain that had fallen so freely outside the building, and longed with all his heart that he could have just a few droplets of it to wet his papery mouth.

He wondered what would be waiting for them when the lift eventually stopped – if it ever would. He had no idea what would lie outside the doors. Would they open, and the lift would be instantly filled with the molten metal of the Earth's inner core? With that thought, he squeezed his eyes shut. Up until this moment, it had never crossed his mind that he might die trying to save Verla. Would that count as a selfless act that would get him admitted to Heaven? Ben's mind went to his mother, his father and his little sister, and he knew he wasn't ready to move on, even if eternal paradise awaited him.

But what if he did die, and was taken to a place where he'd never see his family again? He'd always regret not talking to his father more. They knew each other well enough, but it was his mother that Ben had always had the in-depth conversations with. He wondered if he should have told her about what was going on. A few times he'd considered it, but it had always been easier not to.

At the thought of his mother, he frowned then looked down at his hand, where the piece of parchment had been clenched where the lightning struck.

"Jamie, where's that family tree thing? Did you pick it up?" he called.

Jamie nodded and pulled a torn and somewhat burned crumple of paper from his pocket. He handed it to Ben.

Standing up unsteadily in the dropping lift, Ben smoothed the parchment, held it under the dim fluorescent light and started to study it. Even though he'd looked at it back at the car, it was still a shock to see his mother's maiden name sprinkled so liberally amongst the calligraphic labels. He thought about what she had told him a few weeks back about being born in that little town, and he tried to remember everything else she had said to him about it over the past few weeks.

He eventually relocated with the parchment to the corner of the elevator. He didn't know what time it had been when they first stepped into the elevator, but when he glanced at the watch slipping around on his sweaty wrist he estimated that it must have been over half an hour ago.

"We've been falling for ages," he shouted across the lift at Jamie. "How far can you go in half an hour?"

"I don't know," yelled Jamie. "It depends what you're in at the time! This thing seems pretty solid!"

"Maybe we're going at the speed of light!" shouted Ben, his eyes opening wide despite the dry, scratchy feeling of his eyeballs against their sockets.

"I don't think so. If we'd been travelling at the speed of light for half an hour, we'd have shot right out the other side and be way past the sun by now. I think we're still in the Earth."

"That's one good thing. At least the Earth is solid. It's better than flying around in a lift in space."

Something suddenly occurred to him and he wondered why he hadn't thought of it before. "JAMIE!" he shouted, fear twisting his stomach. "What if we're actually falling? Maybe we're just shooting down a hole with no cables attached! Or maybe they're broken! They'd have to be the longest cables in the world to get us down this far!"

Jamie looked back at him and Ben could see his own apprehension reflected in Jamie's eyes. Then Jamie stiffened and stared around him at the silver walls.

"Are we slowing down?" he yelled.

The lift gradually lost speed, and Jamie and Ben clambered to their feet. Just as Ben was starting to feel like he was back to his usual weight, the lift stopped abruptly and they both lost their footing and landed on the floor again. They stared at each other. For the very first time since he'd met him, Ben saw pure fear etched into Jamie's face.

In front of them, the lift doors opened smoothly and they were hit with a blast of heat.

Still sprawled on the floor, Ben peered out of the doors.

"Finally," he said hoarsely. "This is what I've always imagined Hell would look like."

For the second time in an hour, Ben felt practically weightless; as he stepped forward out of the lift he felt as if he was almost hovering above the ground. Jamie stood unsteadily beside him as they took in their surroundings.

They were standing on a small black platform, with silver metal walkways spidering away from them in all directions. The silver paths were edged with glossy black handrails. Each walkway led to an identical platform, hundreds of them, each connected with other walkways that connected to more platforms. In the centre of each one sat the base of a solid black elevator shaft which disappeared into the ceiling, and seemed to be the only thing suspending the platforms in the air. But instead of a solid ceiling, molten lava swirled above their heads, held there by what seemed like an invisible force field. It cast a strong orange glow over every visible surface.

Ben almost fainted. He legs felt so shaky that he might have fallen if he didn't feel so weightless, and with that in mind he staggered to the edge of the platform to grasp the thin handrail with both hands, afraid he might float away and into the lava above him.

Immediately he wished he hadn't. As he looked over the flimsy railing, he realised that all that was underneath the platform was a massive sphere of bright, swirling colours about ten metres below. What he could see of the surface was the size of several football fields, and it seemed to be made from some sort of thick translucent gas, ever moving and changing, and radiating a heat that he'd never felt before.

If he'd seen it in a picture, he'd have said it looked pretty. Seeing it in person was another thing.

As he stared disbelievingly at the sphere, he noticed something else. The platforms that were dotted everywhere around him didn't stretch into an endless flatness. Along with the lava ceiling, they curved around the sphere in every direction, like the Ozone layer curved around the Earth.

Finally Ben got it.

"We're in the centre of the Earth!" he shouted to Jamie, whose head was swivelling in every direction, fear and desperation in his eyes, searching for a sign of Verla or Mr Duncan.

"That's what I told you!" said Jamie.

"No, really," he replied, his eyes widening as he said the words out loud. "We're in the centre, the actual centre, look!"

He pointed to the massive, swirling sphere below.

Jamie looked hard at the incredible sight, at the spherical shape and the platforms that curved around it, and looked back at Ben.

"That's how they did it," he said so quietly that Ben could hardly hear him over the roar of the lava above them. "They must have found a way to combine their own powers with the laws of Nature."

He gripped the railing and stared down at the sphere.

"Do you think this has always been here?" Ben asked.

"I don't know," Jamie replied. "I'd imagine that that thing has." He pointed at the sphere. "That's Nature's work all right. But this," he gestured around at the mess of steel walkways and elevator shafts. "It looks like they've found a way to use nature's powers in a way that was never meant to be."

"It's something to do with gravity," Ben croaked.

"Yes," said Jamie, the light from the sphere reflecting in his eyes. "I think... I think they're using the central meeting point of the Earth's gravity to tear people's souls apart."

Just as the words escaped his lips, they heard a burst of maniacal laughter from behind them, and Mr Duncan stepped out from behind an elevator shaft a couple of platforms away.

He looked like a man possessed. The calm, controlled exterior of the man who had propositioned Verla was gone. In its place was a man who wanted revenge, and knew he had the Devil on his side.

"I've been waiting for you two little heroes for a long time now," he said, the reflection of the lava above him glowing red in his eyes. "I knew you'd come after her. I thought you might want to watch her go, once and for all, to a place where she won't ever be coming back."

"Let her go, you psycho," yelled Ben, fury building inside him. His anger warred with a feeling of elation borne from the news that Verla was apparently still alive. "Where did you put her? Where is she?"

"Oh, she's here," Mr Duncan laughed. He waved his hand across the sea of platforms and their solid elevator shafts. "Somewhere."

"Give it up, Duncan. She can't be part of your plans!"

Ben sounded, even to his own ears, rather hysterical, and he fought to slow down his rapid breaths. Beside him, it looked like Jamie was having a similar battle.

"My plans?" Duncan asked coldly. "And what is it you know of my plans, boy?"

Ben glanced over at Jamie, who was now gripping the handrail tightly, eyes darting around. Ben sensed that he was calculating the angles and weighing the risks of an attack. He got his thoughts under control and realised that if Jamie was to overpower the man, Ben would have to provide a distraction.

"I know what you're after!" shouted Ben. "I've figured it out, and it's not going to happen, not while I'm here!"

"You?" Mr Duncan's voice had turned silky. "You, boy? This one I can understand," he nodded towards Jamie disdainfully. "One of those ones who thinks he's specially chosen, just because he was given some green card into Heaven for being extra good. But you, boy," his voice lowered. "I have nothing to fear from you."

"You do," Ben replied. "I may be just one of the ones still running the human race. But I know that I was sent to Verla for a reason."

He paused, and Mr Duncan sighed. "I suppose I have to prompt you to get the words out of you, do I? Well, I'm not actually that interested, boy. I have other matters to attend to."

Mr Duncan started to turn and Ben yelled out desperately, hoping his hunch was right.

"What about Susan Diamant?"

Mr Duncan turned back to Ben slowly. A glint of steel joined the lava reflected in his eyes.

"What about her? I suppose you've done some digging into my past, and you think she was of consequence. She's not."

At the edge of his peripheral vision, Ben could see Jamie very slowly backing down one of the walkways to his left.

"Susan was a mere fancy," continued Duncan smoothly. "A foolish girl. I didn't even have feelings for her, and you cannot use her against me now." His head started to turn away from Ben towards Jamie, who slipped behind the elevator shaft on the next platform.

"She's my mother," said Ben, hoping it would come as a shock.

It did. Duncan's whole body went rigid and he whipped his head back around to stare at Ben. "I thought you looked familiar," he whispered. "If she is your mother – then you are a descendant of the Grammaires?"

"Yes," said Ben boldly. "I am."

"If you are of the Grammaire line…"

"Yes," Ben repeated. "I belong to the family whose bloodline you've sought for centuries." He thought back to his recent conversations with his mother and with Verla, and the burned parchment with Verla's family tree, and something clicked into place. He faced up to Duncan and spoke again.

"That bloodline – that same bloodline that has produced nearly all male offspring since you first came into contact with it. Since the time of Marguerite Grammaire in the seventeenth century."

"You know about Marguerite?" Duncan hissed.

"Yes," said Ben, hoping Duncan wouldn't make him elaborate.

"But you don't know why I seek their blood," stated Duncan coldly, his eyes fixed on Ben's face.

"Does it matter?" Ben asked. He needed to keep Duncan distracted while Jamie gradually made his way to another platform. "I know that you need one of her female descendants, but so far there have only been two." Ben swallowed. "My mother, Susan Fletcher. And her distant cousin – Catherine Verla Diamant."

Out of the corner of his eye, Ben saw Jamie reach another platform to his left. If Jamie could sneak one more platform over then cross to the one in front of that, he would have a clear run at the platform behind the one on which Duncan now stood, glaring at Ben.

"How can destroying Verla help you?" Ben asked the man. "You're after the females, but there are only two. Why would you destroy one if they have something you want? Why, Mr Duncan?"

He could see that the man was boiling over with – what?

Anger? Regret?

"Because she did not love me," Duncan hissed back at Ben. "It is the law of nature that there must be love, and I rather think I have missed my chance with Miss Verla Diamant, don't you, boy? Your mother was also hopeless – that Fletcher got to her before I could."

Ben wondered, after all Duncan's talk about not talking, he was sharing this information now.

"But I let her be," Duncan continued. "Why not let her help continue the bloodline? I have plenty of time. And now ..." he stared at Ben and licked his lips. "She has, in turn, produced a female heir of her own."

Ben's heart almost stopped. Tia!

Duncan looked closely at Ben and smiled. "That would be your sister, wouldn't it," he said. "Oh don't worry, boy. I'll keep my distance until she's older, and charm her then. She has to love me, you see."

"Why does she have to love you?" Ben asked desperately, the heat of the lava causing rivulets of sweat to snake down his back. Any minute now, Mr Duncan would surely remember the situation at hand and look to see where Jamie had gone.

"It is the law of nature," Duncan repeated softly. "I didn't know it when I propositioned Verla Diamant. I should not have been so hasty. To harness the true power of the ancestor of Marguerite Grammaire, there must be a bond of love before evil and nature can be combined to produce another."

"What do you mean, nature?" Ben asked loudly.

Mr Duncan threw his hands up to encompass the vast area they were in. "Evil and Nature, boy!" he shouted. "Look what the combination has created here! They said it couldn't be done, but my master combined the forces to create a place that could destroy souls! Can you imagine the combination of evil and nature in a child? Neither my master nor his nemesis has the scope for it, but I! One of Lucifer's most trusted, coupled with a daughter of Nature herself – it would produce a child that could overthrow them all!"

"What are you talking about?" Ben yelled at him. "There is no daughter of nature! My mother and my sister are just normal people!"

"Normal to you, perhaps," said Duncan. "I am probably the only person who realises the potential of your line! It took me centuries to track down Marguerite. I had heard the legends that the Mother had produced a human child, but the line was lost for millennia. I feared it had died out. But then I met Marguerite, and I *knew*."

"How?" asked Ben, desperate to keep him talking.

"Because of one distinguishing characteristic, boy." Duncan narrowed his eyes at Ben. "Something that only someone like myself would ever notice. And something that only someone like me would use to get what I wanted."

He glanced upwards, and smiled at the lava swirling about them.

"Well, what?" asked Ben, trying to keep his eyes away from the figure of Jamie crossing the walkway several platforms away.

"An immunity," murmured Duncan. "Daughters of Nature… they cannot be burned by fire."

Ben opened his mouth, then closed it again. Duncan continued, smiling darkly.

"Fires raged while I searched," he whispered. "I burned down Moscow in fifteen forty-seven and Tokyo ten years later. Towns fell and villages smouldered while I hunted. Many a maiden bore the scar of my errant cigar as I crossed Europe and Asia, looking for the one to complete my plan, leaving a firestorm in my wake."

Ben breathed out slowly. "That's so… evil," was all he could muster.

"It was by chance that Marguerite and I were both in London in sixteen sixty-six," said Duncan, gazing into the lava above. "A fitting year, no? She had crossed the channel to collect English herbs. And while she was there, I just happened to set a bakery alight." He smiled, showing his teeth. "She wasn't so hard to find after that."

"What happened then?" asked Ben, his mouth dry.

"She was easy to charm," said Duncan, returning his eyes to Ben. "What is it you say? Not the sharpest dagger in the armoury."

"Then why didn't you just do whatever it was then?" asked Ben. "Why did you wait, why now, why us?"

"I would have," hissed Duncan. "But I was still finding my way, and Marguerite was not honourable enough to wait for our marriage! Her promiscuous ways led her to marry and bear the child of another, then during another visit to London she met her death – oh no, not at my hands, boy. There were many elements that could naturally and easily claim a life back then, and did. I waited for her child to produce his own offspring in turn, but there were only males from then on. The few females died in infancy. It seemed nature was against my plans."

Ben nodded slowly as Duncan's words sank in.

"Your mother almost went the same way," smiled Duncan. "Luckily I was there to save her. And your little sister? Well, I didn't even have a hand in her successful creation – it was all your mother's doing. I'll be sure to thank her when your sister and I declare our union."

Mr Duncan smiled at Ben, and Ben knew why the man had chosen to share this information with him. Just the thought of his happy little sister growing up to be seduced by this pillar of evil – it made his insides curl up and clench into paralysis.

"Of course," said Duncan, "you won't be at our wedding party. Tragically, you'll be dead."

Jamie chose that moment to strike.

## - CHAPTER TWENTY-FIVE -
# The Devil on His Side

Ben had no time to react as Jamie leapt onto Duncan and the two men toppled back into the railing. Jamie grabbed the man's arms and straddled his body. He looked down, an expression of loathing on his face. "Where is she?" Jamie hissed.

"Ah, it's you again," Duncan spat back disdainfully. "I was wondering what you were playing at while the boy and I had a little chat about my plans for his sister."

"There won't be any plans," Jamie said, his teeth clenched. "The only plan I have for you is a visit to that contraption down there your master's cooked up."

Mr Duncan stared up at him. "For a creature of Heaven, you don't feel as strong as I expected," he said almost curiously, then with a burst of strength, he pushed Jamie off him and onto the side of the elevator shaft.

Before Ben could react, Duncan had slithered up off the ground and was running down one of the walkways behind him. Jamie scrambled to his feet and ran after him, and Ben quickly pulled himself together and followed behind.

Mr Duncan weaved down walkways, across platforms, and around elevator shafts, on and on through the spidery maze ahead, lit eerily by the ceiling of red lava above and the colourful mass below. Finally he came to an elevator shaft, stepped behind it and pulled Verla out, holding her unconscious form in front of him. Verla's dark hair and eyelashes stood out against her pale skin and lips. For a fleeting moment, Ben thought she might be dead – and in another moment, he wondered where her soul would have gone if that was the case.

As that thought crossed his mind, she started to stir. As unconsciousness slowly slid off her and her eyes began to open, she smiled, smiled more brilliantly and more clearly that Ben could ever imagine.

But as she came back into full consciousness, she must have realised that she had her arms pinned behind her back, there was a ceiling of lava above her, the heat was unbearable, and Jamie and Ben stood frozen on a walkway in front of her. Ben saw her smile replaced with an expression of shock and fear, and she twisted to face her captor.

"It's you," she said faintly.

Duncan smiled evilly down at her. "I'm sorry, my dear. But it's a little too late to change your mind about me."

Everything in Ben's mind went fuzzy as Mr Duncan pushed Verla towards the railing, where there was nothing but a steel bar between her and the swirling mass below. Jamie sprang into action, leaping towards the duo, but Ben was paralysed on the spot.

Was this what it was going to come to? That sphere of gravity down there wouldn't be forgiving. Once someone had plunged into it, he knew there would be no going back. There would be – his mind tried to grasp the concept – simply nothing at all.

He knew the moment he met Verla that there was

something special about her, and that he'd met her for a reason. He had no idea the extent he'd become involved; no idea that he would learn more about the world and how it worked that he could ever imagine. Even now, standing in this massive cavern surrounded by lava, he could still hardly believe any of it was true.

Just a few weeks ago, he didn't care about anything much at all. Oh, he cared about his family and having fun and going to a good university and finding a nice girlfriend and getting a good job and making lots of money. But he'd never thought that there would be anything much more than that. He'd never imagined that there could be so much going on in the world.

But then he'd met Verla, who had so much going on behind her dark eyes, who had so much to live for and yet so little. And Jamie, who had made the ultimate sacrifice so long ago, but had been blessed so much since – and yet he had still been willing to give up his immortality for Verla.

Ben squared his shoulders. None of this was worth throwing away in a moment of weakness. There was only one choice here. He certainly didn't intend to die, and he didn't intend to let Jamie or Verla die either. Verla had only just gained her mortality back, and Ben remembered that first, brilliant smile on her face when she woke up free from her hell for the very first time. He looked at the man who had taken that smile from her.

Mr Duncan was struggling with Verla as Jamie launched himself towards them. Jamie was strong, Ben knew, but he didn't have the protection of Heaven anymore. He was back in the human race now, and Mr Duncan had evil on his side.

Jamie tried to tackle the older man around the waist but Duncan was too strong for him, throwing him back against the thin railing. Ben clenched his teeth and ran into the fight, stooping low and trying to grab the man's legs to overbalance him.

But Mr Duncan had a revenge to extract, and it was aimed at all three on the platform. He fought off Ben and Jamie easily as he set his sights on Verla again.

"Verla, run!" Jamie shouted. She was trapped between the elevator shaft and the three brawling men, and she darted around them to reach the nearest walkway.

Ben's eyes widened as he saw Duncan reach out a hand and grip Verla's wrist. Jamie lunged again but Duncan was too quick for him, dragging her out of his path.

"Say goodbye," he said to Verla, and pushed her over the railing. She toppled over the ledge with a scream, and with one last split-second look at Jamie and Ben, she fell into the swirling mass below.

~

Ben's vision went dark, then light again, and dark again. That could not have just happened, it did not, it could not have...

With a howl of rage and grief, he ran at Duncan. Both he and Jamie reached the man at the same time. Mr Duncan must not have expected their reaction times to be so quick, for he was still looking down at the colourful, swirling sphere that had swallowed Verla without even a ripple.

Duncan couldn't understand love, Ben thought in the split second it took for him and Jamie to reach the man who had just destroyed Verla's soul. He doesn't understand that you can care about your friends and family so much that you can almost surpass physical possibilities. Duncan's plan would never have worked, for although he may have been able to convince someone to love him, he would never have been able to love them back. He would have never been able to truly love a daughter of Nature.

Ben and Jamie hit Duncan at the same time, and it was almost too easy. The man was still in the process of turning around, a victorious expression on his face. Upon impact with the two men, his body flipped over the railings and he started to fall.

But he still had the Devil on his side, and as he fell, he took Ben with him.

All of time slowed down as Ben fell towards the swirling mass, Duncan's hands clutching his arms. The evil man was screaming but Ben was silent, overcome by feelings of grief and disappointment. What a pity. He really hadn't ever intended for this to be it.

The duo hit the surface, and everything went black.

# CHAPTER TWENTY-SIX

# Second Nature

Everything was easy, and everything was floating. There were bright colours everywhere, beautiful blues and reds and purples that Ben had never seen before. It was so lovely just to float, and look at these bright, beautiful colours. He had never felt so right, so alive, so at one with himself.

He smiled. Either having his soul destroyed was quite a pleasant experience, or there must have been a malfunction with the Devil's plan and he'd somehow ended up in Heaven. With this thought, he was glad to note that his mind was still working. How convenient. He smiled even wider. He could think! This was fantastic.

His arms and legs seemed to work as well. He looked down at them and waved them around. He was floating! He was still wearing his old clothes, though. His jeans and the same green t-shirt he'd worn the first day he met Jamie. His clothes were scuffed and dirty and Ben frowned. He would have preferred them to be clean and nice.

How pleasant, just to lie here on the air, looking around him at all the pretty colours swirling by his face. He tried a lazy somersault. Ah, this was good.

"Nice, isn't it?"

Ben turned; there was someone else in his swirly little world.

Verla was floating towards him, or was he floating towards her? He couldn't decide as they both seemed to be moving.

"Hi," he murmured. "Are you real?"

"I think so," she replied, wiggling her fingers at him.

"Oh, good," he said. "I'm so glad your soul wasn't zapped into oblivion either."

They floated side by side for a while, reflecting on the convenience of still having their souls.

"Are we in Heaven?" asked Ben dreamily. He rather liked the thought.

"I don't think so," Verla said, gazing around her. "I've been thinking about it. I think we're in the middle of that sphere thing."

"What sphere?" he asked lazily. He was still fond of the thought of being in Heaven.

"The one that Mr Duncan pushed me into," she said. "How did you get in?"

"Oh, we pushed him in too, but he grabbed me on the way down," he explained nonchalantly.

She looked alarmed. "He's in here too?"

Suddenly the impact of what that could mean hit Ben, and he shook his head as if shaking off the last dregs of sleep. When he turned to Verla, there was panic in his eyes.

"You mean we're in that swirly thing?" He looked around and saw the translucent colours floating past were the same ones he'd seen from the platforms. "That means Mr Duncan is in here too!"

"That's what I just said!"

They both looked around anxiously, but the swirling streams of translucent colour meant they couldn't see further than about a metre away.

"There!" said Verla, pointing to the side and clutching Ben's arm.

He looked in the direction she was pointing and saw a dark shape slowly coming towards them. The two stared, frozen, as it drifted forward.

"It's breaking up," Verla whispered.

As they watched, the black mass slowly disintegrated into pieces. The dark scraps swirled around slowly in the colourful currents around them, becoming smaller and smaller.

Ben spotted a stream of pink curling past him, with some scraps of black in them. He reached into the swirl of colour and pulled out a piece of black textile. Verla reached out and caught a few in her hand.

"It's fabric," said Ben, bringing it up close to his eyes. "Verla, I think this stuff may be from Mr Duncan's suit."

"Ugh." She shuddered as a few pieces of green satin clung to her arm, bought towards her by the gravitational pull.

Verla and Ben watched the scraps around them, and noticed they were slowly shrinking and dissolving into nothing.

"I don't think he made it," Ben said quietly.

"How do you know?" asked Verla. She glanced up. "He could be waiting for us somewhere."

"He's not," said Ben, a feeling of certainty settling upon him. He looked around, and felt a deep sense of calm and peace slowly flow through his body. "Not in here. He didn't survive this."

Verla paused. "You're right," she said quietly. "I feel... I know... that he's gone."

The two floated quietly for a minute. Ben breathed deeply in and out. Despite the strange surroundings and the dramatic events of the past few hours, he felt an innate feeling that he was finally safe. That he'd finally arrived… home.

"But we're still here," Verla's voice interrupted his thoughts.

She reached out her arms and began moving around, floating amongst the swirling colours.

"Yes," Ben frowned, "but why?"

"I don't know," she said. "From what I've heard, no one survives this thing. Not even Mr Duncan." She shuddered again, brushing the last of the dissolving black remnants from her arm.

"What makes us so special, then?" Ben mused. "We're obviously still alive. For some reason, the laws of nature haven't touched us."

"Maybe nature just likes us," she suggested, accidentally bumping into him.

"I think you could be right," he said slowly. "Verla, this Marguerite Grammaire. She was an ancestor of both of us."

Verla turned to stare at him. "What are you talking about?" she asked. "Both of us?"

"You never told me your name was Diamant," he said. "That was my mother's name. You both lived in the same town at one point, although you would have been born about eighty years before her."

"I had no idea I still had relatives," Verla whispered, staring at him. "Does that mean we're family?"

"I think it does. I'm your cousin a few times removed or something."

"No wonder you were different," she said. "No wonder you didn't give up."

"Yeah. I'm glad I didn't."

"But what does Marguerite Grammaire have to do with anything?"

"According to Duncan, she was the only known descendent of Mother Nature."

"Is Mother Nature real, then?" asked Verla, sounding surprised.

"Well, I don't know," said Ben. "I only learned about her existence about half an hour ago."

"I did read in one of my books once, that Mother Nature had a human child," she said. "But I thought it was a myth, same as Jupiter and Zeus and all those other stories."

Ben nodded. He's read that somewhere recently too.

"Maybe it's not a myth," he said slowly. "Maybe way back when, it really did happen. And Duncan... Duncan said that the bloodline was lost, until he picked it up again when he met Marguerite."

"Does that mean...?" she trailed off, scrutinising him.

"Yeah," he said, hardly believing what he was saying. "I think that might mean that through Marguerite Grammaire... we're her descendants too."

She stared at him, gently bobbing.

"Is that why we're still, well, alive?" She motioned at themselves, and at the mass around them.

"I can't think of any other reason," he said slowly. "Why else would we survive, and not Duncan?"

"I'm so glad he's gone," she said.

"Oh, man," he said. "I'm so glad Jamie didn't fall in too. I have a feeling it might be too much to think that he could be related as well."

"Do you think that's it, then?" she asked. "Do you think that's why we're okay? We're protected because we're family?"

"Yeah. I do. I think nature's played a hand in a lot of things lately. And I think it's got a lot to do with us being okay right now."

Verla started smiling. "You have no idea how I feel right now," she told him. "We're okay, we're alive, and I feel so good – better than I have in one hundred years."

"I feel pretty good too," he admitted. "Like… like I belong in here."

"So do I," she murmured. "It just feels… right."

"But we can't stay here," he said, regretfully.

"I guess we can't."

"We'd better find a way. I wonder if we can get up to the surface?"

"Look," Verla laughed, striking out, "you can almost swim through here!" And for someone who hadn't swum in at least a hundred years, she managed a passable breaststroke.

"Do you remember which way we came in?" she asked.

"I have no idea."

She shrugged happily. "Then I guess any way will do," she said, and struck off away from the gravitational centre of the sphere.

"Come on!" she called back to Ben. "Jamie will be worried. Let's go find him!"

~

It took a while to locate Jamie once they reached the surface. Ben had forgotten how vast the sphere had looked from above. They bobbed at the top, unable to float any further than the boundaries of the colourful gas, and shouted his name. Then they swam across the surface for a while, calling.

"I hope he hasn't taken an elevator up already," said Ben, realising that Jamie probably thought they were dead. "Or someone might have caught him down here."

"He hasn't," said Verla softly, pointing.

They could barely make out the huddled form of Jamie sitting up against one of the elevator shafts on a platform above them. Hearing their calls, his tear-stained face looked across hesitantly – and when he realised what he was seeing, he jumped up, shouting.

"Verla! Ben! You're... you're alive!"

His face was split by a smile as Ben tried to explain from ten metres below what had happened.

"I just can't believe you guys are still alive," he said, and even at that distance Ben could see him biting his lip. "I'll find a way to get you up."

"Be careful!" Verla called up to him. "Please, please don't fall in!"

They saw Jamie disappear across the maze of platforms. Ben and Verla bobbed at the surface, kicking their legs slightly to keep from being pulled back into the sphere.

Ten minutes later Jamie reappeared above them, and they craned their necks to look up at him. He was holding something bulky, and Ben recognised a blue stripe on it.

"Is that my jacket?" he called.

"Yes, and I'm sorry," Jamie replied as Ben heard a loud tearing noise.

"You can't be serious," Ben said loudly. "Are you trying to a rope out of my jacket?"

"Partially, yeah," Jamie called back. Ben could hear another tear, then another.

Ben thought about Jamie's limited options and for the first time since they'd reached the surface, he felt a stab of fear. What if there was no way to get up? What if they had to float here until they starved to death, or until a Hell worker found them and raised the alarm?

"Jamie, maybe you should go up an elevator," he called. "Maybe there's a place you can get some real rope or something!"

Jamie's face reappeared above them. "Ben," he said calmly. "Can you just give me a minute here?"

Verla put her hand on Ben's arm. She still looked very serene. "He'll be fine, Ben," she said reassuringly.

Jamie's face disappeared then appeared a few seconds later. "Verla," he called. "Were you wearing a coat at any point? Maybe that black one of yours?"

"I don't think so. I was wearing this when I was injected. When Duncan took me, I don't expect he stopped to get my cloak. Sorry."

"That's okay," called Jamie, and disappeared from sight. There was a pause before Ben heard the ripping sounds start up again.

"We should hurry," Ben whispered to Verla. "What if someone comes down?"

"They won't," she replied.

"How do you know?" he asked.

"I don't," she said, taking both his hands in hers. "I just feel... I just know we're all right."

A minute later, Jamie called down to them. "I know it's not perfect," he said. "But it should be strong enough to get you up."

He lowered a long, thick shape over the railing and fed it down to them. Ben caught hold of what used to be the sleeve of his jacket. It was knotted tightly to another piece of his jacket, which was tied to a long piece of white material. The thick knots continued up the line, which seemed to be comprised of Ben's red and black jacket, and a lot of white.

Ben looked at the white fabric and it clicked in his mind.

He glanced at Verla, hiding a smile.

"Ladies first," he said, handing her the end of the rope and gesturing upwards.

"Thanks," she said, and with surprising strength, she hauled herself up. Ben held onto the end, trying to keep it steady for her. When she disappeared onto the platform, he heard Jamie yell, "your turn, Ben!"

He climbed the rope cautiously, hoping none of the knots slipped and the fabric stayed secure. He couldn't get much traction with his feet so he had to rely on his hands to pull himself up. By the time he hauled himself over the edge of the platform, his arms were sore and aching.

He lay on the surface for a few seconds, taking in the scene. Jamie, clad in only a white shirt and blue patterned boxer shorts, was standing at the steel railing holding the end of the rope. He'd looped it several times around the railing for tension. Verla was standing next to the elevator shaft, her cheeks pink.

Ben caught his breath and sat up. He squinted at Jamie, and started to grin. "Are they little aeroplanes?" he asked, pointing at Jamie's shorts.

Jamie pulled the rest of the rope onto the platform. "Yes, they are," he said.

"Flying past little blue clouds?" Ben said, standing up.

Jamie rolled his eyes. "How closely do you want to examine them?" he asked. "Yes. They're aeroplanes. In the sky. Is that a problem?"

"Hmmm," Ben pretended to think for a second. "You just saved us from bobbing around down there forever. I'd say not."

He held out his hand to Jamie, and as Jamie accepted it, he pulled him in for a quick hug. "Thanks. Thank you so much."

Ben turned to Verla. "You okay there?" he asked with a grin.

She laughed in an embarrassed, distracted way. "Yes, I'm fine!"

Ben picked up the end of the makeshift rope. The end of his jacket sleeve, which had dipped into the sphere, had half-dissolved.

"Glad our clothes didn't get dissolved too," he said, touching the jacket sleeve gingerly. "Forget about Mr Pilot-Pants here, at least he's still got his underwear on. Climbing up that rope in the raw would have been pretty embarrassing."

"That would have been horrible," Verla said, blushing at the thought. "I'd hate to be down here with nothing on."

"Yeah, gross," agreed Ben, slotting into his newly revealed role of cousin quite comfortably.

They stood on the platform for a few seconds, looking around at each other. "I don't know about you two," said Verla, breaking the short silence. "But I'm roasting down here. Should we try to find the elevator we came down in?"

"It's over this way," said Jamie. He reached over and took Verla's hand, and started leading them across a walkway. "It took me a while to find it when I was getting the jackets."

"There's so many here, though," said Ben, taking a second to gaze across at the sea of shafts. Suddenly he stiffened.

"Jamie!" he hissed. Jamie and Verla had reached the next platform, and they turned around. Ben was frozen on the walkway. He indicted his head slightly toward the right, and Jamie and Verla turned to look.

About four platforms away, two men and a woman were stepping out of a lift. Ben could see that they were wearing black suits and holding small suitcases.

He squeezed his eyes shut and opened them again. He

couldn't believe it – were they about to be caught?

The suit-clad trio moved down a walkway parallel to Ben's. One of the men turned to the woman and said something, and she laughed. They reached the next platform, then walked across the walkway on the far side.

With his breath coming out rapidly, Ben waited until they had disappeared from his sight behind a shaft. He walked quickly up to the platform in front of him, and he, Jamie and Verla pressed against the far side.

"They weren't here for us," Ben whispered. "They were on their way somewhere. They didn't see us."

Verla peeked out from behind the shaft. "They're getting further away," she reported. "They're crossing and… I can't see them anymore."

Ben sagged with relief. "How far away is ours?" he murmured to Jamie.

"I think it's seven or eight more platforms ahead," Jamie whispered back. "Those people have gone. I think we should move it. I don't think I can pretend to be a Hell worker when I'm not wearing any pants."

Despite the seriousness of the situation, Ben and Verla both smiled.

"Okay, let's go," said Verla.

This time it was she who took Jamie's hand, and Ben could see him grip it firmly before setting off across the next walkway. He followed behind, glancing around constantly in case he saw any more Hell workers wandering around.

"It's one of the ones around here," Jamie said finally, stepping onto a platform.

"How will we know?" Ben frowned. "And what if the lift part has gone back up to the surface? We can't just sit here waiting a few hours for each one to arrive back down here."

"We'll know," said Jamie, leading them down the next walkway. "Because when I got the jackets out of our lift, I wedged your family tree into one of the cracks next to it."

"Smart move," Ben acknowledged. "Very smart move."

They crossed two more platforms before Jamie called, "it's here!"

Ben tore the parchment slightly as he pulled it out of the crack between the bottom of the shaft and the floor. He handed it to Verla. "Check it out," he said. "We're both Diamants."

"Fingers crossed the lift's still down here," said Jamie, literally crossing his fingers as he pressed the small silver button next to the elevator doors. There was a collective intake of breath as the doors stood still for a few seconds, then they all exhaled in relief as the shiny panels opened, revealing the inside of the lift. They stepped inside.

Ben looked apologetically at Verla. "I guess you were unconscious for your trip down," he said. "I have to warn you. It isn't pleasant."

He scanned the rows of buttons on the wall, then reached out and hit the one labelled 'LOBBY'.

The doors closed, and the lift lurched up slowly. Ben was surprised. "I thought it would be faster?" he said to Jamie. "If it goes at this rate, it'll probably take days to – whoa!"

He felt the lift accelerate suddenly, and grabbed the handrail. The strange feeling of weightlessness that he'd gotten used to on the platforms was gone, and despite his best efforts to stay upright, he started sliding to the floor. Across from him, Verla and Jamie were doing the same. They all landed on the floor and scrambled to sit up and lean against the walls. Verla had evidently overcome her embarrassment at seeing Jamie in his boxer shorts, and she huddled against him. He put his arms around her tightly.

"This is so strange," she moaned into his chest. He stroked her hair.

"It's okay," he said. "It's just a lift. A very strange one. We'll be okay."

As the lift sped upwards, the heat increased, and Ben used the edge of his shirt to mop the sweat off his face. "Tell you what," he yelled over the noise of the lift. "I'm looking forward to a shower after this."

Jamie cracked a smile and hugged Verla to him. Ben slid down onto the floor and lay on his back, gazing at the ceiling. He suddenly felt exhausted, and closed his eyes, wishing for sleep.

Despite the heat and noise he must have nodded off. The next thing he knew, Jamie was shaking him gently. "Ben!" he called. "We're slowing down."

He opened his eyes groggily and immediately noticed the air was cooler than it had been before. He pulled himself up to a sitting position. His head was heavy and sluggish.

"What did you say?" he asked loudly. The roar of the lift wasn't as loud anymore, and he was glad he didn't have to shout.

"We're slowing down," Jamie repeated. "We have to be ready when the lift stops. We don't know what's waiting for us out there."

Ben looked up at Verla. She was standing against the wall, her eyes wide and alert. "We need to get Jamie some trousers," she said. "If there's anyone there when we get out, forget not having union stamps – they'll notice pretty quickly if someone is walking around half-dressed."

"Our choices are pretty limited," said Ben, shaking off the last dregs of sleep and standing up a bit shakily. "We may have to just take a leap of faith and hope no one's there."

"We may have no other choice," Verla admitted.

"It's stopping," said Jamie quietly.

"Let's just wing it," said Ben desperately as he felt the lift finally slow to a halt.

Ben, Verla and Jamie stood facing the doors as they opened smoothly, and a burst of cool night air hit their faces.

## - CHAPTER TWENTY-SEVEN -
# Two More Mortals

The scene before them was chaotic. The up-lights around the walls cast a glow over several people scurrying around, shouting orders and speaking in terse voices. Some were wearing full suits but others were still struggling to knot their ties and slide their shoes on. A buxom brunette with her shirt undone and hair flying in all directions hurried over to the elevator bank and stared at Ben, Verla and Jamie with a fierce look in her eyes. They stared back, not knowing what to say.

"Well?" she snapped. "Are you getting out or what? Move!"

The three quickly moved out of the lift and stood to the side as she strode in and punched a button on the wall. The doors closed.

They turned back to the lobby. A man in a blue pinstriped suit was standing in the centre of the room, waving his arms and trying to get his voice heard over the hubbub of noise.

"Kelptorn!" he yelled across the room, and a man stopped. "Kelptorn, if you don't get the locksmith here in five minutes, you're going straight down into the portal, and I don't mean on your way to Hawaii! It's straight over the railing for you!"

He turned and started shouting in another direction. "Lipgore! I don't care what time it is, go get some clothes on!

You can't be wearing a dressing gown when he arrives!"

There was a flurry of activity concentrated around the far side of the lobby, where the doors were. One door was still lying on the ground and the other was hanging from its hinges where Ben had last seen them, and through the vast opening he glimpsed street lights casting a dim glow onto the pavement.

He motioned to Jamie and Verla and started walking quickly towards the doors. He glanced around him, and his heart almost stopped as he saw the pinstripe suited man's eyes focus on Jamie.

"You there!" he yelled, and all three froze. Ben wondered if they should make a run for it, and was tensing himself to start sprinting when the man yelled again.

"Put some trousers on, for goodness sake! What kind of show will he think we're running here?"

Jamie must have thought quickly, because he turned to the man and shouted out: "Right away, sir!" before resuming his rapid walk toward the entranceway. Ben and Verla strode behind him, trying not to catch anyone's eye.

They joined the haphazard stream of people jostling in and out of the entranceway, and stepped past the stone door lying on the ground. A man and a woman wearing hardhats were examining the hinges of the other door, which was sagging dangerously across the opening.

"Careful!" the man admonished someone who bumped against him. "Where's the health and safety department?" he asked no one in particular. "This is ridiculous! Someone's going to get seriously hurt!"

Ben, Jamie and Verla slipped past him. Outside in the courtyard, the streetlights illuminated the water fountains, still bubbling dark water. A man was leaning over the side of the fountain, emptying a bottle of thick black liquid into its depths.

"More, more!" said a woman standing behind him. "It needs to be blacker! It can't be that sludgy grey colour. Use another bottle!"

"Let's just walk away," Verla muttered to Jamie and Ben, and they strode towards the sidewalk. As they reached the road, a truck screeched up beside them and two men jumped out.

"Get the tools!" one shouted to the other, and started jogging towards the Hades Corporation building.

Ben, Jamie and Verla quickly walked down the sidewalk away from the chaotic scene.

"What was going on in there?" Ben muttered to the other two. "You'd think they'd be a bit calmer."

"I have no idea," said Jamie. "But I think we just dodged a bullet. A massive bullet."

They rounded a corner, and Ben let himself slow down a bit.

"You okay?" he heard Jamie say to Verla.

Verla was staring all around her, her eyes wide. Ben glanced up at the tall buildings surrounding them.

"A bit unfamiliar, huh?" he asked.

"They're so tall," she murmured.

As the adrenaline left his body, Ben realised how chilly the air was.

"I think we need to get you some clothes," he said to Jamie. "It's freezing out here."

"I'm all right," said Jamie, but Ben saw him shiver.

Ben's heart was still beating rapidly from their strange adventure and narrow escape, but he tried to push the feeling aside for the moment. "Where's your car?" he asked Jamie.

Headlights loomed ahead, and Ben, Jamie and Verla shrank

back against the side of a building as a car sped by. They heard the sounds of brakes screeching from the direction of the Hades Corporation building.

"I parked it a few streets away," said Jamie. He squinted around him. "If we cut through the lane up ahead we should come out pretty close to it."

As they walked briskly through the dark alley, Ben pulled his phone out of his pocket. He blinked in surprise – it was now a melted blob of plastic. "Hey!"

"Could the heat have done that?" asked Verla, leaning over to look.

"I doubt it," he said, still staring at the phone. "Maybe it melted while we were in the middle of that swirly thing."

Jamie took a sharp right at the end of the lane, and Ben and Verla followed.

"I just keep waiting to be caught," Ben said quietly. He glanced behind them as they walked. "After all that, I can't believe we just walked away."

"Don't think about it," Verla whispered. "You can't. Just keep walking. We're fine."

"I should let my parents know I'm okay," he said. "What time is it?"

Jamie responded. "Just past three."

"Can I borrow your phone?"

Jamie handed it over and Ben composed a quick message to tell his parents he'd lost his phone and would be home in a few hours.

Another car appeared around the corner, and they stepped back into the shadows. Ben kept glancing back in the direction of the Hades Corporation building, half-expecting an angry mob to round the corner and take them prisoner. He shivered. The sooner they got out of the area, the better he would feel.

When the car was gone, Jamie led them to the spot where he'd parked his Aston Martin. He opened the passenger door and Ben crawled into the tiny back seat.

Verla slid into the passenger seat and looked around her wonderingly. "I've always wanted to be in a car," she said softly.

"This is a pretty nice one to start with, then,"Ben commented.

He relaxed against the back of the seat as Jamie started the car, and felt a flood of relief as they started leaving the tall buildings behind.

"How are you going over there?" he asked Verla, who was clutching the hand-rest tightly.

"I'm all right," she replied. "Just feeling a bit dizzy. It's an... unfamiliar feeling."

"I can slow down," said Jamie.

"No, I'm fine," Verla reassured him. "I'm going to have to get used to it." She stared out of the window at the buildings of Sydney, and gave a sharp intake of breath as they drove over the Anzac Bridge.

Jamie finally pulled into his driveway and hit the button on his garage remote. The garage door opened smoothly, and he drove in.

Ben tried to suppress a yawn as he climbed out of the car, but Verla spotted it.

"How long have you been awake?" she asked.

"I have no idea," said Ben. "Since yesterday morning, when I fell asleep at your house? How many hours is that?"

"You can have a sleep up at my place," said Jamie. He unlocked the door at the side of the garage and led them to the elevator. All three stopped in front of it and stared at the doors apprehensively.

"We could take the stairs," Jamie suggested, breaking the silence, and they all laughed nervously.

"The elevator is fine," said Verla, leaning forward and hitting the button. She smiled at them. "I like these buttons."

"You're going to love technology," Ben told her as they got into the lift. "We'll get you a phone and a computer. I bet in a few weeks you won't be able to live without them."

The lift stopped at the top floor, and Jamie led them down the corridor and into his apartment. He flipped on the lights, and Verla looked around in wonder.

"Is this where you live?" she asked, taking in the furniture, the piano and wide glass windows.

"Yeah," said Jamie, heading to the kitchen. He returned with two glasses of water and handed them to Ben and Verla. "Make yourself comfortable."

Needing no further invitation, Ben flopped on the white couch and kicked his shoes off. He leaned back into the soft cushions and took a long sip of water. Fatigue was starting to overtake him, and he stifled another yawn.

Jamie disappeared through a door at the far end of the room, and when he returned a minute later he was wearing jeans and a fresh shirt. He collapsed onto the couch opposite Ben.

"Do all people live in places as nice as this?" Verla asked, walking over to the piano.

"Some do," said Jamie. "But not that many. People live in all sorts of houses. I'm one of the luckier ones though, I guess."

"Will you get to keep this place?" asked Ben.

Jamie looked surprised. "Of course," he said. "I paid for it."

"With your concert money?" said Ben, and Verla looked

over inquisitively.

"Yeah, and I have investments too," Jamie replied. He looked at Verla. "I play piano at the occasional concert," he said by way of explanation.

"Oh!" said Verla, and smiled. "Then of course I will expect to hear you play later."

"I guess so, if you'd like," said Jamie, almost shyly.

"Of course," she repeated firmly.

Ben yawned again, and this time he couldn't hide it. This triggered Jamie, who yawned too.

"Please, you two, you need some sleep!" said Verla.

"Don't you?" asked Ben, who could feel his eyes trying to close.

"Perhaps." She shrugged. "I slept during the day."

"You can sleep in the spare room," Jamie said to Ben.

"I think I'm fine just here," mumbled Ben. And a few seconds later, his eyes closed and he fell into a dreamless sleep.

~

When Ben came to, a bright light was shining through his eyelids and the sun was warm on his face. He slowly opened his eyes.

Sunlight flooded through the windows and spilled across the furniture. On the couch opposite him, Jamie lay sprawled, sleeping. Verla sat on the edge of the couch next to him, gazing out of the windows at the sprawl of the city and harbour. She turned as Ben stretched his arms out.

"Hi," she whispered. "How are you feeling?"

"Pretty good," he whispered back. "What time is it?"

"I'm not sure. The sun's pretty high. You've been asleep for a few hours."

Ben pulled himself up to a sitting position. "I'm hungry," he said. "Reckon Jamie's got any food here?"

Jamie's sleepy voice sounded from the other couch. "What?"

"Good, you're awake," said Ben. "Got any food?"

Jamie blinked and slowly sat up. "Morning," he said. "What time is it?"

"I don't know," said Ben. "Probably around six or seven."

Jamie leaned over and grabbed his phone from the coffee table. "Six twenty two," he reported. "I've got a message. Looks like it's from your parents. It just says 'okay'."

"Thanks. I'm really hungry," Ben said again. "Do you have any food here, Jamie?"

"I've got some bread. Want some toast?"

"Yes, please."

"Verla? Want some toast?"

"I'm not sure," she said apprehensively. "Maybe I'll try a little bit."

Jamie got up, stretched, and headed toward the kitchen. A few minutes later he returned and handed plates to Ben and Verla.

"Thanks," said Ben, taking a big bite of cheese on toast. He watched Verla as she picked up a piece hesitantly. "It's weird that you haven't eaten for so long."

"I hope my system can handle it," she said. "I'd better keep things simple for a while."

She took a bite of toast, chewed slowly, then swallowed with some difficulty.

"What about you?" Ben asked Jamie. "Does your body need food?"

"I can go without if I needed to, but who wants to do without food?" Jamie said, biting into his own piece. "Not any more, though, I suppose. From now on I'll have to remember to do it not just for pleasure but to actually keep my energy going."

"Oh, don't worry, your body will tell you when you're hungry," said Ben. "About every ten minutes, if you're me."

Ben watched Verla tilt her piece of toast up to the light and examine it. As she twisted, her hair fell away from her neck and Ben saw a bandage just below her hairline. He looked below it, where the curly symbol had been marked on her skin.

"Verla!" he said, and both she and Jamie turned to stare at him. "Your tattoo!"

She reached up and touched the place where it used to be. "Has it gone?" she asked, and Ben nodded. "Does the skin look red or anything?"

"It looks pretty normal from here," he replied. "Did it just disappear?"

"Oh no, the Hell doctor took it off just before he injected me," she said. "He had this silver pen thing that he said was a solar-powered laser. I'm not sure what that means."

Ben looked at Jamie. "Could we have used solar power at Verla's house the whole time?"

Jamie groaned. "It didn't even occur to me to try."

"Anyway, he told me that they've only started using the pen thing in the past few years," she continued. "He said up until recently they burned them off with the end of a poker." She screwed up her nose. "Kind of defeats the purpose, if you ask me."

"Ugh," Ben said. "I hope he was joking. But at least it's gone. You're not a number anymore."

She smiled. "Then it's final. I'm free." She turned to Jamie, a troubled look crossing her face. "But I still can't believe you gave up being a Caelun just for me, Jamie. It was an…

incredible thing to do."

She put her plate down and reached over and touched Jamie's cheek lightly, gazing into his eyes. Ben made himself busy by taking his plate over to the sink. He washed and dried it slowly.

After a minute, Jamie walked over. "What do you want to do?"

"Well, I'd better get back to my family at some point," Ben said as Verla joined them. "Verla, what are you thinking of doing?"

She looked uncertain. "I think I'd like to see my house," she said. "There are a few things I'd like to pick up before I go to, well, wherever I end up going. I don't know where that will be."

Jamie looked like he thought it might be a bit forward to offer his own abode, so Ben jumped in. "What are you talking about, cuz?" he asked, slinging his arm around her shoulders and giving them a squeeze. "You're family. You'll stay with us."

## - CHAPTER TWENTY-EIGHT -

# The Last Fire

Jamie's car hadn't even exited the main highway before they realised something was wrong. As they drove towards Carmenton, Verla, Ben and Jamie stared wordlessly at the huge plume of smoke on the horizon. It billowed up then drifted eastwards, dark against the bright blue sky. They all knew where it was coming from.

Verla's street was filled with people gazing up at the fire which was engulfing the porch, roaring out the windows, and licking the chimneys of her house. The members of the local volunteer fire fighting group aimed their truck's hoses at the fire, but the water just disappeared into the flames without reducing them at all. Local townspeople stood a short distance away, some wearing dressing gowns and slippers. Cars were parked haphazardly along the street, and more were pulling up to see the most exciting thing to happen in Carmenton in years.

Jamie pulled over a block before the house. Verla slowly climbed out of the car, her face even paler than usual.

"You okay?" Ben asked, walking over to her. She nodded as Jamie joined them.

They walked the rest of the way to Verla's house and stood

across the road from it, behind a group of people who were talking and pointing to the fire. Verla's eyes were huge as she looked up at the house she'd called home for over a century, which was now slowly being destroyed by high, angry flames.

"How long has it been burning?" Jamie asked one of the men standing in front of them.

"Ages," he replied shortly. "Someone first noticed it a few hours ago, but the fire fighters reckon it'd been going long before that."

"Was anyone in there?" Ben asked cautiously, and he could see Verla glance at him out of the corner of her eye.

"Yeah," said the man sadly. "I think some old lady lived there. The firemen tried to get past the flames to see if anyone was home, but it's too far gone. They reckon anyone would have been long dead by the time anyone even noticed the fire. We can only hope she got out before it got bad, but," he shrugged sympathetically, "the worst probably happened."

"Are you sure, Rod?" another man asked. "I don't think anyone lived there. Place has been empty for years, hasn't it?"

"I thought an old woman stayed in it," said Rod, looking uncertain. "Didn't Mal say he drove past last year and saw someone there?"

"Mal'd probably had a skinful," his friend shrugged. "I guess we might never know, anyway."

Ben led Verla and Jamie past the crowds and up the street, and they finally arrived at the town's oval. Verla's park bench was visible at the edge of the trees, but Ben settled himself on the grass and the other two followed suit.

They sat on the grass for hours, hardly speaking, just watching the flames that were visible over the other houses. At some point Jamie went to get food, and they had a rather sombre picnic on the oval.

Jamie's phone rang as he was finishing the last of his burger, and he walked a short distance away to take the call.

"That was St Peter," he told the other two when he returned. "Duncan's missing and Judas wanted to know if he knew anything about it. I told him to tell Judas we found Verla wandering a few streets away from the Hades Corporation building last night, and she couldn't remember how she got there."

"Will Judas believe him?" Ben asked.

"I don't know," said Jamie. "But at least Duncan's no longer around to tell him otherwise."

"Did you tell him about that place in the centre of the Earth?" asked Verla.

"No, but I said I had some news to share," said Jamie. "He said he'd be at the golf club tomorrow and I can drop by then."

"I don't think you'll have to worry about not being his favourite anymore," mused Ben. "That piece of intel has got to cement your place at number one."

"Thanks," grinned Jamie. "St Peter did say one other thing. Their intelligence network detected that one of the other camp's VIPs arrived in Sydney this morning. Could be why the building was in such shambles when we got out."

"Which VIP?" Verla asked.

Jamie shrugged. "St Peter didn't say. But I got the feeling it was one of the ones at the top."

"Like the...?" Ben started, then trailed off.

"I'm not sure. Maybe."

"Wow," said Ben, trying to get his head around it. He lay back on the grass.

It was mid-afternoon when they noticed the activity around Verla's part of town had died down. They could no longer see any flames, so Verla suggested they walk over and take a look at what was going on.

There was a large fire truck parked in the street; it must have been called from Katoomba. Three firemen were standing next to the house, peering at the damage, while others talked on radios and stood in little groups. A couple of firemen were standing off to the side with two middle aged women who were gesturing and talking loudly. A police officer got into her car and a second later she had driven off down the road. A few curious townspeople were still present; one man had his own camping chair set up, facing the house, and he was drinking from a thermos.

Verla gazed at her smouldering house. The entire right side was demolished; all that was left were a few smouldering walls with piles of smoking black rubble between them. The left side was a curious sight. While most of the walls had been destroyed, a huge cylindrical structure rose out of the debris. Although its brickwork was scorched and the walls leading out from it had been mostly eaten away by flames, the brick tower appeared to be intact.

The three stared at it for a while until Verla spoke.

"That's my library."

She turned to Ben and Jamie and instead of looking devastated, she had a rapt expression upon her face. "It was the only place in this house that kept me sane – my one source of pleasure throughout all those years. The rest of my Hell," she gestured towards the ruin, "is gone."

Ben heard a voice that sounded vaguely familiar, and looked over to where the firemen were talking to the middle-aged women. He caught the word 'books', and under the guise of inspecting the house from another angle, he strolled closer.

"Did you see them?" the brown-haired woman asked

breathlessly. "What did they look like?"

"They were fine, Gladys," said one of the firemen, sounding a little impatient. "They may smell a bit smoky for a while. But the fire didn't touch them."

Ben realised that Jamie and Verla had joined him, and were both gazing innocently at the charred house.

"How many were there?" asked Gladys.

"I don't know. Hundreds," the fireman said. His friend walked off to the truck, and he looked like he wanted to follow.

"Who will they belong to?" she pressed. "We don't know who lived in the house before the big fire. The records were lost years ago. I should have paid more attention! Who will get the books?"

"I have no idea," said the fireman, throwing up his hands. "The local government, I guess, if we can't find an owner."

Gladys turned to her friend. "I'll get Giovanni from the town office right onto this," she said excitedly. "I'll have those books made the property of the Historical Society, quick-smart. I won't let this one pass."

"Where will you store them?" asked her friend. "Your house is already full!"

"I'll clear that good-for-nothing bottle cap collection out of the museum," said Gladys dismissively. "I'll turn it into a historical library instead."

"Yes, you do that, Gladys," said her friend with a smile. She looked at the fireman. "Do they know where the fire started?"

"Looks like one of the upstairs bedrooms," the man replied, and Ben sensed Verla stiffening beside him. "The guys from the city are still looking it over, but they reckon a fire was lit in the fireplace up there, and at some point the rug caught alight."

"Who lit the fire?" asked Gladys, her eyes widening.

The fireman shrugged. "No idea. Probably some kids playing house," he said. "Happens more often than you think."

"Wow," said Gladys's friend. "Hope they got out okay."

"We're pretty sure there was no one in there," the fireman gestured at the house. "Of course, it's all speculation, so please don't quote me in the Carmenton Voice, Gladys. We'll probably never know for sure. No one even noticed the fire until it had taken over the whole house."

"Until it picked up where it left off?" Ben hissed to Verla, and she nodded sombrely, eyes still on the house.

"Let's go," she whispered to Ben and Jamie, and they moved away from the ruin. They passed a couple of people walking in the other direction and overheard a few sentences.

"I've never even been down this street, and I've lived in Carmenton all my life!" the man was saying excitedly. "Look at all these houses! Has this been here the whole time? I never realised there were so many!"

"I know!" The woman nodded. "Could some of these houses be renovated? Some of them still have walls! They just need a roof and a bit of TLC!"

"I can't believe we didn't think of this before," the man admitted just before the couple walked out of earshot.

Ben, Jamie and Verla continued walking. As they reached the car, Verla turned around for one last look at her charred, ruined house.

"I guess your place just caught up with all the others," Ben said, waving his arm to encompass the entire ruined area.

"Yes," Verla agreed, then smiled at both of them; a free smile, rid of the burden it had carried for so long. "Yes. And now the old town of Carmenton can finally rest in peace."

## - EPILOGUE -

# Deadline

"I promise I'll be there. Yeah, the plane lands at seven. Until Sunday. No, because I have a class on Monday morning. Well, you could ask him, but I think he has a concert to do on Monday night and our return flights are already booked. Okay. No, I have no idea, why don't you call her and ask? She has a phone now, you know. Okay. Yep, okay. Will do. Love you. Bye."

Ben hung up the phone, a little exasperated. His mother was sweet, calling every few hours to make sure he had everything under control, but he really wanted to prove to her that he could handle things just fine.

His phone rang again but it was Jamie this time.

"Whaaat?" Ben groaned in lieu of saying hello.

Jamie laughed. "Verla just got here. What time are you coming to pick us up?"

Ben heard Verla's voice in the background talking to someone else.

"I'll be there in half an hour," he said. "I've just got to drop something off on the way."

"Half an hour's good," confirmed Jamie. "Hey, Verla is talking to your mother and she asked her to ask me to ask you if you've remembered to pack toiletries and a jumper?"

"Yes!" Ben moaned.

"Tell Susan that Ben's got everything packed," Ben heard Jamie say in the background. "But he says to make sure there are lots of teddy bears in his bed."

Verla relayed the message and Jamie came back on the phone, chuckling.

"Thanks a lot," Ben told him. "You know she will, too."

"You love it," said Jamie. "I'll see you in half an hour."

Ben hung up the phone and sat back down at his computer. He had to email this assignment to Professor Brightman before eleven o'clock, then stop by the university to pick up a textbook for one of his other units.

His housemate, an attractive redhead called Sarah, rapped on his open door and wandered in. "Shouldn't you be going?" she asked, checking her watch. "You don't want to miss your plane."

"Yep, almost done," he said, checking he'd spelled his name right on the cover page. After a typo on the cover of his last assignment, he wasn't going to risk a second mistake. He swivelled his chair around to face her.

"I just got off the phone," he said. "Things are already going crazy there. My mother reckons Tia has decided to become an astronaut after all, and she turned the entire living room into a space ship."

"She sounds like a lot of fun," smiled Sarah.

"I'm pretty fond of her," Ben admitted, the familiar feeling of brotherly protectiveness nudging at him. "Are you sure you don't want to come with me?" he asked. "A whole week in Perth with my parents, my little sister and the most nauseating couple on the planet – what could be more exciting?"

"No, thanks," said Sarah, smiling. "But I'll be waiting for

you when you come back."

With that, she sashayed out of the room. After a pause, Ben turned back to the computer to send his assignment to the professor. He checked one last time to make sure his list of dates and names were correct – get it wrong by a year, and his fictional case studies could spend yet another century rotting in their own personal Hell. The professor was a stickler for accuracy, regardless of whether someone's life was on the line or not.

When he'd first told Professor Brightman his ambition to become a lawyer for the Sentenced, the professor had been sceptical, but interested. Now, with Ben's first semester of Religion Studies off to a running start and a good chance of being accepted into the law program next year, he was looking forward to seeing if he could make a career of it.

He hit the send button on the email, picked up his bag, and walked out the door.

# ABOUT THE AUTHOR

Katy Scott lives in Australia with her husband Dylan. She loves connecting with readers, so please feel free to get in touch:

katy@katyscott.org
www.katyscott.org
facebook.com/katyscottauthor
twitter.com/katyinoz

7933549R00168

Printed in Great Britain
by Amazon.co.uk, Ltd.,
Marston Gate.